THE ANCIENT RAIN

Also by Domenic Stansberry

The Big Boom

Chasing the Dragon

Manifesto for the Dead

The Last Days of Il Duce

The Confession

The Spoiler

the

ANCIENT RAIN

Domenic Stansberry

St. Martin's Minotaur ❧ New York

THE ANCIENT RAIN. Copyright © 2008 by Domenic Stansberry. All rights reserved. Printed in the United States of America. No part of this book may be used or reproduced in any manner whatsoever without written permission except in the case of brief quotations embodied in critical articles or reviews. For information, address St. Martin's Press, 175 Fifth Avenue, New York, N.Y. 10010.

www.minotaurbooks.com

Library of Congress Cataloging-in-Publication Data

Stansberry, Domenic.
    The ancient rain / Domenic Stansberry. —1st ed.
        p.   cm.
    ISBN-13: 978-0-312-36453-3
    ISBN-10: 0-312-36453-9

    1. Private investigators—Fiction.   2. North Beach (San Francisco, Calif.)—
Fiction.   I. Title.

PS3569.T3335A84   2008
813'.54—dc22
                                                                    2007049768
First Edition: April 2008

10   9   8   7   6   5   4   3   2   1

Death to the fascist insect that preys on the life of the people . . .

—SLA slogan

PART ONE

The Arrest

ONE

The call was one he shouldn't have taken. It was the kind of call, if you'd missed it, you'd never have known, and things would go on as before. If it caught you, though, you would find yourself doing some small thing you hadn't intended, then another, and before long your life had been altered.

It was that kind of call, though Dante didn't know it yet.

He'd been out all night in the Excelsior District on a stakeout, cramped in the back of a Ford Econoline.

So he'd just crawled into bed beside Marilyn. She stirred but did not awaken. She lay in her nightgown, her dark hair spilling over the pillow and her arms strewn recklessly. Dante closed his eyes. As the sky lightened, he skirted the edge of sleep, his consciousness flitting in the shadows. He was pursuing something, or being pursued, it was hard to tell, and he lay on the sheets, his legs twitching. He had a sensation that he was out on the old mudflats, at low tide, with the shore behind him.

Overhead, the sky was dark with birds. He had the impulse to follow them somehow, but he could not lift his feet. His thighs were heavy.

Then his cell went off.

It occurred to him later that if he had turned down the ringer before climbing into bed, like he usually did, then things would have gone on the same as before. There would have been a message on his voice mail when he woke up, maybe, but the urgency of the moment would have passed. Someone else would have been drawn in.

Instead, he took the call.

He smothered the ringer so it wouldn't wake Marilyn, then stepped out of the room. He caught a glimpse of himself. Or something like himself, his angular form emerging from the shadows, from the half light, in the dressing-table mirror at the end of the hall.

"What is it?" Dante asked.

On the other end was a fellow investigator by the name of Bill Owens. Dante had worked with him a couple of months back.

"I need your help," said Owens.

There was something unusual in the other man's voice. A high note that could be mistaken for hilarity, the way the voice quavered in the digital signal. At the same time Dante heard traffic in the background, the sound of someone crying close by—though he wondered later if the sobbing was in his imagination, a detail his memory added when it reconstructed the incident.

As it turned out, Owens was on the Berkeley ramp to the Bay Bridge. Owens had been heading into San Francisco, driving his kids to the private school they attended in the city, same as he did most every weekday morning. Only this morning the cops had blocked off the ramp, then converged from behind.

Dante glanced back into the bedroom, at Marilyn, languorous on the bed. She was a good-looking woman, but she made little pig noises while she slept. Truth was, she snored like an animal.

"I'm being charged with murder," said Owens.

"I don't understand."

"Eleanor Younger."

It took Dante a moment. The Younger murder. It had been a notorious case, some thirty years ago. Owens had never really escaped its shadow. Eleanor Younger had been shot to death, an innocent bystander, during a bank robbery out on Judah. The police contended that Owens had been there on the scene—that it was a part of a spree of robberies connected to the old Symbionese Liberation Army. The case against him had fizzled—but it was one of those cases that circled back into the public consciousness from time to time. Either way, the cops wanted Owens now, his wife was out of town, and he needed someone to drive the kids to school.

"Where are they taking you?"

The reception was breaking up, and Dante receded into the hall. He walked toward the mirror but did not glance up. Dante knew what he would see in the reflection: a forty-year-old man, olive skinned, in white boxers and a sleeveless muscle shirt, standing in his lover's apartment. A man who had a face like some prehistoric bird. With a nose that drooped and eyes that were watery and dark.

"Jill's in Chicago. I was hoping you might get word to her," said Owens. "And the kids, I don't want them sitting around the station. If you could get in touch with Jensen's office, maybe. He's in Chicago, too, with Jill, but . . ."

Jill was Owens's second wife, an attorney who worked in a practice with Moe Jensen, with whom Owens himself had a longtime association. Dante was about to ask Owens again where the cops were taking him. It was surprising that they would let him make the call in the middle of an arrest. Usually that happened at the station.

Then the connection was gone.

Dante glanced at Marilyn again. Her lips were delicately parted.

She was still asleep, still snoring. He touched her and she quieted, and then she rolled toward him. She did not awaken.

They had been lovers for a long time, off and on, but it was only recently that things had gotten like this between them, where he had the key and came and went like her place was his own. She wore a thin, white nightgown that rode up around her thighs. She made a noise like she was laughing, but then she rolled over and he realized perhaps it was not laughter at all.

She snuffled into the pillow and made another indecipherable noise.

Dante pulled on his pants. He went to the window and eased back the sheers and looked out onto the street.

All night he had been on surveillance. To kill time, he had listened to talk radio.

The government had raised the terror alert. People were worked up and they had things to say, one way or the other. About the government. About the war overseas. About the threats here at home.

It's a conspiracy, the CIA, you can't tell me . . . all staged by the Jews . . . the oil companies . . . we've been infiltrated, our water supply, the ports . . . we have to strike back . . .

Meanwhile the city looked the same as ever. It was North Beach as usual out there, the old neighborhood, just stucco-and-clapboard buildings lined up helter-skelter on the old streets, on top of the rocky cliffs, with the Pacific below and the gulls cawing and the scent of morning fog.

Dante went outside. On the car radio, the night talkers had been nudged out by the morning-news people. There were antiwar protestors headed down Market Street, the announcer said, hoping to tie up traffic, but the police were outflanking them. Meanwhile Dante thought of the stakeout from the night before—and the witness they'd been pursuing—and as he pulled away from the curb, glancing into the rearview, he had the impression that someone was following him. That was the way it was these days, everyone being followed by everyone else.

Or at least thinking they were being followed.

TWO

rant Street was empty this hour, the meters untaken, so
Dante slid into a space in front of Moose's, on Washington
Square. It hadn't been his intention, but the square had
lulled him in. The fog had not yet cleared, there was a mist in the air,
and he could hear the pigeons in the cathedral tower. He got himself
some coffee in a paper cup, then sat on one of the green benches that
rimmed the square.

Do nothing.

Dante's father used to come here with a notebook and plan out
his day. Sometimes the old man's friends would wander by, talking
politics—the old feuds, the ancient stuff—and hang around the
benches. Toward the end, the old man rarely left the park all day.

Dante wondered about Owens's kids.

Probably the cops would take Owens down to the Hall of Justice.
So that would be the place to start. Dante knew how the Hall was,
though—how slowly the wheels turned.

Likely he would get stuck there for hours.

Dante knew, too, that police protocol for handling children of an

arrestee was by no means a fixed thing. The arresting officer's obligation was to the immediate situation, to securing and transporting the
criminal. As unlikely as it seemed, there was no requirement to call
Child Services to the scene, and little time to do so, and at any rate it
could be hours, even days, before the agency responded. So it often
happened that the kids at the scene were left to fend for themselves.
The last thing the arresting officer wanted to do was to drag a pair of
kids down to the station. It was a distraction, and there was enough
else to do.

Even if Dante did find them, what was he to do then?

He took out his cell and left a message for Irma at Cicero Investigations. His boss, Jake Cicero, had gone on vacation, and Irma
wouldn't be in for another hour. He left a similar message with Moe
Jensen's office, even though he knew that Jensen and Jill Owens were
doing *pro hac vice* work in Chicago.

Do nothing.

It had been the elder Mancuso's mantra in his later years, his way
of dealing with his wife's slide into madness and the problems down
at the Mancuso warehouse. *If you do not turn your head, you do not see.*
If you do not listen, there is no reason to speak.

A cop pulled up. It was part of the new routine. Over the last
year, ever since 9/11, the cops had been running the homeless out.
For security reasons, supposedly, to protect the cathedral and the post
office, they did a sweep after the bars closed, and another, usually
about an hour before dawn. Even so, by morning there were a number of bedrolls spread out on the grass. An old woman lay sleeping
nearby, under cardboard, oblivious to the dog sniffing her feet. A Chinese family sat bleary eyed near the swing set. At the center of the
square—under the statue of Benjamin Franklin—a black man warmed
himself in front of a can of Sterno. The man dressed as if it were

1977, in a dashiki that had seen better days. He sat with his legs crossed, chanting, words that were almost decipherable but not quite.

The cop's job was to survey the park, poke at packages, look inside paper bags. Survey the area, improbable as it might seem, for biological weapons and explosives.

Dante considered going back up the hill, back to Marilyn. To her body, splayed out over the sheets. To her hips. To her warm breath and the small moaning noises she made in her sleep.

Do nothing.

Ancient advice, words of wisdom. Because how well did he know Owens, really? Dante had worked a case with the man, true. They'd gone a couple times down to Benny's Café, along the Third Street wharfs, and Dante and Marilyn had been out once to his house—but Owens did not talk much about the past. Still, Dante knew the general history. He knew that Owens and his first wife had done a couple of years' time on a conspiracy charge back in the seventies. He knew that the first wife was dead now, and that Owens had remarried and had a daughter and a son. Owens's second wife, Jill, practiced criminal law in partnership with Moe Jensen—high-profile defense work, some of it—but most of Owens's investigative work was for their pro bono clients, people from the projects and the barrios, drug users and stick-up artists, people on the fringes.

In the middle of the square, the man in the dashiki was still chanting. The wind had shifted, so Dante could hear fragments of the man's rant.

I can taste the smoke in the air . . . the rushing wind . . . the black ashes . . . I can taste the flames of the invaders in my mouth . . .

The cop walked around the square, looking under benches, pausing to survey the passersby. The threat level had been raised to Orange, but it was morning now, and the curfew had passed. A businessman with a briefcase wandered through, and a Chinese hipster and his girl-friend started practicing tai chi in the morning light. Across the way, Father Campanella appeared on the cathedral stairs, bent over his cane, and all of a sudden a gaggle of schoolchildren, Chinese mostly, burst around the corner, racing past the Italian Athletic Club toward the old Salesian School.

Do nothing.

His mother had started hearing voices at one point. *So what?* His father had had a different temperament. *You hear voices, don't listen.* He had patted her head, caressed her. But there were things happening out in the ether, his wife had insisted. Voices whispering. Plans being formed, unformed.

She couldn't stop listening, trying to decipher their meaning.

Dante should take the old man's advice, probably, but he couldn't help himself. He headed down to the jail. He took the roundabout way, avoiding the traffic down on the north end of Market Street, taking the streets over Russian Hill, then dropping through the Tenderloin, past the single-occupancy hotels, old men out for the morning, ex-cons, a tired-looking prostitute with her blouse undone. The traffic thickened around the Civic Center, then he got tied up on Market, where a handful of protestors blocked the road, playing dodge with the police. He tapped on the steering wheel, waiting. It was going to be a long morning.

Mind your own business.

His father was right, he suspected, but Dante had never listened to the old man.

THREE

Earlier that same morning, Bill Owens had readied his kids for school. Since his wife was out of town, Owens himself had shaken the kids out of their beds and made their breakfast. Now he stuffed his son's backpack for school. It was a private school, and all the kids had packs like this, loaded down with books and projects and binders, so in the morning they looked as if they were on an expedition to the other side of the world.

His daughter, Kate, entered the room ready to go: fourteen years old, a thin, long-legged girl with her mother's smile—and some of her haughtiness as well.

"Dad," she said, "Zeke won't cooperate. He's only half-dressed—and we're going to be late."

"It's okay," Owens said. "Don't worry about it."

Owens heard her following behind him as he stepped outside, scanning the street. He was aware that the government was considering reopening the case against him, and a few weeks ago he had noticed a gray sedan tracking him sporadically. The car sat parked across the way.

"Dad . . ." she said again.

He saw the vulnerability in her eyes. She was a bright girl, and a year or so back he'd tried to explain to her what had happened long ago.

"I'll go get Zeke," he said.

Then his son appeared at the top of the stairs, ten years old, bent over a handheld video game. The three of them headed for the car.

O wens was in his early fifties, a soft-spoken man with sand-colored hair that didn't show the gray. He wore oval glasses and khakis. He had round shoulders, ordinary shoes. He had been notorious once upon a time—and still was, in some circles, for better or worse—but in truth he was not the kind of man whose looks drew your attention.

To the contrary, he was anonymous by nature. He had a certain blandness, a way of blending in without being seen. He knew this about himself, and when he was younger he had wanted it to be otherwise. At the moment, however, he felt about as conspicuous as could be. He was being watched, he knew, by the cops in the gray sedan.

Moe Jensen, his wife's partner, had told him not to worry.

"It's a cold case," Jensen had said just a few days before. "They don't have any evidence they didn't have thirty years ago."

Owens had known the attorney for a long time—longer than he'd known his wife. Though he trusted Jensen's assessment, Owens knew there were other forces in motion this time. The government's new antiterror laws gave the prosecutors leeway. Most of the agents from the old days were gone, true, but not Leonard Blackwell, who worked as a federal prosecutor now. He carried a special disdain for Owens.

Then there was Elise Younger, the dead woman's daughter. She'd been pushing to reopen the case for years. Pushing to the point of obsession. Once, maybe the year before last, he'd seen her lingering near his house.

The government sedan pulled out, following him. Owens watched the car in the rearview mirror.

"I swear," said Owen.

"No swearing, Dad," said Kate.

She smiled. It was a joke between them.

No swearing allowed.

In the backseat, Zeke sat engaged with his video game. The boy had anxiety issues and could be quick on the trigger. He was a smart kid, with deep brown eyes and a little bit of a stutter, and on account of his differences they had him in private school. The private-school kids, though, were mean as hell.

Money, privilege—all a ruse.

Owens drove up University heading toward the bridge. The gray sedan still lingered. Then a police cruiser pulled up from out of nowhere, it seemed, and rode Owens's bumper. Perhaps it was just coincidence, a cop working the morning traffic, pushy the way cops can be, but Owens didn't think so.

He had the impulse to pull over, to call their bluff. Or, instead, to yank the wheel and punch it down a backstreet.

Years ago, maybe he would have played such a game, but he had his kids with him now.

"When's Mom going to be back?"

"She'll call tonight."

"Can I call her now? On your cell?"

"Your mom's in court this morning. You know she is. I don't think she'll be picking up. She doesn't bring a phone into the courtroom."

"Can I call and leave her a message?"

He could feel his daughter, Kate, reading him, watching the way he moved. She saw his nervousness, and she glanced, too, at the cruiser behind. She was a precocious girl, more practical than her brother, and less temperamental—and a demon for the facts. She had been online these last few days, reading about the case, and he had not yet had the chance to reassure her.

People lied, he wanted to say. They distorted things to serve their purposes.

"Not now, honey," he said. "Now wouldn't be a good time to make a call."

All this time, Owens had one eye on the rearview. The light at Sixth turned yellow as he hit the intersection. He went on through and the cruiser followed. Two more squad cars waited at the foot of University, and they maneuvered behind him as he hit the ramp. The trailing car dropped off, swinging sidelong across the intersection. He was certain now of what was coming. That last maneuver had been designed to keep the civilian traffic from following.

At the top of the ramp, he spotted a couple of cruisers ahead, swung sideways, blocking his way.

He pulled to a stop.

The troopers waited on the other side of their cars, rifles propped over the hoods of their government issue Crown Victorias. Overdoing it, as usual, treating him like he was public enemy number one. Closer by, an officer with a semiautomatic stood on the other side of the guardrail, about ten feet away.

"Dad!"

His daughter's eyes opened wider, frightened. His son seemed absorbed in his Game Boy, still clicking, though with more rapidity.

Owens kept his hands on the wheel. "Don't worry," he said. "These are people I work with. This is a work thing, that's all."

An absurd thing to say, maybe—but there was a certain sense to it. He worked all day with criminals and police and attorneys and judges. So maybe it was true: This was just a work thing. Outside, behind them, a voice boomed over a patrol-car megaphone, telling Owens to get out of the car.

"He has a gun," said Zeke. The boy still hadn't looked up, and it wasn't clear if he referred to the video game or the man behind the guardrail.

Outside the car, behind them, the voice repeated its instructions.

Zeke twitched then, bending deeper over the game. Owens saw something flicker in the face of the man with the semiautomatic.

Owens got out of the car.

He stood with his hands extended in front of him. He stood there for what seemed like a very long time. He stood there with the guns pointed at him, and his kids fidgeting in the car. After a while, the two plainclothes emerged from the gray sedan: first, a square-shaped man in his midthirties; then the other, a Chinese woman, older, dressed all in blue.

Behind them he noticed a third man, watching with his hands on his hips. This one he recognized: Leonard Blackwell.

The man's hair had gone silver, a thick mien that gave him a dignified look, but Blackwell was an aggressive son of a bitch, Owens knew, a prosecuting attorney with a background in investigation who'd worked his way up out of the field. The man swaggered toward him like a cop in a movie who'd finally gotten his man.

"What's this about?"

"Took your time getting out of the car, didn't you?" said Blackwell.

"My kids, you're scaring the hell out of them."

"I want you to come over here with me. I want your ass over the hood of the car."

They marched him over to one of the cruisers. What happened next happened quickly. Owens heard the troopers behind him, moving in around his car—he caught a glimpse of his kids, of his daughter's face—before one of the troopers grabbed him from behind and pushed him spread-eagle over the cruiser. The cop pushed his face into the trunk and held him that way.

"Nose down."

He hoped his children could not see him. He imagined the pair of them, noses pressed up against the glass, watching while the big cop cranked back their father's arms and snapped on the cuffs.

"You thought this would never happen, didn't you?" said Blackwell.

"No," Owens said.

It didn't come out the way he meant.

"Never in a million years, you thought," said one of the others.

"No."

What Owens meant to say was, No, he had not imagined himself immune. He had in fact thought the opposite. Because he knew how the government could be. He had seen the feds go after people years after the fact. Just as they were coming after him now. He had feared this eventuality—while standing in line at the movie theater, in bed with his wife, in so many random moments. He feared not just for himself, but for his kids, his family. There'd been calls sometimes, cranks. Threats.

"Never in ten million, you thought, but here you are."

It wasn't Blackwell talking, but the other one, the younger plain-clothes. The voice had the same self-righteousness to it. A fury underneath. Owens didn't quite understand. From Blackwell, maybe. From someone who had been in the force at the time, associated with the case, this anger might make sense, but from the square-headed cop, too young to remember . . .

He supposed he should understand. He had been young once, full of fury. He had thought there existed a particular enemy you could identify. That you could pin down and destroy. And there were times, he had to admit, that he still felt that way.

This young cop . . . Blackwell . . . all these troopers . . . if the tables had been turned . . .

"Déjà vu, huh?" Blackwell said. "Do you ever think of her, that woman bleeding to death? Do you ever see her goddamn face?"

He heard a noise behind him. He heard his son yelp, maybe. And his daughter cry out. It was hard to tell. There was a traffic chopper overhead, gulls swarming. He strained to look at the kids but the cop pushed his face down into the hood.

Oh, Kate. Oh, Zeke.

He lay over the hood with his ass in the air while the cop patted him down, knife-handing between his legs, emptying his pockets. They took everything—his wallet, his cell.

When they let him up, he saw his kids had been taken from the car. They were being led down the ramp toward a cruiser below, patrolmen walking on either side and another following behind. Maybe his daughter had let out a cry, maybe his son had tried to pull away—but they seemed subdued enough now. His daughter glanced backward, but his son held the hand of one of the troopers.

Blackwell meanwhile rummaged the family sedan, pulling papers from the glove, a game disk from the door pocket, a tube of lipstick. The Chinese officer, the woman, stood next to Owens. Owens asked her name and she told him.

"I'd like to call someone," Owens said. "My wife is out of town, I'd like to make arrangements for the kids."

Leanora Chin was plainclothes, but the way she dressed, she might just as well have been in uniform. She wore blue, dark navy—a skirt the color of midnight and a blouse just as dark. Her hair was black, with streaks of white, and her eyes were gray. Though she dressed like a fed, she did not carry herself like one. She had the bearing of someone who'd been on the force a while.

"Their mother is out of town," he repeated. "I need to contact someone to pick them up from school." What he said next, he wanted to sound confident, but his voice cracked almost shamefully. "It will be unfortunate, you do the wrong thing with the kids. My lawyer . . ."

The woman bowed her head, and it occurred to him that they had known his wife was out of town, and they had chosen this time deliberately, because he would be with the kids, vulnerable, unable to run. And they could get a jump on the pretrial press.

Blackwell returned.

"Let me make a call."

"Why would we do that?" asked Blackwell.

"My boy has a medication issue."

"You can call after you've been booked. Put him inside."

The cops did as they were told, but from inside the cage Owens could see Chin and Blackwell conferring. Owens could see by the way they stood that there was a jurisdictional issue of some sort—there always was with cops—and it was clear Blackwell called the shots. He had been an investigative attorney in the feds' criminal division back then. Blackwell basically ran the office now, if you didn't count the appointed guy from Washington. It was unusual, maybe, an office man out on the arrest, but back then he had been made to look like a fool. Given all this, Leanora Chin must have said something persuasive—raising the specter of the press, maybe—because in a little while the troopers pulled him back out of the car, then rearranged the cuffs, so that he stood bound with his hands in front. The woman handed him his cell.

"One call," she said.

Owens flipped through the phone. His wife was in court, and he did not know how long before she would pick up a message. The same was true of Jensen. He considered his wife's sister, but she was an hysteric, and his brother, and the mothers of his kids' friends. But none of them would have the savvy to pull his kids out of the system.

There also among the names he found Dante Mancuso down at Cicero Investigations.

Mancuso had been to his house once. He had met the kids. Owens did not know him too well, it was true—a sad-eyed ex-cop like a thousand other sad-eyed ex-cops. With his own badgered history, and that impossibly long nose. But Mancuso would know how to get in touch with his wife, and with Jensen. More importantly, though, Owens had worked with him and knew how Mancuso was. Once a notion got hold of him, he had a hard time letting it go.

FOUR

Later that day, Dante found himself on the steps of the Burton Federal Building, on the wrong side of a concrete barrier. It was a low barrier, and he could see over it into the secured area, where the press had started to gather and a young man worked at setting up a microphone. Dante did not have press credentials, and so stood with some women from Code Pink, an antiwar group whose members wore pink T-shirts and black tights.

Earlier, the women had been gathered at the other side of the plaza, where the passing traffic could see their signs: NO BLOOD FOR OIL. NO WAR IN THE MIDEAST. They had been drawn across the square by the television cameras. There were some street people mixed in, yelling stuff just for the fun of it.

The cops were edgy.

It was the kind of job that made you edgy even under normal circumstances. With all the security measures, and the lack of personnel, everyone was working double shift. The public was full of fear, and the cops crankier than usual.

Anthrax in the post office. Poison gas at the Opera House. A terrorist lurking at the Golden Gate Bridge.

The anthrax turned out to be laundry detergent, the poison gas was a woman applying hairspray, and the terrorist was a park employee sneaking a cigarette.

Still, it all had to be investigated, and events like this, a simple press conference, once mundane, required a small army.

Dante himself had spent the morning down at the central jail. At the end of it, he'd learned the feds were keeping Owens under wraps until they could announce the arrest at a press conference. They wanted to make a show for the cameras.

So Dante had come down here to the Burton Building—a tallish, nondescript building, steel girders and blue glass, with a windy, anonymous plaza out front. The vehicle barricades had been put in a few months back to protect the entryway, and now a small group emerged from that entry, gathering in the secured area near a makeshift podium. Dante felt a twinge. He had made the walk from those glass doors to the podium once upon a time, when he'd been on the force, a young man on the cusp. It had not been so long ago, really. There were some new faces but some old ones as well, people with whom he was not on the best of terms. A phalanx of go-getters, in uniform and out. Leonard Blackwell stood at the center, and nearby, off to the side, was Leanora Chin, all in blue, hands crossed at the wrist.

In their midst, a thin, blonde woman—toward whom they were all being quite solicitous, as if she had been injured in some way—wavered from one foot to the other, leaning raillike into the wind. Accompanying the woman, standing close to her, was an older man, out of place with the others, whom Dante recognized despite the fact it had been many years.

Guy Sorrentino, from the neighborhood.

Sorrentino had been with the SFPD at one time, too, and like Dante he did investigative work now. He was some twenty years Dante's senior, but their tenure at the department had overlapped. A long time back, when Sorrentino was a young man and Dante just a boy, he had worked a couple summers for Dante's father down at the Mancuso warehouse.

What Sorrentino was doing here, Dante had no idea. He behaved toward the younger woman in a fatherly way, a hand on her forearm.

On account of the wind and the rustling of the crowd, Dante could not catch her name as she took the podium. She was in her late thirties, with a haircut that was not fashionable, at least not in San Francisco, the hair too high off the head, the blond a bit too much from the bottle. Not unattractive, but with a rawness about her that suggested the regions beyond the city, past the suburbs, where the land was flat and the sunlight caked with dust.

"I have just heard news I have been waiting a long time to hear. I talked to the U.S. Attorney's office here in San Francisco, to Mr. Blackwell . . . Twenty-seven years ago, in 1975, my mother was murdered during a bank robbery. She was shot down, while I waited in the car. I saw the ones responsible," she said. "I saw them leaving the bank. But I was young, and for reasons I have never understood, no arrests were made. Until today."

The woman was Elise Younger, Dante realized, the daughter of the woman who had been shot to death in the robbery out on Judah.

She'd seen the gang through the windshield of her mother's car: four of them in the parking lot—according to her story; and possibly a fifth, a female lookout sitting on a bench at the corner. One of the men had stripped off his mask as he came out of the bank. With the help of a police sketch artist, she'd identified that man as Bill Owens. But she'd been barely eleven years old, and there'd been other, contradictory evidence.

Elise's story—her long struggle to bring the case to court—had been in the papers off and on. She had been portrayed variously over the years: as an innocent victim, a person obsessed with justice; as a woman who had lost touch with reality, casting stones haphazardly, looking for someone to blame. Whose view of what happened was no more reliable now than it had been then. Even those law officials who sympathized—who remembered the case—had grown weary of her. On more than one occasion she had criticized the judges and lawyers, the prosecutors and politicians.

Some of these same people stood behind her on the podium now.

"My mother—" She hesitated. "My mother was just going to the bank—to cash her overtime check. My father had finally just gotten a job, too, our lives were turning for the good, and we were going to have a celebration. But all that changed, in one awful instant . . ."

The woman was not a professional orator, but she had an earnestness that was hard to resist. Still, there seemed something strained, a modulation not quite under control. When Elise Younger left the microphone, she appeared to buckle for an instant, her knees weakening, or maybe just her heel giving way, catching on the concrete. Sorrentino was quick to take her arm, and as he did so, Dante saw the disdainful glances of Blackwell and his assistant. Sorrentino did not have the grace of the others on the stage. He was a working-class guy under it all, with a jacket that wouldn't button and a misshapen hat. And the way he hurried to Elise Younger, there was something a little too hungry there.

Guy Sorrentino was in his sixties, a small man, thick through the shoulders. An ex-cop. He'd lived in the Beach in the old days, but had been pushed off the force. Or had pushed himself.

Truth was, Sorrentino's son had died during the First Gulf War, in the early nineties, and things had fallen apart for him after that.

So what was he doing here with Elise Younger?

At this point Blackwell himself took the podium. He did what prosecutors always do, avoiding the particulars of the case—or pretending to—so as not to jeopardize the trial, but at the same time letting the public know his people were on duty, getting results. Seeking publicity while not seeking. Getting the jump on the defense. "We can't talk specifically about this case, about any of the details, because we do not have the slightest intention to try this case in public. I will just say the simple fact, and that is: Earlier this morning, Bill Owens was served with a warrant for his arrest by officers Leanora Chin and Steve White."

Chin stood at his side, and everyone knew why. They wanted the Asian face in the camera.

The police were happy to oblige.

"But I would like to take this opportunity to make one thing clear. Law enforcement in San Francisco, together with federal officers and Homeland Security, are all committed to bringing terrorists to justice. No matter when the crime happened, no matter if the perpetrators walk among us, or on foreign soil. Decades might go by, but we will continue to be vigilant. We will find you."

In a little while, they opened it up to the press, and it was the usual dance, with reporters pressing for details, and the police having little to offer. It was the kind of conversation he'd heard so many times it was like a voice in his head. *Why now? Are there more arrests coming?*

How can you reconstruct this, after almost thirty years? As the questioning wore on, the Code Pink people began to wander away, back to their signs at the other end of the plaza.

Closer by, a woman cried out, "Fascists!" Then she yelled again, "Asshole pigs!"

She was not with the Code Pink people. Dante had seen her earlier, sitting on a mat just around the corner, an empty tin at her feet. Her hair was unkempt, and she yelled with both hands cupped around her mouth.

"Nine-eleven didn't happen! It's just an excuse to terrorize the people, to fill us with fear!"

Some of the Code Pink people started wandering back. Meanwhile Blackwell backed away from the mike. The press conference had ended. The woman continued yelling.

"Stooges . . . patsies. Don't you know it's just an excuse . . . ? It's oil they want, the oil . . . I have X-ray eyes, I see through you all . . ."

The group at the podium broke apart, heading back toward the building. A couple of the Code Pink women, sensing the police's impatience, stepped in front of the woman, so as to make it more difficult for the police to intervene. The Code Pink women made the police nervous. Many of them were well connected in social circles and had to be handled gingerly.

Dante separated himself from the scene. He wanted to talk to one of the arresting officers, hoping to find out what had become of Owens's children. At the entrance to the Burton Building, he got hung up in security, then caught sight of Leanora Chin leaving through an exit on the other side.

Chin walked briskly and he did not catch up with her until the corner, where she stood waiting for the light.

"Excuse me," he said.

She regarded him, businesslike in her blue skirt and blue jacket, her hair done up in a twist. Likely she didn't remember, but Dante had been in a room with her, maybe fifteen years back, when he was a young cop, at the North Beach Station. Back then she was a homicide cop with notoriety in the neighborhood for having arrested a local man accused of murdering his brother's wife.

"You're with the press?"

"No," he said. "I prefer not to talk with them if I can help it." He identified himself and handed her a card. "Bill Owens called me from the Bay Bridge this morning. And asked me to find his kids."

A couple of patrolmen on mop-up duty lingered up the block. Chin glanced their way, as if she might gesture them over if this man in front of her proved to be a nuisance.

"What did you say your name was?"

He repeated it. If it meant anything to her, she did not show it. She was with San Francisco Homeland, he knew—a division carved up out of the local police force and given federal money. Before Homeland, she had been with Special Investigations. Dante had gotten involved with SI in the past—an ugly business, undercover, growing out of his time in New Orleans. All buried deep in the files. Or it was supposed to be, anyway. Even so, there were other reasons the San Francisco cops didn't care for him. If she knew anything about any of this, it didn't show in her face.

"The kids . . ." he said again.

She stepped back, appraising him, and Dante became aware of the patrolmen still back there, hovering.

"I was occupied with the arrest. At the scene, we allowed the subject to make a call, but apparently he was having trouble with his phone. So I turned the children over to the care of one of the patrolmen on the scene."

"Do you know his name?"

"My understanding, the officer took them to school."

"School?"

"The officer drove them to their school. It was either take them home, or to the station—and the girl wanted to go to school."

Chin smiled, a faint smile, as if bemused or troubled, he could not be sure. Whatever was on her mind, she was not going to reveal it, not to him. The conversation was over. The light changed again, and Chin crossed the street.

The patrolmen followed him for a little while, coincidence maybe, or just for the hell of it, because they'd seen him at the press conference, maybe, then later, talking to Chin. Dante didn't take it personally. Around the corner, now, Dante came across the woman who had been heckling the press conference in front of the Federal Building. She sat cross-legged on her mat on the sidewalk, the tin can pushed foward. Up close, he could see the pockmarks on her face and something off-kilter in her eyes. She had a vague resemblance to his mother.

He put a dollar in her can.

"Pig," she said. "You think I don't see through you, but I do. I know a goddamn pig when I see one."

FIVE

Dante and Marilyn had had no plans for today, not really. Just to sleep late and maybe wander out to lunch.

The night before, Marilyn's dreams had been erotic.

When she woke up, though, Dante hadn't been there. She remembered his returning, she thought—his shadow splitting the gray light over the bed, his weight in the bed beside her, his lips on her cheek—but perhaps she had been mistaken. Perhaps it had been part of her dreams.

There was no sign of him.

For all she knew, Dante was still out on surveillance. Or perhaps he was in that room he kept for himself ever since his father passed, down on Columbus Avenue. Or down at his father's old house on Fresno Street, empty now that the tenants had moved out.

She and Dante had been talking about what to do with the house. They had been talking about going to Europe. They had been talking about their future.

About a lot of things.

She went to check for messages, to find out where he might be, but the cell rang in her hand. It was Beatrice Prospero. Marilyn worked for Beatrice's father down at Prospero Realty.

"Something has come up," Beatrice said. "So now there is going to be an empty plate at Il Cenacolo this afternoon. I can't make it. You know Pop, how he hates empty plates."

Il Cenacolo. The Inner Circle.

Il Cenacolo was an Italian group that met for lunch every week down at Fior d'Italia. Old men, mostly—but old men with money, and Joe Prospero went to their lunches regularly.

"They are going to have entertainment. Susan Ford is going to be there," she said. "The opera singer."

"Is she going to sing for them?"

"A little bit, after lunch."

Marilyn laughed.

"What's so funny? The man who arranged the opera singer, his name is David Lake. His wife died recently . . . and he has property to divest. Very wealthy."

Marilyn understood the opportunity. These were potential clients, men with real estate. Joe Prospero liked to schmooze, but he didn't sit on houses anymore, not at his age, and Beatrice could not handle every listing.

"I have to call Dante."

"Have you got something planned?" she asked. "You have your boyfriend now, so you don't care about Il Cenacolo? You don't care about old men with money?"

"It isn't that."

"Okay," said Beatrice. "I'll tell Pop you don't want to go."

"Of course I'll go."

"Pop won't be mad if you want to throw this chance in his face," said Beatrice, in that tone of voice she had sometimes, walking the edge, so that it was hard to tell if she was joking or being sly. "Don't worry. It's no problem, you treat my father like that."

"I will go. I want to go."

"You want to go?"

"Yes."

"Then put on the dog. A little heel, a little gloss," she said. "The old men like it when you dress up."

The men who crowded the bar at Fior d'Italia did not seem as old to Marilyn as she had thought they might be. Most of them were of another generation, it was true, twenty, thirty years older then herself—gray hair, dark suits, the smell of worsted wool and shoe polish—but they did not seem so old to her as they might have at one time, nor did their age seem quite so unattractive. Perhaps because Marilyn was getting older herself. Or because she did not have, quite as much as some women, an aversion to older men.

Joe Prospero, Beatrice's father, was there at the bar, standing in the midst of them, carrying on in the way that he did.

Her own father had never been part of Il Cenacolo. Whether that was because he had not been interested, or because he had not been asked, she didn't know, but her mother had been Jewish on one side, a German Jew, only half Italian, and that may have been part of it.

But things there were different now, or so they said.

Either way, there were people she knew here, people who had known her parents, and who had known her as a child. For a second she had the impulse to turn heel. She tugged on her blouse, aware of herself in her black skirt, her heels. A man at the end of the bar regarded her. He wore a white shirt and sat a little apart from the others, and the seat next to him appeared to be empty.

"Ah, Marilyn," said Joe Prospero, coming up from behind.

Prospero was somewhere in his seventies and moved in a way that might be described as spry. He had started his real estate firm when he was a young man, and most of the North Beach Italians had done business with him at one point or another.

"This is Marilyn, Joe Visconti's girl, you remember her?" Prospero said.

She shook hands all around. These were people whose essence she recognized not by their faces so much as by their slouch, their smell. Their features she did not recognize until she peered beneath the wrinkles. Then the names came. Frank Besozi and Al Capricio. Liz Francesa and her brother Steve. Nan and Jimmi Tucci. She worked her way through the crowd to the innermost of the inner circle, at which point there was no one at all, just herself, turning one way and then another, standing alone, regarding the newcomers lingering by the wall—the Johnsons and O'Haras and Steins—who maybe were Italian on one side; or had married an Italian; or in some cases, because times had changed, were not Italian at all.

Now Nan Tucci peered into her face.

"Ah, yes, the Goat Girl," said Nan Tucci.

Again with the name. Because Marilyn once upon a time had held the goat by the bridle in the Columbus Day parade.

Marilyn felt her smile tighten. She had never liked the moniker, but more than that she saw in Nan Tucci's face a certain light, a glee. Nan had always been a gossip. They were all gossips. They used to talk about her mother in the old days, she knew, but now she supposed the gossip was about herself. Rumors about how she had gotten along after her parents' deaths. Rumors about how she had managed to support herself, and about the lovers she had taken.

She looked back at the bar.

The man in the white shirt was still there—his eyes skitted away—but in the seat next to him now was Tony Mora. Mora was an estate attorney—a younger, ambitious man whom Marilyn had dated once upon a time.

Mora gestured at her, motioning her over. Prospero saw the gesture, too. He was a bit drunk and put his arm around her.

"Don't talk to Tony Mora, you're my girl now," said Prospero, laughing. "My new girl."

Prospero didn't mean anything by the remark, probably; it was just the kind of thing he said sometimes. Or if he did mean anything, it didn't matter, because he was too old to pay any mind. Besides, she liked the old man. True, he was a fool, and he got excited for no reason, but maybe this was a good thing. Apparently Nan Tucci didn't see it that way. She cut her eyes and turned her back. The woman had something else to talk about now.

Across the room Tony Mora went on smiling. He gave her another wave, gesturing her down his way. Marilyn did not really want to talk to Mora, but she did not want to be impolite—and he was sitting next to the other man, the one who had been regarding her. Tony wore a cashmere polo, thin cut. He was always like that, in love with clothes, in love with himself. The other man was, in comparison, downscale. Just a white shirt, gray slacks. A suit coat draped over his chair.

He wore a Rolex, though, and imported shoes. Up close, his looks were ordinary. He carried, though, a sweetness in his eyes.

She thought of Dante and wondered why he had not called.

"David made the arrangements for our entertainment today," said Tony. "You know David Lake, I assume? He's an opera hound."

"I haven't had the pleasure," she said.

Marilyn realized this was the man Beatrice had mentioned, whose wife had just died. He'd been rich from the beginning, Beatrice said, but his wife, a Getty, had been even richer. David Lake was younger than she had expected, and she caught him, now, studying her hand as they talked, looking for the ring.

"Verdi?"

"Not really," he said. "Wagner."

"David has a box," said Tony. "He's taken Lydia and I, on several occasions."

"You and Lydia—how nice."

"Yes. Myself and Lydia. We were going to Greece this summer, but now, with all the trouble abroad, we'll have to do something closer to home."

"Oh."

"And what is it that brings you to Il Cenacolo?" asked David Lake.

"I work with Joe Prospero."

"Real estate?"

She nodded. "May I ask you, is the singer here?"

"She has been delayed."

Just then, though, as if on cue, there came a fuss from behind, the group grew more animated, and Marilyn realized the opera singer had arrived. David Lake arose, Tony following, and Marilyn expected this would be the last she would see of them. A moment later, however, after he had done the introductions, David Lake came back to her. When it was time to go to the banquet room, he stuck close by.

Fior d'Italia was the oldest Italian restaurant in the country, or so it claimed—a place done up in the old fashion, with heavy tables and ornate crockery. Il Cenacolo had been meeting here for so long that a banquet room had been named for them. The room held two long tables, and on the walls hung pictures of the club going back to the early days, men elbow-to-elbow at these same long tables, napkins stuffed into their collars.

There hung as well pictures of people who had spoken here. Caruso. And DiMaggio. Marconi and Antonietta Stella. And others, perhaps not so well esteemed. Ettore Patrizi, the editor of *L'Italia*, imprisoned for sedition. Rossi, whose son had been taken away for raiding the city treasury. But they were up there anyway, along with Mayor Moscone and Alioto and all the rest.

When the food came, it was heavy, old-school stuff. David Lake leaned over to her.

"I am selling one of my houses. Looking to simplify," he said. His smile was awkward. "You perhaps would like to take a look at the listing?"

"If you would like. Of course."

The others were watching the way he leaned toward her. There would be more talk now. They would go backward in time, talking her over. How she'd been going out with Dante's cousin—when was it, fifteen years ago?—then had switched from one Mancuso to another. How Dante himself had disappeared, down in New Orleans. There were rumors about that, too, and what he had been doing—government work, some said, security—no, drugs, guns, smuggling. While he was gone there had been a string of other men. Young men, old men. Men with money. When you got down to it, she was an opportunist, they said. Or so she imagined them saying. A little plumper than she used to be, though. Looser in the chin.

Now here she was back with Dante. No ring on her finger. Not getting any younger. And her eyes still roving.

Susan Ford, the soprano, sat at the far side of the table alongside

Joe Prospero. The old man was enjoying himself, and the singer was effervescent. Every once in a while her eyes cut toward David Lake. It was apparent that the singer had not expected it to go this way. She had expected to be sitting next to a wealthy widower, yes, but not one so old as Joe Prospero.

It was a meal with many courses, and halfway through, the waiter circled the table, head bowed, as if looking for someone. Prospero gestured in Marilyn's direction.

The waiter came to her.

"There is someone to talk to you."

"Me?"

"In the main dining room, at the bar."

When she saw him, Marilyn felt her heart pull in two directions. It was not like Dante to come searching for her like this. She could see at a glance that he had not slept the night before. He had sharp features, dark eyes, and those eyes seemed even darker now. She liked how he looked, standing alone, waiting for her, handsome and disheveled at the bar—and she liked that he was pursuing her. Even so, she was not yet ready to leave.

"So you want me to go with you. To the school?"

"I think it would be better if it wasn't just me. If there was a woman along."

"I'm not dressed for kids."

It was true. She wore heels and a silk blouse and a skirt slit to the knees. She could not see herself walking into the office of the private school, past all those mothers in the car line.

"Owens's kids'll remember you, from the time we were out at their house. The girl, Kate, you two went for that walk."

"Can this wait?"

"It will be too late."

"Someone else will take care of them. Some friends of theirs."

"I don't think that's a good idea. I managed to get through to Jill Owens, out in Chicago," he said. "They've gotten some ugly calls in the past. I don't think it's anything to worry about, but . . . it might not be a good idea to rely on neighbors."

She saw the weariness in his face. It wasn't like Dante to get her involved in his work, and she figured it was on account of his weariness—and because he could not imagine himself spending the evening alone in Owens's house with the children. She found it hard to imagine, too. She remembered the feeling she had had this morning, not knowing if she had dreamed his presence or if he had been in the bed beside her.

The darkness that emanated from him was too much at times, but she did not like it when he was gone. She did not like lying in bed alone.

"But the kids, they don't know either of us. Not really."

"I know."

"You haven't gotten any sleep," she said.

She reached out and touched his nose. It was in some ways a monstrosity, that nose of his—a handsome monstrosity, from his mother's side of the family. It was the kind of nose you saw in the old pictures, the old Italians, but not so much anymore. It drew attention, sometimes; people stared, pointed, kids laughed. Old women reached out to touch him. Younger women looked him up and down—and sometimes looked again. There was something she liked about the way they would look at him. It excited her—and made her want to keep him for herself.

"I have to go tell Prospero. I shouldn't just walk out."

But it wasn't only Prospero she was thinking about, it was the other man, too, David Lake, a potential client, after all. And as she headed toward the banquet room, she was already taking the business card out of her purse, imagining how she would touch him on the arm when she said good-bye, how his eyes would follow her as she left.

Inside the banquet room, the soprano rose toward the microphone. Marilyn said her good-byes quickly. The sound of the woman's voice, high and tremulous, stayed with her, as Dante held open the door at the front of the restaurant, and as they headed together across the square.

SIX

The Owens's house was across the bay, on Shale Street, at the base of the Oakland Hills. Farther up those hills, the houses were larger, more modern, but the Owens's place stood in the old part of the neighborhood, a two-story bungalow with a wall of bamboo alongside. It had a craftsman porch and a big window and a hedge of wild roses out front.

The business at the school office, picking up the kids, had been somewhat strained. The kids had been subdued on the drive over, sitting up unnaturally straight, knees together. As they walked inside the house, Dante noticed Owens's daughter, Kate: how her lips had started to tremble.

"We'll order pizza," said Marilyn.

"Mom's on the plane?"

"Yes," said Dante. "Otherwise, she would call."

The last time Dante had talked to their mother, she had been on the jetway, headed for the plane. She couldn't get a direct flight out of Chicago, but was being routed instead through Atlanta with a stopover in Denver. The connections were tight, though. She might not have time to call between flights. If everything went well, she would be back in Oakland around dawn.

After the six o'clock news, the house phone started to ring. Most of the calls came from friends expressing concern, but others were strangers, crackpots with an agenda, and one of these let loose with the opinion that Owens had at last gotten what he deserved. After this, Dante adjusted the machine so the calls went straight to message.

Kate left the television and bolted upstairs to her room.

Dante glanced at Marilyn. "Maybe you should talk to her. Get her mind on something else."

"That won't be easy to do," said Zeke. He was playing with the game device and watching a rerun at the same time. "She's obsessive."

A little while later, Dante stepped outside to take a look around. The house had a wraparound porch, so the main entrance actually faced the side, abutting a smaller street, an alley of sorts. A bamboo hedge surrounded the yard, a privacy hedge—but that worked both ways, allowing an intruder to make his way around the property unobserved from the street. The gables were low as well, the lattice work was sturdy and easy to climb, and the boy's bedroom was on the first floor, overlooking the backyard. Outside, beyond the hedge, a car drove past the house. Dante listened as it made the turnaround at the top, then returned the way it came. Likely it didn't mean anything. There was a traffic divide down below, and it was easy to go the wrong way: to end up on Shale Street, when what you wanted to do was drive on up into the hills.

Back inside, the television had been left on, but the room itself was abandoned. Dante found the kid Zeke in his room at the back of the house with the door open—a skinny, loose-limbed boy with his father's looks. At the moment, he played a video game that involved crawling through underground caves and killing men in gray uniforms.

"It takes my mind off things."

"How's your sister?"

"Still upstairs." He shrugged. "My sister likes the Internet. That's the way she relaxes, but I prefer this. The Internet, you run into news, child molesters—that kind of thing. I'm not into that stuff."

"Your father's okay," Dante said all of a sudden. "You don't have to worry."

"How do you know?"

"Some people I know—on the force."

It was a lie. No doubt Owens was alone in an eight-by-twelve, nothing to do but sit on the bunk with his head in his hands. No doubt he'd been pushed and badgered all day and now lay there in his darkened cell, wondering if he'd ever get out. The kid, meanwhile, seemed to understand he was being humored, but did not challenge him.

"I know what happened back then," Zeke said. "I know a woman was killed, but that happened a long time ago. And my father, he wasn't even there." The boy went on with his game, nimble-fingered, deft with the controls, but at the same time the ends of his fingers were raw, Dante noticed, the nails ragged, bitten to the quick. The kid had already polished off the enemies in the cave and was on his way to the next level. "It could be the woman deserved it, too," he said. "That's always a possibility."

Zeke glanced up at Dante through his glasses, hopeful, eyes wide, magnified by the lenses, innocent, and Dante found himself tempted to say, yes, maybe it was so, the woman had deserved to die.

Instead, he ruffled the kid's head.

"I'm going to go check on the girls."

Upstairs, Dante found Marilyn in the master bedroom, lying on the bed. Kate's door was closed.

"She wants to be left alone," Marilyn said. "But she's asked me if I would sleep up here. In her parent's room."

The Owens's bedroom looked comfortable, he had to admit. The bed had a colorful quilt and more pillows than anyone could need. Dante still had not had a chance to sleep since his surveillance the night before, and he felt weariness overcoming him. He went to the window overlooking the street. It was a pretty street, the kind of street people want to live on. Another car pulled up into the twilight, negotiated the turnaround, then went down the way it had come.

Dante felt a sense of foreboding. *La Segazza,* his grandmother had called such feelings, half mocking. The wisdom. It was her name for a particular kind of intuition, but he, himself, at the moment, didn't feel particularly wise.

There were photos on the walls, on the dresser. Owens and Jill on their wedding day. Kate on a pony. At a school play. A family vacation somewhere. Owens and Zeke at the ballpark, caps twisted sideways on their heads.

"Did you lock up?"

"Yes."

"Then lie down."

"I should probably take the couch downstairs," he said. "It makes me uneasy, the boy down there by himself."

"In a minute," she said. "Just rest."

"Their mother must have caught the plane. Otherwise she would have called."

"Unless they arrested her, too."

"There's no reason for them to do that."

"Just lie down."

She ran her fingers down his cheek; she petted his nose. Dante closed his eyes. She took his hand, and the two of them just lay there, very quiet, saying nothing. Despite the circumstances, there was something comforting in it, just lying on the bed, here beside Marilyn. The window was open, and he could hear the evening sounds—but also a vague whispering, as of someone talking just out of range. But when he listened more closely, the sound went away.

"In the pictures, they all seem so wholesome."

"The boy, he likes his device."

"Why are they going after Owens now, after all this time?"

"The woman's daughter. That's part of it. And the feds—they've got a campaign on."

"Do you think he's guilty?"

Dante didn't know the answer, not for sure. Owens's history, and his relationship to the old leftist underground—it was complicated business, as this stuff tended to be, full of names and interconnections that shifted continually, and it was hard to ascertain truth from rumor. There were a few things, though, of which he was fairly certain. He knew Owens and his first wife had worked as legal-aid volunteers out at the prison and were later convicted of aiding in the escape of Leland Sanford, an Oakland stick-up artist who'd gotten a political education in prison. Sanford had hooked up with the Symbionese Liberation Army after he was out, the SLA—the radical group that kidnapped the newspaper heiress Patty Hearst, demanding ransom money from her father to feed the poor.

Old stuff now, newsreel footage, dragged up out of the archives on account of the terror scare. Not too many people remembered the details, but it had been everyday news then, a media circus that made the feds look bad.

Eventually, most of the SLA had died in a shootout with the police down in Los Angeles. There'd been trouble identifying the bodies afterward, some kind of anomaly in the dental records. So the police could not be sure, absolutely, that Sanford was dead—and he'd become a kind of legendary figure on account of it.

You still saw posters of him, sometimes, down in the Haight— collector's items, for those who cared about such things: the radical in his paisley shirt and his beret with a carbine strapped across his chest.

After the shootout in Los Angeles, there had been a series of robberies attributed to the surviving members of the SLA. It was during the last of these that Eleanor Younger had been killed. But Owens's exact relationship to all of this, and exactly how closely he'd been tied to the revolutionary underground . . .

"It was a long time ago," said Dante. "I don't know what kind of case they can make now."

They lay there for a little while, saying nothing. Marilyn leaned over him then and kissed him on the mouth. Her face was flushed and pretty. He reached up to unbutton her blouse.

"Not now."

He put his hand between her legs.

"Not now," she whispered again, teasing him, tongue in his ear.

"When?"

"Soon."

She pulled away.

"Where are you going?"

"To check on the kids."

She was right, of course. Now was not the time, not here on the Owens's bed. Even if he had not been so sleepy.

He closed his eyes.

When he awoke, it was with a start. The room was dark, and Marilyn lay sleeping next to him.

It was past midnight.

It happened sometimes that Dante woke up in this manner, startled out of sleep for no apparent reason, and found himself suddenly sitting bolt upright on the mattress. His jumpiness went back to his time with the company down in New Orleans—those gray years after he'd left the force. He had been involved, seen things, done things—operating in a murky continuum, government approved—that ended badly. That affiliation had ended, or so he liked to tell himself, when he'd returned to San Francisco for his father's funeral. He had developed certain instincts—but as often as not his tuning was too fine. Waking at a shift in the floorboards, a surge in the power.

The light in the hall was off. The girl's door remained as it was, still closed, and so Dante listened from outside, not wanting to wake her, instead waiting until he heard her stir, turning in her sleep. Downstairs, he found the boy's door wide open.

The kid lay on top of the bed, asleep in his clothes.

Dante checked the locks again, examining the yard from the windows. Then he lay on the couch in the television room. The volume had been turned low, and he wondered if this might have been the sound he had heard earlier, coming through the grates upstairs. The station was set to CNN and the news played nonstop. The enemy was on the run in Afghanistan, or so they said, and American troops were gathering in Kuwait. The experts had things to say, almost audible: *conspiracy within conspiracies . . . 9/11 . . . Al Qaeda . . . terrorists in Miami . . .*

Dante turned off the television. He dimmed the lights. Given how little he'd slept these last few days, it should have been easy to fall asleep, but when he closed his eyes, he still heard those voices, it seemed, whispering in the dark.

His cell rang at just past four in the morning. Jill Owens had arrived at the Oakland Airport. She was just at that moment climbing into a taxi, she said, and would be home within half an hour.

"Are the kids awake?"

"No," Dante said.

No sooner had he spoken, though, then he heard Zeke rummaging in the back. Likely he had been awakened by the phone.

"Let them be. I'll be quiet when I come in."

Dante could see the boy had no intention of going back to bed. He came out holding his video game and sat on the couch, leaning his head against Dante's shoulder. He stayed that way until his mother came in the door, smelling of the airplane, red-eyed, tired, full of indignation, fury, and shame. Dante watched the woman struggle to keep all those feelings off her face as she greeted her son. She was a tawny-haired woman in her early forties who had met Owens in her last year at law school. Now she gathered the boy into her skirt, cooing—but she could not keep her anger from hissing out.

"Those sons of bitches," she said. "Those goddamn sons of bitches. This is all Blackwell."

She petted the boy as she spoke, and he nuzzled closer, understanding the anger was directed elsewhere maybe, at the vague forces outside the house—though he glanced up sheepishly for an instant, as if not quite sure. Something in Zeke's expression—the blue eyes, the sudden vacantness—reminded Dante of the boy's father. "The police could have picked Bill up at home, they could have done this a hundred other ways. The people downtown, the DA's office—they know Moe, they know me. They know Bill's line of work. They could have told us in advance and made arrangements. But Blackwell wanted his moment. Grandstanding for the press."

No doubt there was some truth in what she said. The government wanted a jump on the pretrial publicity—to cast the case in the public eye. It was also true, though, that Owens had gone fugitive in the past.

"Bill is innocent. All of this, it has nothing to do with what actually happened back then. The whole point—it's politics. The government doesn't want anyone arguing with them, past or present. It's a way of disrupting our legal practice. Because we defend certain kinds of people. Because the government wants a free hand . . . That woman, Elise Younger, she hired an investigator."

"Sorrentino?"

"Yes, that's the one."

Dante had met Jill Owens once before—that evening here at the house—and she had seemed like a different person, her hazel eyes full of light and confidence. A bit smug about her politics, self-assured, in love with her husband, her kids, dedicated to her work, obsessive, insistent upon its importance, though admitting, too, that some of the people she helped defend, these days, you wouldn't want to bring home.

Now her face was puffy, her hair in a ruff. Her son gazed up toward her. "I want you to remember this," she said to him. "It's how they work. It's how they run us down."

The daughter appeared on the stairs, Marilyn just behind. Kate faltered a moment at the bottom step, her precociousness stripped away: thin and rangy in her nightshirt, only half-awake, regarding them all with a surliness of the type teenage girls usually reserved for their mothers. Then she started to weep. "Come here, darling," said Jill. "Your father's a good man. We are not going to let this happen. Your father will be home in a couple of days. We are not going to let those people do this to us." She rocked the girl back and forth and looked up at Dante. "Bill trusts you," she said. Outside, a car negotiated the turn-around. The passing light rose and fell through the big window overlooking the porch. "When he posts bail, we will have a get-together for the defense. All of his supporters, here. You'll come, won't you? You and Marilyn?"

"Of course," said Dante.

The car was gone now, the headlights passed. The bamboo rustled in the long shadows by the fence.

When Dante and Marilyn drove home that morning, it was just past dawn. There was extra security at the bridge—police and fire vehicles flanking the sides and emergency workers everywhere in yellow slickers. There was a line at the toll longer than made any sense.

A bomb on the bridge . . . an abandoned pickup truck . . . unauthorized personnel on the catwalks . . . On the radio, a talk-show host repeated rumors picked up by callers off the citizens band. The rumors were repeated by the men inside the traffic copters, then retracted, and later repeated like words in a dream.

A policewoman in yellow gear waved them through.

It was a damp morning, and on the other side of the bridge, in San Francisco, there was an antiwar vigil going on. Protestors dressed in skeleton suits. Death masks. Angels holding swords. Sheets covered with blood.

Don't fight their war.

Women on their knees, over dead children.

Or these were the images in Dante's head, later, as he tumbled toward sleep, in Marilyn's bed. He nuzzled up close to her. Over the mudflats, the sky was gray. The flocks were diminishing, wheeling away. His grandmother had once told him the story of the fishermen who lived with the pelicans out in the Calabrian rocks . . . the fishermen, with the big noses, who followed the birds out to sea. Birds who lived in the rocks, birds with brown eyes, beaks in the shape of fish, shoulders hunched like peasants.

Marilyn ran her fingers over his nose. She grabbed his dick.

When she touched him, he forgot about the birds. He forgot about Owens, in his orange suit down at the Hall of Justice. He forgot about the little boy with his raw fingers and his weeping teenage sister, and forgot, too, the woman who'd been shot to death in the bank.

"Let's go somewhere far away," said Marilyn.

"Okay."

She blew in his ear. The sound of it was like the sound of the ocean inside a seashell.

"Don't leave me," she said. "Promise me."

"I won't."

"Promise me you'll love me forever."

"I will."

They made love. Afterward, she got up and checked her answering machine. There was a man's voice on it. Dante thought he heard the faintest wistfulness in that voice, or that's how he would remember it later. But he could not be sure. Because he was already on the shore again, out on the mudflats. The skies were empty, and the tide was rolling in.

PART TWO

The Explosion

SEVEN

As of yet, Guy Sorrentino was not concerned with Dante
Mancuso. There was no reason why he should be. He had
known Dante, from their time on the force, and it was true
their paths had intertwined briefly. It was true, too, that they were
about to get intertwined again, but neither man knew this yet.

Whatever violence lay ahead—whatever enmity—neither man
was aware.

Maybe Sorrentino, himself, had felt a flash of recognition when
he'd seen the hawk-nosed man milling around in the crowd in front
of the Federal Building. But he had not put the face with the name,
and had no way of knowing that Dante might have a connection
with the Younger case.

And the Younger case was the only thing Sorrentino was concerned with these days.

Sorrentino had met Elise Younger three years ago. She was like a
daughter to him, and it was on account of her he pursued the case.

Or so he told himself.

It was on account of her, on account of the case, that he had been fishing around North Beach these last few months. It was on account of the case that he'd left his apartment in San Bruno this morning and drove down to the Serafina Café. The café was a place from his past, down in the old neighborhood, and he would not have gone there, he told himself, if not for the case.

These days, down at Serafina's, the television played continuously above the bar. It was an older television, a cathode-ray tube with a convex surface. It had been hooked up to cable somehow, but the color was off, and the picture had a glassy, funhouse look.

Stella, the owner, had put it up there a few years back.

Her husband would never have agreed, Sorrentino knew. People didn't come to watch television, he would say, they came to talk, to eat—but things were different now. Stella's husband was dead, and it wasn't the old days anymore. The Serafina's clientele had always been from the neighborhood, and they were getting old, their numbers dwindling, here on the border of Chinatown and Little Italy. Those who came now were mostly from streets close by—old Italians who lived in the Florence Hotel or the apartments above Columbus. There were some who still came down from Telegraph, but it was not an easy walk down the hill. If you had the money for a taxi, then you would not eat at Serafina's anymore.

Stella's husband may not have approved of the TV, but things had changed. Stella had to compete with the bar around the corner and also with the flophouse lobbies.

It wasn't the old days, no.

It wasn't like when Rossi was mayor, and people lined up in the streets smoking cigars. Not like when they had fresh tomatoes delivered every day, and you could smell the produce in the trucks as they went by the orchards of San Jose, the cherries and the prune plums, and also the broccoli from San Bruno.

But people did not grow broccoli in San Bruno anymore. As far as Sorrentino could tell, there was no such thing as prune plums.

When Sorrentino walked in, the regulars did not pay him much mind. Or it did not seem so to him. A couple of old men sat at a table by the wall, and they glanced up at him the way they might glance at anyone. Maybe they paid him some mind, maybe they didn't. There was an old bastard who kept his eyes on him, and an old woman who whispered to herself, and some shadows at a table in the back, but Sorrentino didn't recognize anyone, at least not from what he'd seen so far, and he assumed it was similar the other way around. When he sat down, Stella peered across the counter at him.

"Guy," she said.

He started to smile but knew better. There was nothing like joy in her face.

"Spaghetti."

She nodded and walked away. Ten years since his last visit, and that's all it came down to. He was sixty-one now, and Stella was seventy. They had grown up in the neighborhood, and he remembered when she'd been a blousy young woman standing around with her thick brown hair at her father's produce stand. Sorrentino had known her husband. He'd gone to her wedding and to her husband's funeral. She'd been there, too, when Sorrentino had put his own son in the ground—and this was what it came down to: Stella walking back to the kitchen wearing a dress like his grandmother used to wear. Then returning with a plateful of noodles and sauce.

"Wine?"

"No. I don't drink anymore."

"Some people can't take it, I guess."

"No. Some of us can't."

Sorrentino had left the SFPD not long after his divorce. His wife had said the divorce was on account of his drinking, but the truth was that after their son had died, he didn't have much stomach for his wife anymore. Nor she for him.

The boy had been killed when his truck toppled over on some road in Kuwait, some weeks after the fighting had ended, in the aftermath of the First Gulf War.

There was a photo of his boy along Stella's counter, under glass on the countertop along with photos of lots of other people from the neighborhood. He knew the exact place where the picture lay, farther up along the counter, but he didn't glance toward it, and neither did Stella.

That wasn't why he had come.

Very faintly, as if in the distance, he heard Chinese music, a pop song, and also the sound of running water, dishes rattling. Sorrentino wanted to talk to Stella, but she had her back to him now.

The old ones watched the television. It was way up in the corner and the sound was off, but they watched anyway. On screen, firemen were digging out the rubble at Ground Zero in New York. The World Trade Center had gone down some time ago, a little more than a year now. It looked like old footage but you couldn't be sure, and anyway the media liked to show it over and over. And the faces had started to become familiar. Like they were people Sorrentino knew out there doing the digging. Then the scene switched and switched again. Other parts of the world, men being held hostage. Then bombs—artillery in the desert. Protestors in a European city, upset over the expanding American retaliation—but then, no, this last scene was here.

Downtown San Francisco.

Local jackasses. A-number-one idiots. Wise guys against the war.

"It's over." The man who said this was old, maybe a million years. Maybe a hundred million. He sat with another old man at the table by the wall.

Sorrentino did not recognize either man at first, but the longer he looked, the more he began to see something familiar about the pair—their faces before gravity had lengthened their chins, before the moles had grown ulcerous, when the skin was still tight and there was not so much hair growing from the nostrils and the ears. The older of the two men wore a black shirt. He coughed and lit a Pall Mall.

Johnny Pesci, he remembered. And the other one—George Marinetti. Pesci was Marinetti's uncle, something like that, and the two were always arguing. Together, they looked as if they'd crawled up out of the crypt.

"It's over," Pesci said again.

At a table nearby sat Julia Besozi. Guy recognized her now as well. She wore a hairnet, with blacking on the scalp underneath, like the old women used to do when their hair thinned. She sat alone, sipping tea, legs crossed, wilting into the wallpaper.

She smiled. Her eyes were black like pebbles.

Meanwhile Stella had retreated into the kitchen. You could hear the Chinese dishwasher in the back, laboring in the sink. You could hear him humming along with the radio and dishes clattering in the background. Then he dropped a dish, and you could hear Stella scolding him in Italian.

It was an old routine. Stella enjoyed it, yelling at the Chinaman. It went on for a while and then there was silence.

In the recesses of the café, in a rear booth, one of the shadows moved. Franceso Zito, he thought. Mollini. Ettore Patrizi. Or men who resembled them. Sorrentino remembered obituaries, but maybe he had been mistaken. Or maybe not. Maybe they *were* dead. They raised the grappa to their lips and grunted, but that didn't prove anything either way.

"It's over," said Pesci.

"What's over?" Marinetti wanted to know.

"The whole business. America—all of it."

"I don't see how you can say that."

"They should beat their heads in."

"Whose heads?"

"All of them. All their heads."

"That's not a thing to say."

"Once upon a time, things were not this way."

"'Once upon a time,' what does that mean? When was that, anyway, once upon a time?"

"It's not now."

"When . . ."

"They should beat them on their heads."

"Once upon a time, they should beat them on their heads. This is what you mean, once upon a time?"

"Once upon a time, this was not permitted. You have to lay down the law."

"Don't fool yourself, there's plenty of beating going on now. Everywhere, people are getting beaten."

During this, old lady Besozi was sitting there with her tea, her legs crossed, and that pinched face—but sitting upright, upright as could be, with that same vague smile on her face. Looking right at him.

He smiled back, but she didn't respond, and when he swiveled away, her eyes stayed fixed on the same spot.

The old woman was blind.

Meanwhile, Pesci asserted himself. He did not mean to let it go. "Blah . . . you let the world get away with murder, you let them stick a flower up your ass, it's what you get."

"What's wrong with sticking a flower up your ass?"

"What's wrong is that stuff is supposed to come out of your ass, not in. You reverse the process, you do things ass backwards, it affects the brains. You get some funny ideas."

Marinetti shrugged.

"Airplanes start falling out of the sky."

"I don't get the connection."

"Poison in your mail."

Above, the television cut to a picture of Owens in his orange jumpsuit, hands cuffed in front of him, appearing for the arraignment. It had happened several weeks ago now, and the hearing for bail was coming up later this week. Then the image of Owens was gone, off to something else—fighter jets, a girl in fatigues. A car exploding in a market.

Pesci started to cough. Julia Besozi still grinned her black-eyed grin, and there came the sound of running water again, dishes clattering, and in the back, Stella thumping on her cutting board.

Sorrentino lowered his head.

Why am I here?

The old men were right. Everything had gone wrong, but he was going to straighten it out—his own little part. He had a mission.

He glanced down the counter and thought of his son's picture and felt the darkness seize him.

No . . .

The bail hearing for Owens was coming up, and soon the trial itself. As far as the feds were concerned, the case was their baby now. But Sorrentino did not trust them. Arrogant bastards. Especially Blackwell—a spider in his web. You could never tell who the son of a bitch would bite next.

Regardless, he hadn't come to Stella's to hang around at the counter. To fall into this Italian gloom. He had come for a reason.

Sorrentino got up and walked into the kitchen. Stella stood there pulverizing chicken with a mallet. There was the smell of garlic and of dough, and of tomatoes in the corner, overripe, and of wine that had been spilled a long time ago, and of kitchen smocks dampened by steam and sweat. Of dishwashing soap. All of the smells of this place were stronger here, and stronger the closer you stood to Stella.

She was a tough woman, wide ass, tits like a Cadillac, who backed off from no one. Nonetheless she flinched, maybe, just a little, as Sorrentino moved up closer.

"What do you want, Guy?"

She didn't back off though. He stood up close, and the smell of her was in his nostrils, Stella Lamantia, seventy years old, with hair like a wire brush, unflinching in her flowered dress, with her big breasts and her hands on her hips and sauce on her apron. Ten years ago, one night, after her husband was dead and his own son was in the ground and his wife had thrown him out—that night—he and Stella had had their moment together. He had pulled up her skirt and leaned her against the wall and she'd grabbed his ass with her strong hands.

Their moment had not lasted long.

"This," he said.

He showed her a picture of someone they both had known some three decades back, a Japanese woman by the name of Cynthia Nakamura—a slight woman with long black hair, maybe thirty-five years old in the picture. She stood with a cigarette in her hand. Next to her was a black man, African American, in a turtleneck. Stella clucked. He had his arm around Cynthia, but his eyes were closed and his head was tilted back. He looked to be in a trance.

"Do you know who she is?"

"That's Cynthia Nakamura. But why do you ask me? You know her already. She lived just down the street."

It was true, he knew Cynthia's history. She was a war orphan who'd been flown back from Tokyo after World War II, when John Panarelli married Cynthia's aunt.

"Do you know where I can find her?"

Stella walked away from him. She picked up the pulverizer and began beating the chicken again. "It has to be thin," she said. "All the chickens today, they are too fat."

"What's wrong with fat chickens?"

"I saw you on the television. I saw you standing in the back while that blonde was talking—there with the prosecutors and all those people. That young woman, the blonde, tell me, is she paying you anything for the work you do?"

"Of course," he said, but he was lying.

"Cynthia Nakamura, what can I tell you? You know her story. She left the neighborhood a long time ago. Who knows where. Married again, divorced. The last I heard, she had the cancer. But I don't know. No one tells me."

The fact was, Sorrentino had already found Cynthia Nakamura, but he didn't tell Stella. Sorrentino had found her about a month back, living in the South Bay, but now she was in Laguna Hospice. He knew because he had moved her himself, with help from Blackwell's people. She was part of the reason why the original indictment against Owens had failed. She had provided an alibi. Now, after all these years, she was willing to renege. And the government was trying to keep her alive.

Stella hit the chicken again.

"The trouble with fat chickens is that they are stupid. The head is too small for the body. A chicken looks like that, who wants to eat it?"

"Do you remember the man, here in the picture?"

Stella shook her head. "After her divorce—the first divorce—back then, the time of that picture, Cynthia hung around with some different men for a while." She shrugged. "Black men, white. There was a time she would sleep with anyone."

Stella looked Sorrentino over, with his fat belly and his bald head. He knew how he looked, but there wasn't anything he could do about it. He thought about what had happened between them here in the kitchen. Probably they both had looked different ten years ago. Or maybe it had just been dark.

"His name was Kaufman," he said. "Bob Kaufman."

He could see Stella's bile rise. He could see her irritation. "If you know the name, why do you ask? You can find him on your own." She spoke loudly, same as when she used to scold her husband in the kitchen, loud enough for everyone to hear. "You come to play the big shot? You want to show everyone in the neighborhood you aren't sitting around in your room drinking anymore? That you have this big case, with this woman on television . . . ?"

"Kaufman's dead. He's been dead since 1986."

"Then why are you talking to me?"

Sorrentino hesitated, then said, "He was a poet."

Stella scowled.

"He lived in the neighborhood here. He used to stand on the street corners. He was one of those—"

Stella interrupted—"You know I know nothing about poets." She spoke with disdain. Stella had never liked the bohos, with their beards and their books and their all-night squaloring. "Those people. You want to know about them, you have to go someplace else. You know that. Go around the corner."

She made a motion with the back of her hand. The truth was, he had been to those places. He had been to Spec's and Vesuvio and the Sleepy Wheel, all the bars where the old bohos hung out, or used to hang out, because there weren't so many of them anymore.

"So all this, it has to do with your case? Is this why you are poking around?"

For a second, he was tempted to explain, but it would lead into that gray plethora of names that ultimately surrounded anything to do with Owens, so it was impossible to separate the instigators from the sympathizers from the people who had just been standing around. The inability to do that was what had foiled the government's case thirty years ago.

Ultimately, it wasn't Kaufman he was after, but one of Owen's cohorts Leland Sanford. Sanford had been the key, the man the government couldn't find. Rumor was there'd been some kind of association between the Kaufman and Sanford. Sorrentino, out of leads, hoped that the people who'd known Kaufman—if they would talk to him—it might somehow lead him to Sanford: to confirm the identities of those four Elise had seen scampering from the bank.

A goose chase.

Meanwhile, the way Stella watched him now, as if she suspected he had some other reason for being here, something he would not admit to himself . . .

He thought of his son's picture out there, pressed under the glass countertop.

Stella turned back to her chicken. The Chinaman was humming to himself. Stella was humming now, too, thumping at the chicken.

Sorrentino went back into the restaurant.

The picture of his son was at the other end. He and the boy fishing out at Shasta. Right before the kid had been shipped off to the Middle East. They'd eaten here after they got back from Shasta, him and the boy and a couple of his friends from the SFPD, and he'd given the picture to Stella to slide under the glass countertop. Nine months later, the kid's truck flipped, out there in the desert. Sorrentino hadn't looked at the picture since.

And he wasn't going to look now.

They're all watching me, Sorrentino thought. *The old Italians. They know who I am.*

Marinetti and Pesci. The three dead bastards back in the shadows. Julia Besozi and her teacup, sitting with her knees crossed and her face pinched. Smiling right at him.

She kept right on smiling—at the same dead space, even after he moved.

It had been a mistake to come here. He threw his money on the counter and out he went.

EIGHT

After the arraignment, Dante had gotten a call from his boss, Jake Cicero. Cicero was on vacation, on a cruise boat somewhere off the coast of Italy—one of those small liners that worked the port towns. It was high season, but the occupancy was low, on account of the terror threat and the American buildup in the Middle East. He and his wife, Louise, had taken the trip anyway.

"How's the cruise going?"

"Wonderful," said Cicero. "I'm having the time of my life."

"And Louise?"

"Everyone should take a trip like this."

The truth was, Dante knew, Cicero had not wanted to go at first, but he and his wife, Louise—his third wife—had been on the brink of divorce. Cicero had taken a second mortgage in order to afford the trip. And in the time leading up to the journey, his boss had changed.

Cicero started playing tennis. His skin was tan. He bought a sports car.

Meanwhile, the business slid downhill.

"I've been talking with Moe Jensen," said Cicero. His boss had known Jensen for years and done work for his firm in the past. "They want me to put you on this."

"My impression, they're going to be strapped for cash."

"I don't know about that," said Cicero. "We've got a retainer, for now."

"What do they want?"

"Someone to shadow the prosecution case. To go back through the witness list, the discovery material."

"And Sorrentino?"

"Yes, they'll need to know what he's been doing. And Elise Younger, too. Apparently she's a little off in the head."

"I saw her speak."

"What do you think?"

"I don't know."

"You don't sound excited about this."

"The bail hearing—it's still pending."

"Bail or no bail, they are going to need legwork."

"Unless Owens cops a plea."

"I don't think that's going to happen. You don't like this case?"

"Who's going to take care of our other work?"

"I have other investigators for that. I would think you would jump at this. You have trouble with Owens?"

Dante had his doubts, but there were always doubts. Half your job in a case like this—any case, if truth be told—involved undermining the attacker, maligning the accuser, impugning not just the evidence, but the person who brought it forward. In this case, that would mean going after Elise Younger, and probably Sorrentino as well.

"Marilyn and I were thinking of going away for a while."

"Are you getting married?"

Dante hesitated.

"Okay," said Cicero. "You don't have to answer that. But listen, this isn't a good time to travel, anyway."

"I thought you said it was beautiful."

"All the saber rattling . . . It's not a good time."

"That's not what you said earlier."

"I'm just making the best of it. You're better off where you are. There on the home front."

"You're lying."

"Of course I am."

There was a pause, and in that pause Dante imagined the blue sea slapping up against Cicero's boat. He saw the coastline out there, and all those little pastel houses falling down to the sea, and the goats higher up the hills. He thought of Marilyn. He thought of Owens in jail. He heard the clink of cocktail glasses on the other side of the line, maybe, and a tennis ball bouncing on the deckside court.

"But I like these European cell phones," said Cicero. "They're cheaper—and they don't ever go dead."

"I didn't know that."

"Besides, I already told Jensen yes. My understanding, this case, there's deep pockets in the wings."

NINE

On the second day of Owens's bond hearing, between ses-
sions, Guy Sorrentino went with Elise Younger out to Judah Street. The bank itself had been torn down five years
back, and a construction site now stood in its place, with a wooden
fence ringing the block. Every year, on the anniversary of her mother's
death, Elise built a sidewalk memorial here. The anniversary had passed
several weeks ago now, but Elise maintained the sidewalk memorial
on account of the coming trial. The shrine had grown quite ornate
with the publicity, strangers adding bits of ribbon, notes of apprecia-
tion, pictures of their own deceased. While Elise replaced the flowers, Sorrentino walked over to the wooden fence, gazing through a
hole at the construction.

Elise's mother had been wearing a checkered blouse and black
slacks, Sorrentino knew, because he'd seen the evidence bag, still in-
tact after all these years. According to witnesses, she'd been standing
in the queue when the gang rushed in through the glass doors at the
side of the building. She'd turned abruptly, too abruptly, purse sliding

from her shoulder, and one of the gunmen had let loose. She'd crumpled then, shot in the stomach.

Sorrentino turned away. It was just workers down there now, concrete and rebar. He couldn't look anymore.

When Elise was done with the flowers, they walked to a dincr down the way, and as they walked Sorrentino could see her agitation. Part of the reason had to do with the bond hearing. Originally the court had scheduled an additional session this morning to hear from people who might be affected by the bail—and that included Elise as well as members of the Owens family.

At the last minute, though, the session had been pushed back till the afternoon, while council convened in chambers.

"What's this delay about? I don't understand," said Elise.

She was skeptical of Blackwell and the other government attorneys. Sorrentino couldn't blame her. She'd been through a lot trying to get the case to trial. Even so, she seemed a little too obsessed on the matter of the bail. Now that Owens had been jailed, she didn't want him back out.

"Don't worry," said Sorrentino. "It's the usual thing."

"I got a call from one of Blackwell's assistants. She told me not to wear yellow. Or talk to the press."

Elise scoffed, and he did, too. They both took pleasure in scoffing at the feds, at Blackwell and his obsequious assistants. Part of him understood, though. Elise had a tendency to go off sometimes.

"Well, anyway, what you are wearing now," said Sorrentino, "I think you have made a nice choice."

Elise was in gray—a longish dress with pleats and a faux collar. The collar was white. He didn't know much about these things, but the gray wasn't so dark as to be funereal, and it gave her a touch of dignity. She had bought a rash of new outfits, and part of him wondered about the money for it all. Regardless, the shadows under her eyes were plain enough. She had not been sleeping, he knew. Partly this had to do with the trial, and the events surrounding it, and her desire to keep the case in the public eye. Also, there was the Remembrance Day march, upcoming in Sacramento, a victims' event at which she'd been asked to speak.

"I don't think I can take it if they let Owens out on bail—if they just let him walk out of there."

"If he gets bail, it will be high," Sorrentino said. "That's the important thing."

"They can't set it high enough."

He reached out and put his hand on hers, trying to reassure her. At an adjacent table, a woman saw the gesture—saw, maybe, how Elise smiled at him—and he could see the disapproval on the woman's face. He didn't care.

Anyway, it wasn't like that. People could think what they wanted.

Sorrentino had met Elise maybe three years ago at one of those grief groups, or survival circles, whatever they were called. Sorrentino had not been there by choice, but on account of a road-rage incident on the El Camino. To avoid charges he'd agreed to see a counselor, and the counselor had sent him to the group.

Elise had told her story that first night, or part of it anyway, and she'd told him the rest sitting with him in his car in the parking garage under the psychologist's office. Maybe she had told him because he used to be a cop, and she thought he could do something. Or just because he listened. No matter, she told him how she'd spent years trying to ignore the past, but there had been a gaping hole. After her father had died, she tried to fill that hole. She became obsessed with the case—with trying to reopen it. Until eventually the victims' advocates and the state legislators and the people in the DA's office went cold at the sight of her.

She'd gotten divorced in the process. She'd had a breakdown. At one point, she'd followed Owens and his family on the street . . .

"It's all about career with these people, the prosecutors, all of them," she said now. "Whatever's expedient. I have seen them operate. I heard the promises made to my father, but nothing ever happened."

"It's different this time."

"If they let Owens out on bail, what that means to me—it means they are getting ready for a plea bargain."

"That's a leap."

"What?" Elise snapped.

"The atmosphere," he tried to explain, "the political climate, it's not the same as it was thirty years ago. They won't just let him walk."

Elise glared. She was angry and did not like to be contradicted, and she regarded him as if he had somehow joined the enemy. It wasn't fair. She got up from the table, pushing her chair back. For a second, he thought she might leave him there—but no, she just went outside and stood there smoking, looking toward the site where the bank had been.

He wished she wouldn't act that way. He did not like how the woman at the next table smirked at him now, as if a point had been proved.

Still, he understood Elise's skepticism.

He understood how dead this case had been—how far out in the cold. He'd felt that coldness, firsthand, when he'd approached Blackwell on her behalf, maybe six months before 9/11. But now things had changed. After the towers went down, there was a different atmosphere. Antiterror laws, public fear. People out to settle old scores. So Blackwell had reopened the case.

When Elise came back, he tried to apologize.

"It's okay," she said.

Her mood had shifted. Elise was like that. She smiled at him, and he felt his heart leap. She was a young woman, and he couldn't help the effect she had on him sometimes. She had blonde hair, more freckles than you might expect on a woman her age, a gap-toothed smile. The old biddy was still watching them, making her assumptions, but Sorrentino had seen the expression before: the same slant-eyed look, full of suspicion, that people gave to anyone who wasn't content to die alone in his room.

"I want to pay you, for all you've done," she said.

"No," he said.

They'd been through this before. He knew her financial situation.

"I told you. I got a check recently for the fund. There are people who want to help. And the first thing—"

"There's always strings, those donations."

He didn't quite believe her. Her father had set up a legal fund years ago, but it had gone dry a long time back. Her attempts to raise money, they never worked, and it wasn't necessary anymore, now that the state was involved. But before he said any of this, she squeezed his hand a little harder.

"Not this time," she said. "I've got the money."

She pushed her food away. She hadn't eaten half of it. She seldom did. The first time he had gone out with her, he'd had to fight the impulse to finish it for her.

"I want to pay you back. I know how far behind you are—on your alimony, on all that. It isn't right, you shouldn't have done all this work for nothing."

She wore new earrings, new shoes. The other day she'd been wearing a yellow dress, matching heels—a new wardrobe as well, though at the time he hadn't thought about it much. Most of the women he'd known, no matter what their situation, somehow always managed to come up with money for clothes, and anyway he didn't begrudge her. He hadn't done this for money, but it was true, he'd worked a lot of hours with little reward.

"All right," he said. "But not now. Maybe later. You can pay me, if that's what you want to do."

When they entered the courtroom, Sorrentino could feel Elise prickling beside him. Murder trials were not the friendliest of things, but there was an enmity here between the attorneys as well: Blackwell and his assistants on one side of the aisle, stiff-necked and earnest, court briefs stacked in neat folders; then Jensen's blustering crew on the other. Elise had her supporters, but the defense had filled the room with people who had worked with Owens these last years, old friends and cohorts, and the looks she got—and Sorrentino as well—were sharp-eyed and accusatory, bemused, full of condescension. Or this was how it seemed to him. Owens's wife, by contrast, they regarded with compassion—she with her copper-colored hair and her demure skirt, carefully chosen, and the two kids on either side of her looking battered and forlorn. In a little while, the bailiff brought out Owens himself, dressed in a suit and tie, his hair trimmed. He nodded to his wife and children, and by the way he leaned, you could see for an instant his desire to embrace them.

Sorrentino felt a stab of sympathy, but almost immediately that emotion was superceded by a wave of disgust.

Owens's manner was too deliberate, too staged.

Sorrentino had no interest in hearing about what a good father Owens was, what an upstanding member of the community. How he worked long hours in a dangerous profession, searching for the truth on behalf of those who otherwise might be abandoned. He knew Elise did not look forward to it either. She sat stoically, suppressing her anger, face flushed, the red blooming from beneath her collar.

The judge took the bench and engaged in the usual paper shuffling. Called counsel to the bench. Shuffled some more. Then addressed the courtroom.

"After meeting with the attorneys, the prosecution has waived their right to further testimony in regard to this issue. Bail is set in the amount of two million dollars."

The noise rose and the judge gaveled it down.

The amount was high enough to cripple the defense. Sorrentino saw Owens hang his head, and the wife slacken in her seat, and the two kids glance around in confusion. On the other side, Blackwell smirked into his assistant's ear. Elise, though, sat stone-faced. Then she buried her head into his lapel and started to weep. The judge gaveled again.

A little later, out in the hall, she seemed under control. Her makeup was ruined, though, the mascara running.

"I am going to take care of my face," she said.

She seemed calm enough, but you could never tell with Elise, and Sorrentino sensed a fury underneath. She was not satisfied. She had wanted her chance to speak all these years. She had not wanted Owens out on bail at all.

Then he saw.

Elise headed toward the reporters congregated on the steps. Sorrentino went after her but it was too late.

"This is a travesty," Elise said. "My mother's murderer has been

let free again. The way things are in this country, today . . . I can understand why people might take justice into their own hands . . . I
can understand . . ."

Sorrentino put a hand on her shoulders. "Don't, Elise, no . . ."
Blackwell's people were a step behind, attempting damage control,
but the exchange got into the paper anyway, along with a picture of
Sorrentino and Elise, earlier in the courtroom, in her moment of rage
and grief, when she'd collapsed onto his lapel.

On his face, in the picture, he noticed, oddly, a look of pleasure.

TEN

The next afternoon, Dante and Marilyn headed down to his father's old place on Fresno Street. The tenants had cleared out rather abruptly, and Dante had not made any effort to fill the vacancy. Partly he blamed the case—he had already begun his work, digging backward in time. Meanwhile, he and Marilyn had discussed posting the listing on one of those swap boards, where you traded places with someone in a foreign city, but he had not, in fact, stepped inside the house for some time.

On the way there, Marilyn's cell went off.

"Damn."

"Ignore it."

"I should," she said.

Instead, she took the call. She turned her back on Dante, huddling against the noise from the street. As she did, he glanced down along the sidewalk: at a woman standing flat-footed on the corner; at a man in shades; at a pock-faced drunk sneering his way down the block. It was his habit to look, to study the street—but there was another reason.

Yesterday there'd been a call to the office. A crank—displeased that Cicero had taken the case.

"Real-estate business," Marilyn told him. "I need to swing by Prospero's office, just for a minute."

"I'll walk up with you."

"It's client stuff."

"Then maybe not."

"I'll meet you up there, on Fresno. I shouldn't be too long."

"All right."

"I'll bring some pictures off the swap board," she said. "That place in the Costa Brava, down along the Spanish coast . . ."

Dante left her at the corner of Vallejo Street.

Prospero's was just a few blocks away, but as he watched her turn the corner, disappearing into the crowd, he felt a vague misgiving— as if she might disappear forever.

Probably it meant nothing.

Such feelings were common enough these days.

The house on Fresno Street was not what you might call tidy. His tenants had taken most of their belongings, but not all. The most conspicuous item was a large restaurant booth they had somehow gotten through the front door and into the living room. Maybe the original idea had been to put the booth in the kitchen, but they had not made it that far.

The restaurant booth was the kind of thing you picked up at salvage somewhere, and did not look like it could be easily disassembled. Likely it weighed a thousand pounds.

To make up for it, they'd left him a bottle of wine.

Dante wandered downstairs to look among his father's old things.

Dante had moved them down there after the old man died. The stuff remained there, untouched—though he would have to do something with it someday, one way or another. In one of the cabinets, he found his mother's old keepsake box. Inside there was a picture of his mother and father on their honeymoon, and a picture of himself as well—one of those two-by-two miniatures that had been popular, himself as a baby, no more than a few months old.

His mother's wedding ring was in the box, and his father's ring as well. Dante had put them there after the old man died.

Dante found a corkscrew. He opened the bottle of wine and sat down in the booth in the front room.

He wondered how long it would be before Marilyn would return.

Dante . . .

On the day they'd committed his mother, it had been raining . . . People were conspiring against her, she insisted . . . She had gotten her information from the dead . . . from the fish on its plate . . . from noodles covered with sauce . . . Her husband and the film star Ida Lupino were having an affair . . . Mussolini was sleeping with Jackie Kennedy . . . The Chinese had taken over the family warehouse . . .

Dante . . .

The house creaked, and in that familiar noise, the creaking, he imagined his mother's voice. Outside, a motorcycle went by, and he heard the singsong of a Chinese woman scolding her children on the street. A siren died away in the distance.

He remembered his mother, head to the sidewalk, to the walls.

Listen . . .

Maybe it was true, the inanimate world conspired with the living—but the tracings were hard to read.

A shopping bag on the bank floor.

Bullet casings. A woman's blouse, bloodstained, held in a plastic evidence bag for twenty-seven years.

Had Owens been inside that bank?

Dante didn't know. From what he could tell so far, the government's case was weak. Meanwhile he had started tracking Sorrentino, and the man left a path a mile wide.

Nakamura . . . Kaufman . . . Elise Younger . . .

Where did it lead?

Finally, Marilyn returned. She carried a folder she had not had with her before, full of listings, maybe, from Prospero's office. Now, standing in the living room, she regarded the big booth with its maroon vinyl.

"What's this?"

"A place to sit."

"Most charming."

They went around the house, from room to room. There was something cautious in her manner. When they had talked about the house—about the possibility of moving in—it had not been about the house as it was but as it might be: if this wall were gone, a door here, the kitchen opening onto the back porch. Now her manner grew remote, a little sad. And he saw at the same time her professional side, a real-estate agent examining a property.

"What did Prospero want?"

"I have a client," she said. "He's considering selling his place. And he wanted to look at the multiple listings—to get an idea of the market."

"The man on the phone?"

"Hum?"

"The man who left the message the other day—that was the one?"

She looked distracted.

"Oh, yes," she said. "The market is hot, you know—all of a sudden."

She had tried to explain it to him earlier. On the surface, it might not make sense, given the papers were full of doom—stories about how easy it would be to poison the water at Hetch Hetchy, to gas the crowd at Candlestick, to make a dirty bomb, to kill us all—but for some reason, in the midst of all this doom, houses were selling. People were frightened, nesting in.

"Did you bring the photos?"

She nodded then and laid them out on the table: pictures of an apartment somewhere in Spain. A place with a balcony and a view of a city street. Then more pictures behind those.

Marilyn sipped at the wine. "I read in the papers," she said, "Owens has been granted bail."

"He still has to raise the money. We've been invited to the defense party—when he gets out . . . remember?"

Marilyn faltered. "The kids . . . ?"

"They're okay."

"Sure."

He glanced again at the pictures.

"You and I," she said.

"That's not the Costa Brava."

"Someone snapped that place up."

"Madrid?"

"Yes. I spent some time there, just after college."

"I hear it's different now."

"There's still the backcountry, all those little towns. The women in black . . ."

"That was a long time ago."

"Franco . . ."

"The peasants, they are all gone."

"No, they just dress differently," she said. "More like here."

They sifted through other possibilities. A cottage in the hills near Dublin. A house with a tin roof in Baja. A thatched veranda. Ceiling fans. Lava rolling to the jungle coast.

More pictures.

Saigon and Copenhagen and Casablanca.

Landscapes in which to imagine yourself.

Marilyn, with her green eyes and her skirt up around her knees, lying by the glass coffee table, next to the red sofa from Milan, her hands inside his pants, that first time making love, years ago, on the floor of his cousin's house.

"How much do you think I could get for this place?"

"Do you think you could let it go?" she asked.

Empty now, stripped of artifacts, it was just a house, but the emptiness had its own grip as well.

"I think so."

"If you did sell, what would hold you here?"

"In North Beach?"

"You could go anywhere."

"We could, yes."

She was smiling, her eyes had a brightness to them, but there was a dark sheen over the luminosity. He saw her sense of vulnerability but also a toughness, a determination not to be taken in. She liked things, he knew that. She liked clothes, hotel rooms. Men with money.

He thought about his mother's box with the rings inside.

He was tempted to get the box—to show her the rings—but there was a next step following that, an implication.

"Let's go," she said. "Let's get some decent wine."

She smiled then and kissed him, but she carried a reserve about her that he could not quite read. Or did not want to read.

Everyone had their secrets.

They left the house and walked down the street, hand in hand. They said nothing. They stopped at the end of the block, at the Iron Horse, where they drank in a reckless way despite the hour, straggling out at dusk, then stumbling up the hill, into bed, into each other's drunken arms.

ELEVEN

A week after the judge had set bail, the money had not yet been raised—and Owens was still in jail. He sat in a meeting with his attorney and his wife and the legal representatives of a liberal financier by the name of Walter Sprague.

"It's a lot of money," said Owens.

The guards had retrieved Owens from his cell about a half hour earlier and had brought him down the long hall to this gray room. In the three weeks since he'd been arrested, he'd been out of the cell a number of times—for the arraignment, for the bail hearings, for the indictment—but a kind of disconnect had happened. He felt himself in a kind of nether land, a gray zone in which he could not accept the reality of his immediate situation. The world outside felt increasingly remote. He had done time before—almost two years, for his alleged role in Sanford's escape from prison—and had not found it easy.

No, he was not someone who did easy time.

Owens knew the labyrinthine turnings of the justice system, especially in a case like this, with its political overtones, the rulings and counterrulings, a world populated by documents filled with names, pictures, connections imagined and real, arranged and rearranged.

All of those names . . . those photos and affidavits . . . the details of the trial, then the appeal . . . The longer you were on the inside, here, the more your other life vanished, the more you became one of those names on paper.

This meeting today had been hastily arranged, and the guards had not let him change clothes. He wore an orange suit and his leg was cuffed to an immovable bar below the table. His wife and the others had been searched before they came—and he would be searched again before they took him back.

"Yes, the bail is high. It's a lot of money," said Jensen.

Jensen had been his attorney back then as well. A burly man, hair in a ponytail, wide hazel eyes that seemed to take in everything you said. The first time they'd met had been in a basement in the Haight, and Owens had spoken freely, maybe more than he should have. But he had been underground then, he and Rachel, his first wife—both of them wanted for their association with Sanford, with the SLA, various antigovernment activities, pipe bombings—every unsolved crime in the book including, as it happened, the robbery in which Eleanor Younger had been killed. As a result, Jensen knew things that no one else knew.

Names . . . affidavits . . . More names . . .

Meanwhile, Jill focused on the attorney who had come here on behalf of the financier. "As far as the bail," she said, "we don't have that kind of equity in our house—and even if we throw in our retirement money—"

"It bankrupts us," said Owens.

"And there's no money left over for the defense."

"None."

Everyone at the table knew this already, including Sprague's lawyer and his assistant. Their boss had liberal leanings, it was true—he'd funded something called the Sprague Foundation—but his interest in this case, Owens knew, was on account of one of those names from Owens's past.

Jan Sprague.

She'd had a different name then, before she married Walter Sprague, but that didn't matter now. Like Owens, Jan had been affiliated with the old radical underground. A tall, good-looking woman with a desire to speak out—to prove herself. She had been captured on a surveillance film at a suspected SLA safe house. She and a friend of hers, a San Francisco radical by the name of Annette Ricci.

They were always together. Annette and Jan. Jan and Annette.

Annette with the wild hair and the barking laugh. Jan with her honey-colored hair, always in denim. Earnest eyes. Earnest as could be.

Names from the past.

The government had tried to hook all their names together at one time, linking them to the robbery, pieces in a puzzle the feds could not quite put together, examining one suspect, then another, subpoenas and evidence trails confounded by misinformation, political maneuvering, a fog in the press, part of which issued from Jensen it was true, Owens's own friends and cohorts.

Owens did not see them anymore, but Annette and Jan were still around. Annette Ricci ran a theater group in the city. Jan had gotten a job at the Sprague Foundation, as communication director. Eventually, she had married Walter Sprague.

But Owens had known her before that. She hadn't been a name, but a woman who'd kept him company, with whom he'd been intimate on the floor of the Berkeley safe house, her long legs wrapped around him. Before Jill. Before Walter Sprague.

"This is the situation," said Jensen. "The state came to Bill with a deal."

"What kind of deal?" asked Sprague's attorney.

"The government's seeking indictments on a broad range of unsettled cases. Not just the Younger case."

The lawyer shifted uneasily. There was something unsaid here, and Owens understood what it was. Part of the government's goal was to hook cases together—get one suspect to tumble and the others would fall as well.

To link the names.

"What kind of deal?" the attorney repeated.

"We haven't gotten the specifics. The government's playing cat and mouse. But this case isn't just about Bill. The government is trying to set a precedent here, with that new antiterror legislation. Any kind of dissent—past or present—it makes you suspect."

Owens understood what Jensen was doing now. Establishing a larger cause—demonstrating the political dimension behind the charges. *Felony robbery . . . conspiracy to commit a felony . . . second-degree murder in the process of felony robbery . . . seditious endangerment . . .*

Sprague's attorney peered at Owens, as if trying to decipher what the truth might be. Owens went black inside.

"My kids . . . ," he said.

Jill covered his hand with hers.

"The government is compiling a list, that's what this is all about," said Jensen. "One name leads to the next. These indictments—they won't stop with Bill. Our feeling: We have an obligation to fight back, to resist. So long as we can find the money to proceed."

The attorneys went on, discussing the intricacies of the case, possible strategies, more names, and Owens felt himself disappearing into that netherworld.

Pretty soon, though, the meeting was over, and the others filed out. He saw Jensen take his wife by the arm. The guard unshackled Owens, then pinned him to the wall, running a hand up his ass, looking for a smuggled cigarette, a penknife, anything. The guard unlocked the door and pushed Owens toward the lower block. As he stumbled forward, all the names were in his head at once.

The guard pushed him again.

He descended.

TWELVE

It was a nice day out, beautiful really, and Marilyn found herself with David Lake, driving across the Marin Headlands through the dry hills that fronted the Golden Gate. The cottage was farther on, in Tomales. Though it was out of her territory—up the coast, in a market she did not know—Marilyn had nonetheless agreed to go take a look.

He wanted to sell the place, he said. He never got out here anymore, and he had too much to look after.

Usually, in situations such as this, it was customary for the real estate agent to do the driving. Beatrice Prospero had offered Marilyn the loan of her father's Mercedes, a second car that the old man did not drive anymore, but it turned out the car was in the shop, and so they were riding in Lake's car: a Mercedes as well, as it happened, an upscale model, newer than the one Marilyn would have driven, with more appointments.

And also a top that rolled back.

The redwoods were thick at the summit, where the fog piled up against the hills, but the western slopes descending to the ocean were mostly scrub: old grazing land now covered with Scotch broom and thistle and the occasional oak. The clouds rolled overhead, building up along the ridges.

At one point along the way, Lake asked if she would like to have the top down.

"No," she said.

Lake had a boyish, transparent face, and a look of disappointment fluttered across his features. Marilyn felt some small regret. She wouldn't have minded, really, having the top down, but it did not seem quite appropriate.

The house itself stood in a sheltered cove overlooking Tomales Bay, down in the banana belt—a smallish cottage on the bluff just below the settlement, in a cluster of older homes. The house possessed not only the advantage of being sheltered by trees all around, but also a footpath to the dock and the small beach below. Wisteria grew over the fence, busting apart the pickets, and the pampas grass grew wild in the yard.

"It used to be a fisherman's cottage," said Lake. "And when my wife saw it, she fell in love with it. Now, well . . ."

He continued her tour of the property. He showed her his wife's shed, where she had done her ceramics. Some of her work sat on the redwood shelves—fanciful vases, oversized plates glazed in bright colors. Mugs too large for anyone to use.

Impractical, functionless work that nonetheless communicated a certain domestic joy.

"This was her special place. She used to be out here a lot. But to be honest, I haven't spent a whole lot of time here lately . . . These days, it's just me and the dogs, at home in the city."

Afterward they walked down to the town, so that she could get a feel for the neighborhood, and he insisted on buying her lunch.

He told her then he was willing to sign the contract, giving her exclusive rights to sell.

It was apparent to her he was interested in more than just the house. This should have made her uncomfortable, but it didn't. Lake was harmless, likeable enough, and he seemed to take a small thrill out of holding the door for her, and she enjoyed having it held. In the car, on the way back, he talked more intimately. This happened sometimes with clients. A house was an intimate thing.

He loved the house, he said, but it was a burden. Emotionally. The place brought back memories, and he couldn't imagine himself living there alone. And what if he did remarry? The house had been too much their place. Her place. He couldn't imagine another woman being comfortable with all that.

"I guess not," she said.

When they got back to the city, they stopped by the office for the paperwork so he could get a copy of the listing agreement. He wanted to sign right then and there, but she told him to take it home first, to look it over. Outside, he seemed reluctant to let her go.

"Do you need a ride?"

"I'm just up the hill."

"I'm happy to take you."

"No. I have a couple of places I have to stop at along on the way."

"Friday, at the War Memorial, they are doing *Tosca*. The final performance."

She understood what was coming next.

"Do you ever go to the opera?"

"Let me get some comps on your house. Then we'll talk again."

He gazed at her with his blue eyes. She had ignored the question and was afraid he might repeat it, and she did not want to embarrass him.

"Okay," he said. "I'll look this over. And be in touch."

He smiled then.

She walked up the hill alone.

Dante was not home.

She made herself dinner and afterward rummaged herself some cigarettes from a pack Beatrice Prospero had left behind. There were three left in the pack. She smoked two of them and stood in her nightgown looking out at the street.

There was nothing out there. She was tempted to turn on the television, but she didn't want to hear that chatter.

The unease of the world is the unease of the self.

But how true was that, really?

Probably Dante was out on assignment.

She envied Prospero and his ability to be at harmony with himself. To care about nothing but his cigar and his wine and the moment.

She thought of the way David Lake had looked at her.

He was right to sell the house.

She took another drink and lay down on the bed. When she woke up again it was just before dawn. Dante's jacket lay across the chair.

She found him downstairs, at the window, smoking the last cigarette.

They weren't going to Spain, she knew.

He was already too deep in the case.

THIRTEEN

Two days after Owens made bail, the defense held a gathering at his house on Shale Street in Oakland. Though he and Jill had expected otherwise, the oddball phone calls had let up after his release, so there'd been no ugly messages. Just good will, just friends. Now cars lined the street down past the corner and people filled his home—more friends and sympathizers and legal types—and a long table of food, buffet-style, had been spread out in the backyard.

It was a coming-home party of sorts, but more than that it was the launch of his defense.

It was the way Jensen often did things, Owens knew. When there was a case, it was not just a case, it was a cause, and Jensen made it into a family kind of thing, with everyone gathered around. The approach was a carryover from the old days—from the Panther trials, the Berkeley Eight, the Free Speech Movement—and though Owens had been around this before, it nonetheless felt odd to find himself at the center of the spectacle, here in his own house, under the gaze of his wife and kids.

Jensen put his wide hand on Owens's back. By the man's side

stood a new paralegal, a young blonde who followed his every move. Twenty-five pounds and two divorces later, Jensen had the same weaknesses.

"The Spragues are here," said Jensen. "Go mingle."

Owens treaded through the crowd, smiling sheepishly. He shook hands with his brother-in-law. He pressed his cheek against the cheek of his neighbor's wife. He looked into the uncertain eyes of his children and headed for the white-haired man in the kitchen, Walter Sprague, whose generosity was making all this possible.

Among the visitors were some he had not seen for a long time, whose names dwelled with his other self, back in the cell. Jan Sprague stood alongside her husband—as well as Annette Ricci, the director of the San Francisco Street Troupe.

"So here we go again," said Annette Ricci.

Jan met his eyes cautiously, but not so Annette. She had directed the troupe since as far back as he could remember. Now, like always, she placed herself at the center of things. An attractive woman, in her early fifties, energetic—red hair, green eyes—she regarded him with her chin tilted, imperious and vulnerable at once. Her boyfriend was maybe ten years younger, and had fought in the Sandinista Revolution.

"Yes," said the Sandinista. "But it is not surprising. The American people are so placid. Like sheep."

"Bah," said Annette, rubbing her wooly hair. "Bah, and bah again."

Owens had seen the routine onstage years ago, Annette wrapped in an American flag, bleating like a sheep.

The group laughed, but it was an uneasy laughter.

Annette had a certain flamboyance, it was true, a brightness in the eyes, but there was a darker spirit underneath. There always had been. The point of street theater was to push things to the edge, and she was always orchestrating, controlling.

"How are things with the troupe?" asked Jan.

"No one has come after us yet . . . we are still operating."

Though Sprague helped fund the troupe, Jan and Annette did not see much of each other anymore, Owens guessed. There was, at any rate, a certain tension between them. He and the two women had been involved with the SLA at about the same time, and they knew things about one another that it was better perhaps not to know. Even so, Jan Sprague was still a handsome woman. Her honey brown hair had gone white, but in a glamorous way. Even when she was younger—dressed in denim, a man's work shirt rolled up at the sleeves—she'd had an air of sophistication, of breeding and money. She looked down into her cup now, and her husband put his hand on her shoulder.

"Bah," Annette said again.

Though Walter Sprague was a powerful man, and very wealthy—and outspoken in his support of liberal causes—he had one weakness. That weakness was Jan. He was in his midseventies now, and she was twenty-five years his junior.

"I have to thank you, Walter," said Owens. "I would like to say again how grateful I am."

Jan's glance acknowledged nothing. The Sandinista, on the other hand, looked at Owens wryly, smirking, as if he understood it all. Rumor was that he had been a foot soldier in the street wars of Managua and had gone door to door, rooting the wealthy out of their beds. The Sandinista made Owens uncomfortable. Today he and Annette had been among the first to arrive, bringing with them a man from a restaurant in the Mission who carried in several trays of Honduran tamales wrapped in banana leaves. The other man was gone now, but Owens remembered him lingering out by the bamboo.

The Sandinista held one of the tamales.

"Have you tried these?"

"Yes. They are quite good."

Supposedly the Sandinista had, for a while, held a high post in the party back home. Owens supposed it was possible. The man had rakish good looks and political assuredness. But since the Sandinistas had fallen out of power, he was here in the States, living with Annette Ricci.

Persona non grata back home. A romantic figure among the aging politicos of San Francisco.

Blood on his hands, maybe. But who could talk?

O wens spotted Dante then, lingering by the back door. He had brought Marilyn, who was talking real estate, something about Europe, as she helped Jill at the counter. They talked, too, about the Honduran tamales, the banana leaves, the unusual texture of the corn. Meanwhile, Jill was exhausted, Owens could see that. He could see the strain in her face.

"We are working on a play, for Columbus Day," said the Sandinista.

"Shouldn't we be moving people outside?" asked Annette. "We are going to do a little preview—for the kids."

Dante approached and Owens introduced him all around. Annette Ricci regarded the man carefully, holding her chin a little higher, putting her head in profile the way she did, waiting to be admired. The Sandinista, on the other hand, went on talking as before: "This game your president is playing in the Middle East—cowboys and Indians all over again."

"They'll never get out," said Annette. "They will create what they fear."

"It's an excuse, this war on terror. To bury the political opposition. If the American people had any gumption, they would fight back."

Owens didn't necessarily think otherwise, but the Sandinista puffed his chest out disagreeably. Though the man did not look at Dante, the remarks seemed to be directed at him, testing him, perhaps. Jan and Walter Sprague had the look of tremulous relatives at a family party they intended to leave at the first opportunity. Walter Sprague leaned forward.

"You are right," he said. "We must fight, in the ways that we can."

They are afraid, Owens thought. All of them.

Even Annette, brassy and laughing, and her Sandinista boyfriend. He could feel the fear coming off of them.

What happened to me will happen to them.

Dominoes in a line . . . one flick of the finger . . .

"So what kind of play are you doing for Columbus Day?"

"Just a little skit," said Annette. "A tribute."

She laughed then, big-throated, full of herself, and Jan Sprague laughed too. There was a fragility in the laughter, an awkwardness. Her eyes skittered over to his but did not linger. There were things they all remembered, but did not want to think about.

Owens shook the ice in his glass, ill at ease.

It was a typical Berkeley gathering in some ways. Here they were under the eucalyptus, under the oak, with the light filtering through the blue haze, at the moment when the afternoon turned into evening, and the air was suddenly very still, and the kids started to yearn for their electronic devices. There was a smell like marijuana burning, the sound of a motorcycle in the alley, of cars in the distance. Just a backyard barbecue, friends around the table, complaining about the government, growing boisterous, loud, before the talk turned to schools and real estate. Owen wished this were simply that—friends reminiscing together under the cloud of current events before the inevitable ride home. He wished he could turn upstairs after it was all over and lie on his brightly colored bed with its million pillows and his hyperactive kids roaming the Internet, playing with gadgets. He wished he were just some ordinary dad cursing under his breath the foul gloom of the government, distant events, and news-hour commentaries. If only it were that simple for him, and the face he saw on the news was not his own, displayed split screen with Elise Younger, seeking revenge for her mother's death.

Now Annette Ricci stood in front of him blocking the way inside.

"Can I get by?"

"Everyone's out here now. I herded them out."

"I was going to get a jacket . . ."

"We are going to do a toast," she said.

"To my innocence?"

"To the task ahead."

She was being rather coquettish, flirtatious. Insistent. A hardness underneath. For Annette, always, everything was a show. He had learned a long time ago that she always had plans of her own, and there was little you could do to interfere. He remembered then a moment at the SLA safe house, Annette and her boyfriend at the time, a Chicano kid, Naz Ramirez. Another name the feds would have been tracing as well, if not for the fact he'd been dead ten years. But Annette, she'd liked the Latinos even then. Doing the Ché thing. All in khaki, dark brown, a blouse with military sleeves. Jan at the window, sober-faced, working up her courage. The cache of weapons on the floor. If only he could go back . . .

I am innocent.

"Be quick," said Annette.

He got the jacket. When he came back, Annette stood as before, waiting on the stairs. She pulled the door behind them, and he saw her pause at the threshold.

"Did you just lock that?"

She put a hand on his wrist.

"We are giving a little performance. For the kids. I don't want everyone running in and out."

They walked down to the table. Dante was there, and Marilyn, and his wife, and all his friends and his kids, and they made their toast.

"To a free and happy world."

"To the end of these dark times."

"Free Bill Owens."

They did one toast, and then another, his old friend Moe Jensen at the head of the table, a big man with a soft voice, gray in his beard, eyes dim. Jan leaned against Walter Sprague as if this occasion had more to do with her philanthropist husband then herself. She looked at Owens, doe-eyed, as if she were not really there, but they both knew the reason for her husband's involvement: to erase her name from Owens's past. He would not see her again after this, he realized, unless it was at the trial, and there, too, she would keep her distance. In a little while, Annette turned on the boom box, playing Andean flute music, then she and the Sandinista disappeared by the bamboo to change into wardrobe.

"I'm chilly," said Kate. "Can I get my sweater?"

Marilyn leaned toward the girl. "I'll get it for you. I need mine, too."

The back door was locked, as Owens suspected. It was just like Annette, the way she tried to control everything—and so he got up and walked with Marilyn, key in hand, to let her in himself.

"Oh, thank you."

"My pleasure."

"I don't want to miss the play."

"They'll wait."

He stood in the kitchen, in the hall, and watched Marilyn go into the living room. Marilyn bent over, picking his daughter's sweater up off the couch, then looking for her own on the rack by the window. She had her back to him, and he stood in the doorway admiring her. She was not of their group, no, with her silver blouse and her jewelry and her dark hair that smelled of the salon—and maybe Owens found her more attractive for that reason, for her wide hips and her tight skirt. But at the same time there was something else, darker maybe— and he suspected Marilyn was conscious of his looking, that there was something studied in the way she lifted her head, gazing out the window, curious, as if something out there had drawn her attention. Then the window imploded.

There was flying glass and a sudden burst of light. Then smoke, thick smoke, and in that smoke, as he struggled forward, Owens caught a glimpse of Marilyn, just ahead, a shadow illuminated by fire, a figure in flames—but then he could see nothing.

The smoke overcame him. He fell to his knees.

PART THREE

Code Pink

FOURTEEN

The cocktail had been well made. It was Finnish-style, the police said later—made in a vodka bottle, with a Bengal light strapped on each side. The Bengals were slow-burning flares, of compacted powder, that emitted a small blue flame. Whoever had thrown the cocktail had likely stood inside the hedge, invisible from the street, and hurled it through the window. The cocktail ignited when it hit the glass and the contents splattered out—a mixture of gasoline and grease and tar.

When the glass broke, the liquid splattered. The flames followed the mixture. The curtains were sheer and ignited easily, and smoke issued from the couch. It was noxious smoke. Where the mixture landed on flesh, the effect was like napalm—a tarry mixture that generated its own heat and burned through the clothing and onto the flesh and kept burning.

Some of the mixture had hung for a split instant in midair, droplets of gas suspended in vapor.

Then there was a burst of flame and light.

Marilyn felt a searing in her lungs, as if she were on fire from the inside—a burning across her face, her chest, her thighs.

The flames leapt from her dress.

At the moment of the explosion, Dante had been at the table in the backyard, watching the Sandinista and Annette Ricci move in pantomime, puppetlike across the lawn.

Then he was on his feet.

At first he could not enter the living room, the smoke was so thick. Back in the kitchen, he ran a dish towel under running water, then held the wet cloth over his face. He entered the living room on his knees, close to the ground, where the smoke would be less dense.

He saw Owens—down low, on his elbows, struggling along the carpet.

Dante pulled Owens into the kitchen. He left the man gasping on the tile and went back after Marilyn.

The towel slipped and soon he was gagging, his eyes streaming from the smoke. He saw her in the center of the room, where she had collapsed on the carpet, apparently trying to roll out the flames. He put his body over hers, smothering the fire. The air was better down low, and he grabbed her under the arms, pulling her along the carpet, but it was too slow, and so he cradled her over his back, stood up in the heat and roiling smoke, and stumbled forward.

In the kitchen, Jensen was helping Owens. Dante staggered into the Sandinista at the top of the stairwell, and there was a minute when all three of them might have fallen if Dante hadn't shifted himself into the wall, bearing their weight. Then Dante brushed him back. He collapsed with Marilyn on the back lawn.

Her clothes still smoldered.

Dante knew something about burns and that the first step was to strip off the burning clothes and cool the body. He called out for ice, for water. He did not notice Annette Ricci already on her knees beside him in her outfit from the play, a peasant dress embroidered with peacocks. Later Dante would wonder about the backyard door and why it had been locked—but at the time he did not reflect on that, noting instead in the back corner of his mind the glance she exchanged with the Nicaraguan—as if something had gone terribly astray—and noting, too, the hardness, the steely calm in them both, as the Nicaraguan headed out to reconnoiter on the street, and Annette dipped her hands into the Styrofoam cooler she'd brought from the table. She dumped the ice, wrapping the soda cans and beer bottles as compresses for Marilyn's wounds.

Marilyn's cheeks were blistered, her eyelids singed, the hair frizzled back to the scalp on one side. Dante placed a damp rag over the side of her face, hoping to cool the burn, while Annette Ricci put compresses about the thighs and abdomen.

"No," he said, waving her off, worried that Marilyn's temperature would drop too fast.

Her breathing faltered, her chest did not move.

He placed his fingers in her mouth and cleared the air passage and put his lips over hers.

She came to consciousness, moving spasmodically beneath him, muttering, then she was gone again.

"Get me the hose," said Dante. "Get me some water."

Dante wanted water to lower her temperature. Marilyn had burns over a good part of her body. The wounds should be iced, but drop the body temperature too far, and she would go into shock. Her face was red, and it was already starting to puff up, and there was a string of postules across her face where the tar grease had spattered. There were holes in her skirt from where the tar had burned through, and an ugly cinch around her waist where the elastic had melted into the flesh.

When she came to again, she twisted painfully on the ground, clawing at the dirt. She was delirious and uttered a stream of obscenities.

"Fuck me . . . no . . . I can't see . . ."

She started to shiver, and Annette came now with the cloth from the picnic table. There were sirens in the distance. He did his best to cool her burns with the water, and at the same time keep her out of shock, keeping her warm under the cloth.

"No," she moaned. "My eyes . . ."

When the paramedics arrived, they started working on Marilyn even before they had her on the stretcher. They hooked her to an intravenous and put on an oxygen mask. The paramedics were young and lithe and had the ability to keep their voices calm, offhanded, in a way that was both reassuring and detached. They covered her eyes with a thin gauze and then loaded her into the ambulance.

Dante stood alone on the sidewalk. He had made a mistake bringing her here.

He felt now the ache and rawness in his own lungs, the effects of the smoke, and felt, too, the rawness on his cheeks, the blistering on his forearms and thighs where he had brushed against the flames. Standing there on the street, he looked back at the house—at the bamboo hedge, at the sidewalk, the alley of garages that led out to a busier street below.

An incendiary device. Loaded with gasoline and hurled through the window.

Who?

Likely the perpetrators were gone. But sometimes, if you moved quickly, you got lucky . . .

One of the paramedics took him by the arm.

"Your turn," said the paramedic.

"No."

Something happened then.

On account of the smoke inhalation. Or his mind just let go. Either way, the next thing he knew he was lying in the darkness, in the ambulance, Marilyn moaning beside him.

"You're beautiful," he said.

Then it was dark again, and in that darkness the paramedic slipped an oxygen mask over his face.

Sometime after midnight, Leanora Chin showed up at the hospital. The last time Dante had seen her had been at the Federal Building, the day Owens was arrested. She wore dark blue, same as before, the same outfit, it seemed, with her black hair gathered in the back. She had come to Mercy, as far as Dante could tell, to see if the medical report would offer any insights as to the cause of the explosion. She talked to the emergency staff for a while and then came to find Dante. He had been treated and sat now in the waiting room. Chin, he learned, had already been out to General, where Owens was being held for observation. Marilyn, though, had been brought here, to Mercy, on account of the burn unit.

"Where were you at the time of the explosion?"

"Marilyn went inside, to retrieve a sweater. Then the cocktail came through the window."

"Cocktail? Why do you say it's a cocktail?"

Chin's voice was flat, devoid of innuendo, but there was suspicion underneath, he knew. There was always suspicion underneath.

"There were grease splatters on her clothes," Dante said. "Hot grease and tar. And I could smell the gasoline."

"How about the people in the backyard?"

"What about them?"

"Who were they?"

Dante told Chin as many names as he could remember. He watched her write the names down. She did so slowly. Likely she had gotten these names already, or most of them, and was just writing them down to crosscheck. Still, the cop dwelled over the names. Asked him a little bit about each. Went back over the incident again, wanting to know if Dante had seen anyone on the street. If any of the guests had come and gone. If anyone had been there before, maybe . . . someone . . . Dante realized the implication. The people at the scene, you always had to consider them. He would do the same.

"No. They were all in the backyard."

"There was a man earlier, who came with Annette Ricci and her boyfriend. He brought in the tamales."

Dante shook his head. "He was gone before I came."

"Were any of these people in the drug trade?"

"What are you trying to say here?"

Chin put her pen down.

"The Oakland investigators, they told me they had a case like this, last year—some kind of drug dispute. So the dealers put a cocktail through the window. Little girl burned to death. These kinds of things, they happen in Oakland."

"I don't think this incident was drug inspired," Dante said. "This isn't that kind of crowd."

Chin held any expression from her face.

"Sometimes they get the wrong house."

It was a dumb idea. Likely Chin knew that—she was not dumb herself—and suddenly Dante had a sinking feeling about the direction of the investigation. He knew how the people upstairs didn't like Owens and how things rolled down from the top. So he told Chin about the threats against the kids and did his best to connect the dots: to suggest that someone had come after the Owens family but had gotten Marilyn instead. "This case, there's also a political dimension."

"That aspect of it . . ." Chin paused then. Something in her manner, it reminded him of how cops lined up together. "You work for them, don't you? You're working for Owens?"

"What's that have to do with it?"

Chin said nothing.

"That's my fiancée who was burned."

"I'm sorry," Chin said. "But—"

"But what?"

Chin looked him in the eyes. Dante understood the implication. She didn't say anything, but Dante understood. *It's too bad, but what were you doing working for these people, anyway? What were you doing bringing your fiancée to this kind of gathering? What did you expect?*

When the phone rang, Dante was in a deep grog. Cicero, calling from somewhere in the Mediterranean, farther east. Past the Aegean now, off the coast of Cyprus, and in Dante's imagination he saw the narrow straits, the sheer cliffs, the islands where the giant seabirds hulked on the shore under the moon, as if Cicero were calling from someplace back in time.

"Dante?"

Dante suspected Cicero knew everything, as he always seemed to: that he had been in touch with the office, with his numerous sources. Dante himself had been back and forth to the hospital. He'd slept little. He'd broken away once to visit Shale Street—walking the scene, knocking on doors—but had been chased away by the Oakland police.

On the news, there were contradictory reports. One of these said a neighbor had seen a man lurking outside the house just before the bombing. A Latino in a red shirt.

Meanwhile, the stars were out in Cicero's faraway world. Out there in the cell-phone darkness. Off a black coast. The waters stretched out forever, ink black under the moon. Somewhere in that blackness was the Jake Cicero he had known—the leather-skinned man with the white hair and the white shirt, sleeves rolled to the elbows.

Dante missed Cicero.

"How's Marilyn?"

"In pain."

"Can't they give her something?"

"A lot of it's nerve damage," Dante said. "The drugs don't do a lot of good. Then there's the surgery."

"Already?"

"This morning. There's more scheduled."

These days, they started the grafting process early with the theory that early grafting promoted healing. Marilyn had a combination of second- and third-degree burns, and there would likely be some scarring. She suffered from smoke inhalation, but the thing that concerned the doctors most were her eyes. The fire had singed the lids, and the cornea was damaged. And some of the deeper ocular mechanisms as well.

"The Oakland police are swamped. To them, everything's a drug case. And the feds . . . the way the cops feel about Owens, I don't know if any investigation . . ."

"Dante?"

"Yes."

"You know what I am going to say."

He did know. It was a cardinal rule. When something like this happened to someone close to you, you didn't go after it yourself. Chances were, you'd fuck it up. "I talked to Moe Jensen," said Cicero. "Walter Sprague, the financier, he'll cover Marilyn's medical. As for the bombing, that part of the investigation—they've offered one of his people."

"His people?"

"A man like that, Sprague, he has people. Also, the financial aspect, if there's a money trail—if someone paid for this—Sprague's people know that world better than we do."

"They're throwing us off?"

"What they want you to do—us—hasn't changed. Go through the discovery material, everything the prosecution presented at the indictment, the witness list, all that. And stay with Sorrentino. Figure out what he and Elise Younger have been doing. The bombing, that part, leave it to the others."

Dante didn't say anything. It seemed Sprague was paying not just for Owens's defense, but for Marilyn's recovery, and, he supposed, for the retainer that kept him on the case.

"There's something else," Cicero said.

"What?"

"Owens, his place is ruined. He's got his family in a hotel."

"Yeah."

"There's media outside. And the hotel is pretty upset about it."

Dante knew about this. He'd talked with Jill Owens on the phone and had seen the circus on the news.

"Your place down on Fresno?"

"Yes?"

"It's still empty? I know it's a lot to ask . . . but it would just be for a little bit. There aren't too many other places for them to go right now."

Dante thought about the empty house, with the restaurant booth in the living room and his father's furniture in the basement and the keepsake box he'd left on the mantle beside the empty bottle of wine. He thought of his mother going nuts in the attic and his father dying in the bed upstairs and the creaking in the stairs every time the house shifted. Part of him blamed Owens for what had occurred, but he remembered, too, the kids and their ashen faces. Also, if he wanted to know what had happened on Shale Street, it might be wise to hold Owens close.

"Sure," Dante said. "They can stay."

"You're a good man," said Cicero.

"A prince," said Dante.

FIFTEEN

The next afternoon Lieutenant Leanora Chin went out to Shale Street to walk the crime scene. As usual, she was in blue. Middle-aged blue. Steel blue. Gun metal blue tucked into a straight skirt that hit, uniform-style, just below the knees. Fifty years old, twenty-three of them on the force. Again with her hair tied back, black hair streaked with iron. It gave her a severe look—except for her eyes. They were gray eyes, not warm exactly, no one would say that. There was in fact a certain coldness there, an analytical sweep— but there was an intelligence as well, and it was this intelligence that animated her face and kept the severity at bay. This, and the under- standing, inherent in the way she held herself, that intelligence itself was not the final factor in anything.

At this point, the case was still under the jurisdiction of the Oak- land police. So far they were viewing it as a local crime, but if it con- nected to the Owens case then SF Homeland would get involved. Logically speaking.

Of course, there was no saying that logic would have anything to do with it. That was always true when it came to jurisdictional issues, but even more so lately, Chin knew. She had spent most of her career in Homicide, then been transferred over to Special Investigations, to work in the Gang Unit. But then 9/11 came along, and everything shifted.

She was under Homeland now, a local unit, recently created, carved out of SFPD and federalized for the sake of national security. At first glance little had changed except the lettering on the door. Only the organizational lines were not clear, or the funding. Mandates changed daily. Fact was, SI wasn't an investigation unit anymore. It was an escort service for visiting dignitaries.

And her Gang Unit was in shambles.

A year ago, they'd had a half-dozen agents out tracing gang activities in the San Francisco ports. They were on other duty now. The new byword was "terror." Domestic terror. Sleeper cells. People with agendas, hidden among us, waiting for the word from abroad. The leads came from hotlines, from disgruntled employees, public servants with a bug up their ass. To put it mildly, the leads rarely panned out. "Never" was more like it. But you couldn't say that. You had to pursue.

An Iraqi grocer. A college professor with relatives in Iran. An evangelical minister sending money to a church in Basra.

You had to bring these potentials in for questioning, so people could see you were doing your job. And once you brought them in, you had to be careful about letting them go. Because if you made a mistake . . .

So the tendency was to hold them forever, evidence or no.

Meanwhile, there was pressure to turn back the clock—to go after people who had slipped away in more lenient times.

Owens.

It was an old file, a grudge file, minded all these years by Leonard Blackwell and given to her at the last minute because they wanted a local face on the investigation. But Blackwell was still running the show. Since 9/11, in the organizational vacuum, his presence crossed departmental boundaries.

Not that she thought Owens was an illegitimate target necessarily.

But even if Owens was guilty, it wasn't supposed to come to this: a Molotov cocktail tossed through the window while the family gathered with friends, raising money for the defense.

The Oakland cops had secured the area. They had done well enough, she supposed. The firefighters had stomped all over the place, of course, and there were a million footprints, trampled bushes, broken glass, debris everywhere. They had managed to secure the scene by nightfall yesterday evening, putting up the yellow tape and posting a cop car out front—though the cop had been called away because of a robbery down on Fruitvale, and the scene had been untended half the night.

That could be a problem later, if they needed to take evidence to trial.

Meanwhile the Oakland police had pulled in the usual suspects, guys out on arson charges, drug freaks, and fire junkies. They'd pulled in as well a half-dozen Latinos in red shirts, based on a neighbor's description—including a gardener who had been working across the street earlier that morning.

The guy had been playing soccer when they arrested him, but he was illegal, and Immigration had him now. There'd been another Latino at the scene apparently, at the time of the party—a friend of

Ricci's and her boyfriend, from the Tamale House—but the preliminary description did not match. Either way, so far, Oakland had not
tracked him down.

Chin walked the scene. The forensics team had arrived, working
the perimeters now that the ashes had cooled. It was clear they didn't
want her around. She'd gotten the same response earlier when she'd
called downtown with an offer to coordinate resources. They did not
like that she had been out to the hospital the evening before, muck-
ing around in their investigation.

Today when she returned to the office, there was a call from
Blackwell.

"You were out at the scene."

"Yes."

"I want you to put out a statement for the press," he said. "Tell
them San Francisco Homeland stands ready to support the Oakland
Police. But at this time there is no evidence of any national security
threat. Rather, this is a criminal matter, under investigation by the
Oakland Police. I've talked to the Bureau, and they are putting out a
similar statement, saying the FBI will assist as needed."

"Jensen says his client was targeted."

"The defense is going to say a lot of things. The best thing to do
with this kind of nonsense is to ignore it."

Chin understood his logic but did not necessarily agree. Back in
the seventies, the case had gotten tangled in side issues, baited by the
defense and a media cross fire that had forced the investigation inward, the agencies turning one upon the other. No doubt, Blackwell
did not want to see that happen again. Still . . .

"We have some profile sheets, known firebugs—"

Blackwell cut her off.

"Leave it to Oakland," he said.

SIXTEEN

Owens was restless. It was early evening, two days later, and he and his family were trying to get settled in the house on Fresno Street. His restlessness was natural enough, he supposed—given all that had happened. At the moment, the kids were upstairs. Owens and his wife sat in the living room, in the vinyl restaurant booth Dante's previous tenants had left behind.

"Dante's on his way," he said.

"What does he want?"

"The case— he has some questions."

"What does Moe say?" She looked at him with concern. "Is it wise to keep Dante on? I mean . . ."

"It would be less wise to throw him off."

"Is he eating with us?"

"We're going out to someplace in the neighborhood."

"I don't know . . ."

"Don't worry."

"I just wish we could get the hell out."

Jill was on edge, the kids disoriented. The kids wanted their backyard, their things. Not this claustrophobic row house on an alley of row houses tilting haphazardly on the hill, laundry hanging out the windows in back, all over the fire escapes, and Chinese music till all hours of the night.

Meanwhile the police had set up surveillance.

For the family's protection, they had said. The real reason, though, was because Jensen had pitched a fit in the media, accusing the prosecution of fostering a climate of retribution. It was good theater, maybe—designed to gain public sympathy—but Owens did not enjoy the scrutiny.

"I feel trapped," said Jill. "I feel like I am under house arrest."

"It's just for a little while."

"This place is musty—I can't get the musty smell out. And this furniture . . ."

"Jensen's looking for another place . . . maybe you can—"

"Me?"

She put her hands on her hips, indignant. Since his arrest, she had spent time on one crisis after another. To defend him, she and Moe had had to give up the case in Chicago and had thinned their docket here as well. It cost the firm money, putting them in the hole. Sprague had engineered their bail and helped with other things as well, but with Jill at home, and he, himself, unable to work, their household was running on empty. Also, there were things Sprague wanted—and it wasn't clear, exactly, how much further his generosity might extend.

"It's how the government works on you," Owens said. "Pitting one against the other—so even those people who are on your side, your friends, you can't be sure. I remember—"

"I don't want to hear about what you remember," she snapped. "I don't want to hear about any of that."

He couldn't blame her. Earlier today, they had taken care not to be recognized at the corner market: Jill in dark glasses, her hair pulled back; himself wearing a wool beanie and a 49ers shirt. She'd accused him of enjoying it. *Like the old days, yes. You and your gang.*

Now Jill stomped upstairs.

Owens sat alone in the restaurant booth, studying the alley. In a little while, he saw a darker shadow emerge from the other shadows in the alley, a black silhouette cast on the walkway, under the street-light, in the pool of light, growing larger; then the shadow became corporeal. Dante knifed out of the darkness and into the light.

O wens did not wait for Dante to knock but instead joined him out in the alley. He could see the surveillance car still there at the top of the alleyway. The cop was watching, no doubt. Owens knew this. No doubt the man inside the car had taken note of Dante's presence, of the comings and goings, but the man did not follow them. Dante walked with his head down and his hands in his pockets, and Owens walked beside him. Fresno Street was really nothing more than a cobbled path up the hill with row houses on either side. In the day-time they were all faded pastel, but at the moment, with the fog and the cadmium lamps, the clapboard looked fog slick and damp, all but colorless. As they clomped downhill, their pace quickened, and Owens had to admit, at least part of him wished he could just keep going.

"They're watching the house?" Dante asked.

"For our protection."

"Yes."

"I don't know which idea scares me more—the nutcases, or the cops perched outside my door."

"Jensen insisted?"

"Yes. But I want them gone. It's an intrusion."

Dante didn't say anything, and Owens found himself wondering if it were wise to push the matter. But no, he wanted the surveillance gone. In the first place, it was not 24/7. It was sporadic. If someone wanted to get them, they would get them.

And for all he knew, the cops and the loonies were in league.

They walked on Grant Street now, headed toward Columbus. Owens knew this neighborhood from his time underground, when he and Rachel, his first wife, had skitted from house to house—and he also knew it from his many years working as an investigator in the city. He caught a glimpse of himself in the window walking by, he and Dante under the electric light, himself with his wool cap pulled tight over his head, looking like he belonged here, slicing through the neighborhood. His wife was right—he enjoyed it, the street, walking the edge.

They worked their way across Columbus to one of the old-line restaurants on the slope of Russian Hill. The food was old-style—the noodles wet and heavy, the meatballs full of eggs and crumbs.

"It's good that there are still some places around like this."

"Elise Younger, as I'm sure you know, she claims she identified you, those years ago, coming out of the bank. You've seen the police sketches—the renderings they did back then."

Owens nodded.

"The likeness is good."

"I know," said Owens.

He smiled awkwardly, but the truth was, this turn in the conversation, it was not altogether unexpected. Meanwhile, a waitress sauntered over with their wine. Owens welcomed the interlude—watching her pour the glass, nodding his approval—but at the same time felt something darken inside himself. He tried not to let it show.

"Jan Sprague and Annette Ricci," Dante said, "what were their roles in all this?"

Dante was quick, Owens thought. *Maybe too quick. Perhaps Jill was right, and he should speak to Jensen.*

"It's true that I gave material support to the SLA—to Sanford after he escaped," he said. "That was why Rachel and I went to jail. Jan and Annette, they were around, but their roles . . ." he shrugged. "Annette was into guerrilla theater, Jan spoke at rallies against the war. We were fervent, But none of them, none of us . . ." Owens hesitated. "That drawing—Elise was ten years old. The police put ideas in her head. That whole time they were whispering in her ear."

Dante said nothing, not following up. Owens recognized the technique, having used it himself. You raised a question and let it sit there. Often as not, the interviewee would circle back, sometimes unexpectedly, and reveal something from the other side of that veil, from within the darkness.

"How's Marilyn?" he asked.

"They moved her out of the burn unit. But the fever, it's higher than they would like."

"The delirium?"

"It comes and goes."

Something about the way Dante regarded him, he felt a shift in the man, though maybe it was only the light, the way his eyes retreated, peering at him from the shadows of that enormous nose. Owens thought about the old North Beach, the one he'd never quite experienced, the saxophones blaring, the old beat poets howling, Lennie Bruce sniggering in front of the Hungry i. But there was another North Beach—the one with the old ones and their pasta and their Knights of Columbus meetings and their flags pinned to their lapels.

Dante, he realized, did not really belong to either one. It was hard to know which way he might fall.

"You know I appreciate you taking the case," Owens said. "I appreciate everything you have done. And if you want to back out, I would understand." He smiled. "I wouldn't be happy about it—but I would understand."

"No," said Dante. "I want to see this through."

Owens felt sheepish. He had opened the gate, giving Dante an avenue out, but the man wasn't going to take it. He hadn't suspected he would.

"I've been looking into the discovery material," Dante said. "The initial evidence and witness list that the prosecution submitted with the indictment. It includes an affidavit from the original indictment, back in '75, outlining your activities with the SLA."

Owens had seen the old affidavit—put together by Blackwell himself—chronicling his antiwar activities. His participation in the rally that had shut down the MacArthur Tunnel. His presence in the room when Sanford and a handful of others had cast their lot with the SLA. His alleged involvement in the kidnapping of heiress Patty Hearst.

According to the affidavit, contrary to the original reports, Leland Sanford had not been killed during the gun battle with the SLA in Los Angeles. He had survived, and together with Owens and the remaining members of the SLA they'd gone underground. To raise money for their activities, they'd engaged in a spree of robberies, including the one at Crocker National, where Eleanor Younger had been killed.

But the government had never been able to prove this, partly because they'd never found Leland Sanford.

"How about Cynthia Nakamura?" Owens asked now. "Is her name on the discovery material?"

"No. But Sorrentino's been looking for her. Nakamura—she provided you with an alibi, correct?"

Owens thought of all the times he had been on the other side of the table, listening to the stories of defendants on their way to trial. A junkie who'd shot a grocer in the Tenderloin. A Vietnam vet who'd been running a welfare scam for fifteen years. A farmworker who'd poured lighter fluid on his schizophrenic wife. They didn't remember their crimes, or changed the memories in their heads. Because to recognize them was to dissemble, to collapse into nothingness.

"Yes—we were in Aptos the day of the robbery. At Cynthia's parents'—down the coast. I was there. So were Jan and Annette."

"How about Leland Sanford?"

"No."

There were still stories, all these years later. Sightings in Tangier. Bali. In Castro's Cuba.

"Did you ever see him again?"

"No."

"He wasn't with you in Aptos?"

"No."

"I heard differently."

Owens shook his head. There was confusion about this, he knew, because the police had raided Cynthia's place in the city after their departure. Who they found was Cynthia's boyfriend, the poet Bob Kaufman. They had taken Kaufman into custody, not being able to tell one black man from another, and there had been stories ever since . . . a rumored correspondence.

"What happened next?"

"There was this swirl going on . . . The police . . . the feds . . . I realized . . ." Owens hesitated. "We feared the police would shoot us on sight, and so we made arrangements to meet with Jensen down in the Haight. Rachel and I, we were tired of running. So we took his advice. And we gave ourselves up."

SEVENTEEN

Earlier that same day, Dante had gone to the sidewalk memorial on Judah. What he thought he might learn, it was hard to say. The bank had been torn down, there was construction in progress, but he walked the perimeter of the site, trying to understand the eyewitness reports from decades before.

Dante had studied the newspaper accounts and the depositions. He'd seen the picture of Elise's mother: thick glasses; hair in short, tight curls; a face wide-boned and without glamour—German Czech by way of Oklahoma; a part-time department-store clerk recently moved to the city from the Central Valley.

Here, on the north end of the lot, Eleanor Younger had parked, leaving her young daughter in the car. She'd walked past a woman seated on a bench—a woman in a sundress and a straw hat—then four people had emerged from the alley at the back of the lot.

The alley was gone now, and the people who had emerged from it had been variously described. Two women and two men. Three men. A woman with curly hair. The woman with the curly hair was not a woman at all, but a man, African American, light-skinned. Or maybe Latino. Wild hair jammed up under a baseball cap. Regardless, the four had burst in through the side entrance, masks pulled tight, yelling the SLA slogan.

Death to the fascist insect . . .

Dante stepped past the shrine to the hole in the wooden fence. He peered at the excavation where the workers in their blue helmets and yellow jackets were laying concrete and rebar for the building that would go up where the bank had once been.

A thin man with a shotgun had stood at the center of the melee. The eyewitness accounts were contradictory. Not a man, but a woman with a husky voice. A woman giving orders in military fatigues, wearing a mask that muffled her speech. Not fatigues, camping clothes. Two of the gang moved swiftly toward the tellers while the one in the center shouted orders, and another paced back and forth, shouting, too, so it was hard to know whose voice was whose, which commands to follow. One minute, business as usual, the customers queued up between the velvet ropes—then, chaos, the line dancing backward, snaking away, people falling to the floor at the intruders' commands. Noses down to the linoleum.

Eleanor Younger had moved too slowly. Or too suddenly. When her purse slipped off her shoulder, the shooter misread the motion, maybe—panicked. Or maybe the shot was accidental. The suspected weapon had been recovered later, at an SLA hideaway. Forensics showed the shotgun's mechanism had been filed too fine, amateur work—a hair trigger so close it would go off too easily, at a sudden movement, a jerk, the waving of the gun.

Accident or no, the gun had fired. Eleanor Younger teetered a moment in her checked blouse and black slacks.

Hush up, hush up.

A man on the floor next to Eleanor as she lay whimpering implored her, *Shh! Shh!,* not realizing she'd been shot, he testified later. Fearing her cries would attract the gangsters' attention.

Hush up!

Dante turned away from the fence now, from the men down there in the blue helmets.

He all but tripped over the memorial. He got to his knees, straightening a vase that had fallen over.

As he did so, he felt the kind of prickling on the back of his neck that you feel when there is someone watching. *La Seggazza.* When he stood up, he saw a woman at the corner. Happenstance, perhaps, but no, she was often here, tending to the shrine; he knew this, because he'd tracked her himself. Now she stood at the corner, a half block down, flowers in her hand, watching.

Elise Younger.

The manner in which she'd hesitated gave him the impression, unlikely as it seemed, that she had recognized him, too. Perhaps he had the feeling because he had been digging into her past himself. He'd seen the pictures of her as a girl, and knew about her divorce, her breakdown, and a lot of other small things that he would eventually pass along to Hansen. He knew also that she had filed for a gun permit some time ago, but never actually purchased the weapon. Now she stared back at him—as if she had something to say. As if she had indeed recognized him as well, seen him hovering at the corners of her life.

Then she turned away, as if offended by his presence.

Now, back in North Beach, Dante turned the key and walked inside the apartment. The light flashed on Marilyn's machine, but Dante ignored it. He called the hospital to check on Marilyn's condition. She was sleeping quietly, the nurse said, and advised him to do the same.

"How's the fever?"

"Under control."

He stripped down to his underwear and lay on the bed. Then he went back to listen to Marilyn's messages. Well-wishers, friends. One of these messages was from a client of hers, David Lake.

Dante deleted the message and went back to the bed.

He did not sleep.

EIGHTEEN

Marilyn was floating, dreaming. Time was a nonsensical thing. They had taken her out of the burn unit earlier that day and removed the bandages from her eyes. Or maybe it was the day before. Either way, they'd had to remove the bandages carefully because in cases like this the lids themselves might peel off when the cotton was removed—and also the explosion had left bits of glass in her face. Periodically they changed the dressing and irrigated her eyes and examined them, but the doctor said nothing definitive either way, and during those brief interludes the room was a disconcerting blur of light and shadow. The cornea had been singed, and she felt as if she were peering up through some kind of scabrous jelly, so it was almost a relief when they replaced the bandages. Or would have been if not for the itching—and for the darkness.

They gave her more drugs.

One of the surgeries had been for preliminary grafting. Or maybe that was happening tomorrow. "Don't worry," the doctor had told her, "these burns are all show biz. You'll be healed up in no time."

Meanwhile, the side of her face felt as if it were on fire. The tar had splattered in a scattershot fashion over her chest and thighs and had soaked through the silk fibers of her blouse and burned through the raglan sleeves and left hot swamps of damaged nerves that transferred pain helter-skelter in ways that made it feel as if her flesh were in perpetual contact with molten iron.

She lay in the bed and listened to the television.

The drugs helped. They didn't make the pain go away, but instead moved it into the distance—as if it were a barking dog made bearable by shutting the window and cranking up the music and closing your eyes.

Just sing along. Just float.

Dante.

During surgery, the eye doctor had taken out the shard of glass that the paramedics had inadvertently jammed in deeper when they immobilized her eyes at the scene.

One side of her face was covered with bandages, and her skin oozed. She wondered how bad her scars would be.

All show biz.

On the television, a cartoon hound had just been hit over the head with a frying pan by a horse named Quick Draw. She couldn't see the cartoon, but she could hear it and in the darkness her mind made a picture. The hound was purple and the horse wore a holster.

She laughed.

Her mother stood next to the bed, dressed in a blouse with a fluted sleeve like it was 1966. Her mother had been dead for ten years, but it didn't matter. She'd dressed like that until the day she died.

Marilyn felt dispassionate and somewhat amused. It was the drugs, maybe. Dante came into the room. He had been here a lot, in and out. She was asleep, but she heard his footsteps or maybe she dreamed them—she had been delirious for a while but the fever and chills went away. Then they returned. She was lying on the Owens's lawn, under the blanket, chilled and burning at the same time. She was in the ambulance.

"We'll go to Spain," Dante said.

"Yes."

"We'll go along the coast."

"I'd like that."

"Just you and me."

"It's not safe to travel these days."

"We'll go along the Moorish coast, and then over to Sardinia by boat."

Along the coast there were white breakers, the sound of which was soothing at first, drowning out the sound of the dog outside the window, of the television laughter, and then the sounds of the waves became a white static that grew louder and more menacing. It pricked at her and danced on her body. Dante was trying to explain something.

"Owens . . ."

"Your father's house?"

"It's empty."

It made sense, she guessed, but something about the situation made her want to cry. She was in this hospital, and Dante had let them move into his father's house. Those strangers were living there as a family.

The room filled with noise now, as if someone had opened the window. She slammed it shut.

"Where are you staying?"

"At your place."

But she knew that he wasn't there, not really. Dante was never anywhere, even when he was by your side. He was like a reflection fissioning in the glass, everywhere and nowhere all at once. "We have to leave," she said.

"We will."

"Right away?"

"Right away."

"We have to get on the plane and go to Europe."

He didn't say anything, but she knew his logic. She needed to heal first. Visiting hours were almost over. There was a case to finish. But she couldn't wait for all that.

"Let's go now."

"All right."

She touched his nose. She reached out into the darkness and touched his nose and ran her finger over the hump in the middle.

"Go close the door."

"It's already closed."

"Go close it again."

He did as she told him. Humoring her, maybe. The pain had receded. Maybe the nurse had come and gone, administering the drugs. Or maybe the pain reliever was in her IV. But it was also true that the drugs only worked intermittently.

"I want you to fuck me."

"This is a hospital."

"I don't care where we are."

"You have burns all over your body."

"I want you to fuck me."

She thought he might laugh, or go away, but instead he leaned over and kissed her with those dry lips of his. She was in her hospital gown, no panties, and she guided his hand between her burned thighs, and in a little while he put his lips to her ears.

"I want you," she said.

He was a shadow in the dark corner of the room. He was not here. She thought of Cadaqués. The sound of motor scooters in foreign streets in a movie she did not quite remember, people pushing one another to get a look at something on the street. Technicolor water splashing against the sea walls, and the Arabs pushing to get a better look. The smell of intrigue, salt spray in the air. She reached out and touched Dante's shadow and felt the gun underneath his jacket.

"Your nose," she said.

He had his finger in her vagina.

"No, not your finger."

He moved away but that was not what she meant. She pulled him from the dark corner of the room and took his head between her hands.

"Your nose," she said again.

He understood then. She pushed his head down toward her midsection and ran her fingers through his hair while he hovered over her, on his knees, facedown between her thighs. His nose was inside her now, expanding, wet like a tongue.

His nose like the Italian peninsula. His noise like the hull of a ship. She was arching her back and tugging at the hospital bedsheets, clawing, and he was up inside of her, and she itched all over.

He ran his fingers over her body and her skin sloughed off in handfuls, and she heard herself moan in a way that maybe resembled pleasure.

But then it was over. The moment was gone. She was in some kind of haze lying on the bed while out in the hall there was the murmur of the hospital, the nurses at their station, footsteps down the hall. The sedation took her under.

When she awoke, the bandages were sticky, and there was a clamminess between her legs.

"Dante," she said.

But there was no answer. She slept for a while and then was awake again. Wide awake. The medication had worn off, and the door had broken down, and the window was flaring open, shattering—and she was in pain again, on fire, crying out his name.

NINETEEN

Over the next several days, Dante spent an inordinate amount of time tracking Guy Sorrentino. It was what Jensen wanted. There were other things on his mind: Marilyn, for one, and also the rumors, coming out of Oakland, saying the investigation into the bombing had gone flat. Meanwhile Jensen had him nosing through the discovery material, the endless list of witnesses the prosecution had put forward, but mostly, he had him tagging Sorrentino, trying to see if he could find a lead on Cynthia Nakamura: Owens's alibi.

Sorrentino lived on the side of the hill, in San Bruno, overlooking the freeway, so Dante found himself parked across the way, waiting and watching. The complex itself was nothing to look at: short and squat—a series of fourplexes, really—two-story affairs built in the fifties: white siding and aluminum frame windows and outside stairs. The stairs were concrete, with iron handrails that led up to open balconies where no one ever sat.

At the moment, Sorrentino was inside.

Dante knew this because he'd been around back and seen the

man's car, a Ford Torino, parked under the carport in the space marked 2C. Apartment 2C was nothing fancy—a one-bedroom that held a green sofa and mottled carpet and a kitchen sink full of take-out cartons. Dante knew this because he had surreptiously entered Sorrentino's apartment the day before, but that visit had been cut short.

So today, Dante would have to try again. He would go back up the stairs, and back through the sliding window.

Right now he had his eyes on the postal truck at the bottom of the hill. The complex was at the top of a cul-de-sac, and Dante could see the truck working its way uphill. In a little while, the driver would pull into Sorrentino's complex, toward a bank of mailboxes near the carport. The boxes had keys, but they were cheap locks and opened with a fingernail file.

Dante knew because he had rifled Sorrentino's box as well.

Fact was, Dante knew more about Sorrentino then he cared to know. He'd seen unwashed laundry on the closet floor. He'd staked out the apartment and knew the man was up at all hours. Inside 2C, the flickering light of the television played against curtains until well past midnight, and Sorrentino would appear every hour or so on the balcony to smoke a cigarette. Then in midmorning he would reappear on the concrete stairs—in his polo shirt, his gray slacks, a shapeless sports jacket—and then drive his Torino down to the Lamplighter Café on the El Camino. Not until after the postman came, though. Sorrentino always waited for the mail.

The afternoons were another matter. Sorrentino was not predictable. Sometimes he returned immediately after lunch. Other times he was gone for the duration.

Now the postal truck crept into the lot. The driver sorted the mail into the line of boxes. The truck crept out.

Dante waited.

Sorrentino did not appear.

Dante sat in his car behind the hedge in the lot across the way and listened to the birds in the trees and the sound of the freeway below. More time passed. A fly skittered across the windshield, and Dante sank lower in his seat. Then Sorrentino emerged. He had on his hat and his sports jacket and was also carrying a briefcase.

This was a new touch, the case. Dante didn't like it. Sorrentino was not the type to be carrying a case.

Yesterday, he'd gotten in without much trouble. He'd found Sorrentino's files easily enough as well, in a cabinet inside the bedroom closet. Jensen wanted information on Cynthia Nakamura and her whereabouts, and whatever else might be there. Dante's mistake had been to scan the files instead of simply lifting them all. Or maybe it wouldn't have mattered either way. Because no sooner had he begun than he heard the keys at the door.

Sorrentino, he thought.

It turned out to be the cleaning lady. It didn't matter. Dante had slid the file drawer shut. Then he stepped onto the bedroom balcony— and dropped over the side.

Now Dante watched Sorrentino walk across the lot with the briefcase in his hand. He waited until the green Torino disappeared down the hill, past all the flat-roofed apartments, turning onto the four lanes below, and then he went back up the concrete stairs.

This time, Dante decided, he would not dally. But he was too late.

When he went to the file cabinet, it was all but empty. The yellow pads, the files, the folders—they were all gone.

Dante searched the apartment. A handful of papers lay scattered on the kitchen counter—old mail, circulars, a statement from the bank. That statement did not suggest that Sorrentino was getting rich on the case.

Other than this, nothing.

Dante headed down the hill. Apparently Sorrentino had cleared out his files and taken them with him in his case. The timing seemed suspicious, as if the man had known Dante had been after them. It didn't seem likely. Regardless, Jensen wouldn't be happy about it, and Dante needed to see Marilyn. She was feverish one day, better the next, then feverish again, and the doctors kept changing their minds about whether to send her home. Dante had been down earlier but they'd sent him away.

Meantime, he still hadn't located Cynthia Nakamura, and the path back to her, to whatever had happened that day of the robbery, seemed to go through this dead poet. He could not see why else Sorrentino would be searching the man out.

He would go to North Beach, he decided, and pick up the trail there.

B ob Kaufman had been a figure on the streets, once upon a time, up and down Columbus Avenue. Dante himself had some vague memory of the man—thin, shadowlike, skin dark as an old saddle, muttering and gesticulating on the sidewalk in front of the Co-Existence Bagel Shop—though it was hard to know if the memory was genuine or something reconstructed from photos he'd seen in cafés and the stories people had told.

Bob Kaufman was part of the local lore, one of thousands who'd come to San Francisco after the war, when the shipyards were booming. Jewish father. Black mother. Youngest of fourteen children. He wrote his poems on paper bags. On toilet paper and advertising circulars. On scraps of dissolving tissue that fell from his fingers as he read. Stumbling around in stinking rags, holding forth inside bars full of Italians who did not want to listen.

The American Rimbaud, the French called him. Genius.

But the French were far away and did not have to deal with him sleeping in their doorways, or pissing all over their cars.

Kike. Nigger. Schizoid pain in the ass.

The locals had their own opinions. During the Vietnam War he had taken a Buddhist vow of silence. Truth was, people would tell you, he'd kept talking the whole time, muttering up and down the street, wailing in the park. He'd done a couple of stretches out at the local laughing farm, wrapped in a white jacket.

Sorrentino had been all over the Beach, Dante knew, with the picture of Kaufman and Cynthia Nakamura. Stella from the Serafina Café had pointed Dante here, to the Sleepy Wheel, and now the bartender directed him toward the couple at the end of the bar. The woman looked to be in her midfifties, and the man somewhat older—though it may have been that their faces had aged with drink and smoke. Dante ordered a beer.

"Bob Kaufman," Dante asked, "he used to hang around here?"

The woman jostled the man next to her. Her face was bloated and her eyes were blue.

"Hey, it's another one."

"Another what?"

"You a tourist? The tourists come in here all the time. Looking for Bob. And Ginsberg. Jack Kerouac. Hey, I tell them—those guys are dead."

"Give the guy a break," said the man.

"I'm just saying, he looks familiar."

The woman looked familiar to Dante, too. Not in a particular way but more generally, with her print skirt and the graying hair tied back in a ponytail. The man wore a vest and wire-rim glasses and a wide-collar shirt that had been fashionable once upon a time. The shirt was frayed, and the couple had a vague odor, as if it were not just the style that had gone unchanged.

"No," said Dante. "I'm not a tourist."

"I knew Kaufman," the man said. "I'm a poet myself." He put his chin out as he spoke, watching Dante, judging his reaction. "I can't say I knew Bob really well—nobody really did—but he was around here, just like I was around. Like everyone was around."

The man introduced himself then. His name was Jack. The woman smirked sadly into her glass.

"I slept with Bob Kaufman," the woman said. "Up on Montgomery Street. We fucked all night long."

Jack grunted, as if he'd heard this before, and the woman went on smirking. The bar was tucked into a side alley and a hard patch of light fell through the open door but did not penetrate to the interior. On the walls hung San Francisco memorabilia: Hack Escalante, Joe DiMaggio, a 1940s scare photo of a Jap plane circling the city.

"You a cop?" the woman asked. "The other one who was in here, he was some kind of cop."

Jack shot him a glance as well, and Dante felt their suspicion. On the other side of the room, a handful of locals engaged in conversation about politics, about an election that had been rigged, conspiracy theories. Tubes of nuclear fuel smuggled out of Russia via Korea, into Baghdad, as an excuse to go to war.

"I fucked Bob Kaufman," she said. "Jack doesn't believe me, but I did."

Jack acted as if he didn't hear. He had a story he wanted to tell

Dante, about the old days. About all the poets who'd been here once upon a time—Ginsberg and Corso and the rest, Ferlinghetti, DiPrima—of all of them, Kaufman was the only one who mattered, Jack said. For Jack, Kaufman's fingers bled ink, tissue paper still hung from his pockets, he recited not from memory or craft but read from the inside of his eyeballs. All the rest of them, they were pretenders as far as Jack was concerned. In their Nehru jackets, with their flowing robes, their whale poems, you could see them trying to figure out a way to steal it, to copy Kaufman's jazz rhythms.

"I fucked Bob Kaufman," the woman insisted. "Allen Ginsberg, Ferlinghetti, I fucked them all."

Jack turned to her. "Ginsberg was gay."

"What are you saying?"

"I'm saying he liked boys. Skinny boys."

"You saying I'm fat?"

"No."

"You're just jealous. That's always been your problem. But I was skinnier then, I admit. Rail thin. Ginsberg liked them skinny."

Of all the boho poets, Ginsberg was the big banana, even Dante knew that. Jack shook his head.

"Allen liked boys."

"My hair was just like it is now. Very blond. And I had big eyes." Her eyes were still big, and but the blond part, that was an act of imagination. "The poets couldn't resist me."

"You don't have a dick."

"Why should that be a matter of prejudice?"

"You have tits, but no dick—that would be a problem for Allen."

"Allen had tits himself—old-man tits that sagged down. Anyway, it was dark and he fucked me in the ass."

"You don't have a dick," he repeated.

"Bob Kaufman did," she said. "Bob had a big dick."

The woman slapped her glass down on the table and the place fell into silence. You could hear the toilet running in the back. After a while the bartender went back to jiggle the handle, but it didn't do any good, and the men at the other table resumed their talk. Something about the current government and the end of times. About the collusion between the CIA and the Israeli government. How the planes that crashed into the World Trade Center had been piloted by computer drones controlled by the Pentagon. Same way they killed Kennedy.

"The other man—who was in here the other day?" Dante asked at last. "The one who asked about Kaufman?"

Jack raised his eyebrows. The woman scowled.

"I told you," the woman said. "This one's a cop, too. Another goddamn cop."

"No," said Dante. "I'm a private investigator."

The man hesitated. "He wanted to know about Kaufman, same as you. He wanted to know if I had ever heard him talk about Leland Sanford."

The way the man stood, Dante got the impression he knew who Leland Sanford was. Apocryphal founder of the SLA . . . friend of the Panthers . . . declared dead in the ruins of the Los Angeles firefight, then resurrected, now vanished . . . maybe dead, maybe not . . . Rumors were that he'd had some kind of correspondence with Kaufman.

"The woman in the photo, the Japanese woman," Dante said, "did the man who was here, Sorrentino, did he ask about her?"

"She wasn't part of the conversation. Us girls, we were never part of the conversation."

"Did you know her?"

The woman shook her head.

"Bob wrote a poem about Sanford once," said Jack. That's all I know."

"Where can I find that poem?"

"He read it—some reading. But it's one of those scrap-of-paper things. Those papers that he just let flutter."

Jack smiled, as if he knew something he was not telling, though it was hard to tell if the look was purely for effect. Regardless, Dante bought the couple another round. Jack leaned over the bar. That particular reading, it had been at the library, he thought. Or maybe it had been down the coast. There was a guy with an eight-millimeter camera. Maybe he'd captured something. There was a Kaufman collection, down at the local library.

The woman sighed all of a sudden, a big, weary sigh. "Ginsberg had it wrong. The center of the universe is the vagina," said the woman. "Not the anus."

"That's not what the Buddhists say."

"What do the Buddhists say?"

Jack shrugged his shoulders. "Buddhists don't talk. Real Buddhists, they don't say a damn thing. But Ginsberg, you know, he couldn't shut up."

They were silent for a long moment.

"Kaufman, he didn't say anything. We just fucked."

"How did you know it was Kaufman?" asked Jack.

"Haven't you been paying attention? Kaufman. Not Kaufman. It's all inside our heads. We create all this shit ourselves."

TWENTY

It was true: Before leaving the apartment that morning, Sorrentino had taken a little more care with himself than usual. Upon rising, he took out a clean polo and newly pressed slacks. He hung his sports jacket on the towel rack as he showered, steaming out the wrinkles, then sat on the edge of his bed and punched out the dents in his felt hat. Instead of going out to breakfast, as he often did, he scrambled himself some eggs and ate in his undershirt, so as not to take the chance of spilling anything on himself. He polished his shoes, then washed the polish from his fingers. He dressed carefully, but when he was done and he examined himself in the mirror—slump shouldered, holding the briefcase by his side—he couldn't help but feel disconsolate.

Sixty-one years old. Divorced. Gut hanging out over his gray slacks.

Sorrentino had a meeting with the prosecutor's office later that afternoon in the city, but that was not the only reason for his preparations. He had another errand first. He drove north on the El Camino for a while, then headed west over the hills toward Daly City.

There was an envelope in his pocket, with a check inside.

Years ago, it had been truck farms out this way. It was all box stores now. There were people who longed for the old days, but he couldn't go with that. A person could only eat so much broccoli, so many tomatoes. He liked the box stores. They were cheap, and you didn't have to struggle all day for parking. You didn't have to deal with the no-goods on the city streets, or worry about running into someone you knew from the neighborhood, because there was no neighborhood.

But there was too much damn traffic. Too many damn cars.

He snaked his Torino up over the hill and down into Daly City.

His ex-wife still lived here, in the middle of the fog belt—in the little house that he had bought on his policeman's pay back in the late seventies. The idea had been that they would keep the place for a few years and then step up to someplace bigger. It hadn't worked out. Then a few years back there had been a rash of break-ins, so his wife put up iron bars on the door and the windows.

Now, whenever he drove by the house, he was taken aback by those iron bars.

Sorrentino parked a little ways up the street. His intention had been to go up and knock on the door, but he had had that intention before. Instead, he pulled out the check in his pocket, examining it.

Elise Younger had given the check to him a few days back—when they'd met, once again, at that diner out in the Sunset. Elise was out there two, three times a week, tending to the flowers on the sidewalk, the notes people left, the small commemorations from passersby. Cleaning up, too, the trash and scrubbing the graffiti from the sidewalk.

"No," Sorrentino had said. "I can't take your money."

"You must. You've done too much work for nothing. I don't feel right."

"Where did it come from?"

"That's not all of it," she said, embarrassed.

"A donation?"

"To the justice fund. The person who gave it, he wants to remain anonymous."

"You need it yourself. There's Sacramento coming up."

"That's taken care of," she said sheepishly. "I bought myself some clothes. Presents for the kids."

"Does Blackwell know about this?"

"It's none of his business."

She was right about that, maybe —and if people wanted to help her, well, it wasn't like there had not been expenses . . . but it made him uneasy.

"I'll go to Sacramento with you," he said. "To the Remembrance Day march. Just like last year."

She glanced away. Put her hand over his the way she liked to do.

"Take it."

Five thousand bucks.

It wasn't so much money, really, not for all the hours he'd put in, and though she wanted to give it to him, and he had his needs, there was something sad in her eyes. All through the conversation, it was like they were skating around something.

"That man who works for them—the investigator," she said. "I saw him out by the memorial."

"Nosey son of a bitch." He shook his head. "Nothing's sacred."

He took the check. He had his reservations, but he took it anyway. Then the next day, Blackwell called. The prosecution wanted to see him—and they wanted him to bring his files. He had half a mind to say no, but if it helped Elise, then OK. They needed him on the case, he thought. They had work for him.

Now Sorrentino held the check between his fingers. His ex-wife was home, he was all but certain. Her car was in the driveway. It was always in the driveway. What his ex did with her days, he didn't know anymore. She didn't work. She didn't do anything. With the divorce settlement he had given her half his pension, so he was always broke, and the house had gone downhill. The roof was leaking. She'd embarrassed him by calling up Leo Malvino's kid and asking him to do the work on account, till her husband caught up with his alimony.

His intention had been to walk up and ring the bell and give it to her. A way of exonerating himself somehow. He had gotten a hint of the kind of stories she told about him, and he wanted to clear his obligation. And maybe more than that, for her to see his name on this check and know that he was not a fool. He'd done a job and he had gotten paid.

But he had been at this point before, sitting in the car out in front of her house, with some offering or another. He'd been out to Colma, where his son was buried, but in the end, whether he sat in the car or went up to look at the grave, what difference did it make?

He couldn't bring himself to get out. No doubt, she still blamed him—because he had encouraged the kid to enlist. No doubt there were still pictures of their son on the mantle, in the tiny hallway, on the bureau in their bedroom. If he knocked on the door, he would have to look into her eyes, he would have to see all those pictures. There was no telling where things would go.

He couldn't do it.

He drove around the corner to the local post office and dropped the check in the mail. His wife would see the postmark, he told himself. That was good enough. She would know he had mailed it from nearby.

The prosecution had scheduled the meeting for just after two. Sorrentino was not sure exactly what they wanted from him, but he had brought his files, as requested. He parked the Torino in a cyclone lot up Polk Street, even though it meant walking past a boat-load of junkies and an asshole transvestite. *Hey fat boy, what you got in those pants?* Still, it was better than paying the higher fees at the Union Street garage.

Outside the Federal Building, there were protestors. This wasn't anything new. There were always protestors outside the Federal Build-ing. This particular group, Code Pink, he remembered from the press conference, the day they'd brought in Owens, though their numbers had grown. Older women mostly, dressed in black tights and pink T-shirts, continuing their vigil, protesting U.S. troops massing in the Middle East. "All for oil!" they chanted, "All for greed!" There were maybe seventy five of them chanting in the north end of Federal Plaza and a smaller group on the sidewalk, just outside the square. At the fringes, a number of the woman stood passing around cartons of milk—and a number of these looked quite pale, as if seized by a sudden illness. As he walked into the plaza, the chants echoed more loudly against the building. Meanwhile, the cops watched placidly.

Sorrentino couldn't believe this city.

Everywhere else in the country these days, people had flags out their windows, bunting everywhere. Anywhere else, loudmouths like these would be stuffed in the tank.

But here . . .

The women looked harmless enough, but Sorrentino knew better. Lesbians. Professors from Berkeley. Women on the edge of menopause, too uptight to get laid. He had a sister-in-law like this. College teacher, so used to laying off her opinion on her students, she'd gotten the idea that the world was her soapbox. If you disagreed with her, if you so much as twitched, then there was something the matter with you.

Eventually, even her husband had gotten sick of listening and left for another woman. One of her students, as it turned out. A girl with big eyes and no opinions.

Sorrentino reached the security barricade at the front of the building, and there joined a line that snaked back into the plaza, to the image of the federal seal embedded there in concrete. The line moved slowly. Up ahead, there was some kind of problem with the scanning machines.

Across the plaza, the protestors fell quiet. The group did not seem as cohesive as it had just a few minutes before, lingering now in smaller groups, loosely knit—like a flock of birds, flamingoes in their pink shirts and spandex leggings. They started to move then, as if by some common signal. The police moved, too, in an arc outward from the center of the plaza. Since 9/11, protestors were restricted to the far end of the square, and the police moved now in such a way as to keep the women toward the periphery. The chanting started up again. One of the women broke from the others, dashing forward toward the police, then all of a sudden falling to her knees. Another woman did the same. Similar scenes, more or less identical, played out around the plaza—a woman bolting toward the statue of justice, another holding her stomach as she ran, heading for the security quay, straight toward Sorrentino, her face contorted, as if she meant to leap into his arms. A cop ran to intercept her. At the last minute, she pulled up short. The policeman stopped, too, regarding her warily. The chanting went on in the distance. And as the cop stepped forward, his club drawn, the woman grabbed her stomach, doubled over, then vomited violently onto the federal seal.

Pink puke, bubbling and frothing. Pink blood.

Around the square, the same scene played itself out, women rushing forward, falling to their knees. *America makes me puke! The blood of America is in my belly!*

The plaza smelled of curdled cream.

We are vomiting up the blood of America!

The policeman leaned over the woman now, struggling to get her cuffed. She gazed up at Sorrentino. Her eyes were bright with hatred. Her lips were pink.

The security guard emerged from behind the barricade and started herding the line. He glanced at Sorrentino's trousers and shook his head.

"A vomiting agent," he said. "They put into milk, along with pink dye. One of them got into the lobby this morning."

The milk was on his pants legs, all over his shoes. Meanwhile, the woman struggled with the cop. "Since when is it against the law to get sick?" she said.

Then she vomited again.

Sorrentino danced backward on his toes.

Inside, Sorrentino dampened a paper towel, cleaned his shoes, blotted his pants legs. After the incident, it had taken him another twenty minutes to get through security. He was going to be late as it was, but there were tiny flecks on his jacket still, and on his shirt.

Dabbing these only seemed to make matters worse. As he rode up in the elevator, he noticed the damp spots still visible under the fluorescent light. Worse, he feared, was the lingering smell.

The smell seemed worse inside Blackwell's office when he leaned over to shake hands. Mike Iverson, the assistant prosecutor, sat at the table, too, and also the Chinese woman from Homeland Security.

Blackwell had a stack of trial folders at his elbow, and paperwork lay scattered about the table.

"I'm sorry I'm late," he said. "There was an incident outside. The Code Pink . . ." He started to explain, then decided, no. It made him look like a buffoon. "I got tied up in security."

Blackwell and the others did not respect him, he knew that. Never mind that he had practically dumped the case in their laps. Never mind that he was the one who had chased down the remaining witnesses after thirty years and told the prosecution about the new forensics that would link the Younger murder to the ammunition at the SLA safe house. More than that, he was the one who'd found Cynthia Nakamura.

He only hoped she didn't die before the trial.

"I brought all my case notes, like you asked."

"We appreciate your cooperation."

"Well, any way I can help."

Sorrentino had never worked with Blackwell on the force, but he remembered department people grousing because he was always getting into their business, trying to federalize local investigations. A glance at Chin told him she understood the situation. Blackwell didn't work in the field so much as he once had, maybe, but behind a desk—and from that desk he pulled a lot of strings. But there was a string hooked to him as well, and that string went down the long corridor all the way back to those assholes in Justice. The only reason this was going to trial was because there was a certain spectacle the feds wanted everyone to see. *Don't fuck with us, do everything we say.* In some ways, these people were just as bad as those women out in the streets.

"I'm sure you know—in fact, we had this conversation once before: The government has its own folks on this now."

"Yes."

"But you've still been out fishing, haven't you?"

"Just some loose ends."

"What kind of loose ends?"

"Leland Stanford, if you remember. I've been looking into the notion that he communicated with Kaufman, all that confusion about whether Sanford died in that raid. I mean, the first time around, the case never recovered from that."

It was the wrong thing to say.

Blackwell had been involved in all of that, ridiculed in the press back then, and again more recently.

"You understand what you've been doing?" asked Blackwell. "Walking around North Beach, with a picture of Cynthia Nakamura? There's a reason we are holding her in protection, you know."

Sorrentino hung his head a moment. How they knew about his efforts, he had no idea, but it was true he had not been particularly discreet. He tried to explain. "Those women, Annette Ricci, Jan Sprague, they were at the farm in Aptos." He hesitated, unsure where he was going. "If Owens doesn't have an alibi, then neither do they."

There was an exchange of glances then, between Iverson and the others, and Sorrentino got the impression he'd touched upon something. What? Identifying Sanford, locating him, had been integral to their case thirty years ago, and more recently as well, but now they seemed more concerned with keeping Cynthia Nakamura under wraps.

He didn't quite get Blackwell, the man's angle, his point of view—but he was starting to understand, whatever that view, it did not include Guy Sorrentino. His own interviews with Nakamura had been preliminary. She had not told him everything, he knew that. Blackwell came in later, and he wondered what he had gotten her to say.

"You are the ones who sent me after Kaufman," he said. "It was your—"

Blackwell snapped now, cutting him off. "Are you trying to tell me that you are going to accomplish what the FBI hasn't been able to accomplish for thirty years? That you are going to pull Leland Sanford out of a hat?"

"All I'm saying—"

"You're out of your league," snapped Blackwell.

"I know you are well intended," said Iverson.

"Fuck his good intentions. You interfere with this case, Mr. Sorrentino, it's obstruction of justice."

"I'm working for Elise," he said.

"This isn't up to Elise. She interferes, we will file against her, too."

Blackwell leafed through the file in front of him, pulled out an envelope, then pushed it across the table. Sorrentino opened it. Inside, he found pictures of himself—on the landing outside his apartment, on the streets of North Beach. In some of the pictures, items had been circled. A gray Honda Accord. A man's face. The same man later, on a street corner. Sorrentino in the foreground, oblivious.

"The man's name is Dante Mancuso."

"I know who he is."

"Another ex-cop. Not one of our favorite people."

"He's been following you for a couple of weeks," said Chin.

"This one was a lousy cop." Blackwell pointed at Mancuso's picture. "And he was shitty undercover, not knowing when to back off. That nose of his, that face—how could you not notice somebody like that following you, a face like that?"

Sorrentino felt his own face burning. He thought of the check Elise had given him, and the little kiss on the cheek, and the vague look of sadness in her eyes. He had felt disloyal, not telling her about this meeting, but now he suspected she had known.

Meanwhile, he noticed a fleck of pink on his jacket. He brushed it from himself as the others watched. The damp spot on his polo had left a vague stain, and his pants legs were still damp.

The air around him smelled of sour milk.

"Listen, Guy," said Iverson. "You've been invaluable, but we're moving past the investigation now, into the trial. And one of the things we are concerned with, like it or not, a case like this, is controlling the pretrial publicity. The firebombing—that works against us. It gives them sympathy. Meanwhile, Elise has this thing coming up in Sacramento . . . It's going to be very high profile."

Sorrentino knew what was coming. They were prepping Elise for the final push. They were going to take his files and freeze him out. She had known.

Five thousand bucks.

"We think it would be better, for the case, for Elise, if you kept your distance."

"Elise agrees?"

"Yes," Blackwell said. "Elise agrees."

PART FOUR

The Parade

TWENTY-ONE

Maybe it was the next afternoon, as Dante pulled out of the hospital lot, that the car first appeared behind him. Or maybe it was a little farther along, on Cathedral Hill, as he negotiated the long swoop down Gough Street, past churchyards and playgrounds and the sidewalk nobodies who slumped along in the shadows. Either way, he did not notice the car at first, preoccupied as he was with other things.

Marilyn would be released the next day. At the moment she was in session with a medical cosmetician—a woman who specialized in makeup for burn victims. "Girls only," Beatrice had whispered to him in the hospital corridor, arms loaded with packages, clothing from Dazios. "Why don't you come back later, when she's all dolled up."

Dante had promised to return.

In the meantime, he headed across town toward Annette Ricci's. He had tried to get access to Jan Sprague earlier, but the reception at the Sprague mansion on the Heights had been pretty chilly—and Jensen had called afterward, telling him to back off. It didn't make sense to Dante. Partly, he supposed, the sensitivity had to do with some of the stuff running in the paper lately, wide-swinging attacks from the law-and-order people, hyperbole suggesting the bombing was some kind of ruse, that the police had not looked hard enough at the people on the scene. Still, if the defense wanted him to find Nakamura, well, Sprague had known her back then. And so had Ricci.

Dante kept driving.

He remembered Annette and her Sandinista boyfriend chatting it up in Owens's kitchen. He remembered the Honduran tamales and the taste of the corn. He remembered Marilyn writhing on the lawn.

Dante had some questions for Ricci. He wanted to ask her about Cynthia Nakamura, true. But he had some other questions as well.

Halfway down Gough, rolling down that long hill, Dante spotted a green Torino in the traffic behind him. The car kept its distance—not rushing to make the light, but not falling off either, rising over the crest, disappearing again into the trough at the inter-section. Then reappearing.

Sorrentino, he figured, but the car was too far back to tell, and San Francisco was a big city after all. There was likely more than one green Torino still on the road.

Near the McAllister projects, in the sump at the bottom of the hill, Dante pulled over. The Torino kept coming. It was a one-way street, and the car switched into the far left as it approached, but Dante got a good look at the man, anyway. It was Sorrentino. He drove with his hat on and his nose up, both hands on the wheel, eyes ahead.

Dante stayed put for five minutes, ten, waiting. It was possible, he supposed, that Sorrentino's appearance was coincidence.

Dante circled the block once, then parked again, waiting—but there was no sign of the Torino. He pulled into traffic. Then it was there again in the rearview, tagging him across Market Street into the Mission.

Annette Ricci's house was in the Inner Mission, in the old Irish neighborhood. When Dante was a kid, his father used to take him to the Longshoreman's Hall down on Mission Street, and sometimes after those meetings they went to Mackie's, a restaurant full of old micks, but the place had been an island even then. Irish waiters in their tuxes and their brogues, hostesses named Molly and Catherine and Margaret, hair gone gray, freckles gone to moles, long dresses wrapped in the middle with green sashes. The last of those places was long gone, the Irish having trundled south to Daly City, then vanished altogether, as far as you could tell, taking their potatoes with them and their kids and their green beer.

It was a Latino neighborhood now—Salvadoran and Guatemalan and Nicaraguan—refuges from Central America, dissidents, some of them right wing, some left, but mostly just villagers following their relatives north, working to send money back home.

Sorrentino followed him past Mackie's, then down Folsom. Toward the end, the man gave up on being inconspicuous and tagged up right behind him. On Ricci's street, Sorrentino swung a circle and parked halfway up the block. Dante could guess what had happened. Sorrentino had figured Dante as a tail, and now he wanted a few words. The man sat in his Torino, as if he expected Dante to walk over. Instead Dante walked the other way, toward Ricci's place on the corner. The son of a bitch could wait.

Annette Ricci's place was a large Victorian, a decaying house in the Eastlake style that had last been painted a couple of decades back—a painted lady gone to seed, the lower story done up hippie-style, bright colors, sunbursts in the friezes. The upper story, beyond the easy reach of ladders, was an older style, a muted brown, so there was a kind of schizophrenia to the place. A large magnolia tree grew in the yard. A canary palm. Boston ferns.

It had been a co-op at one time, Dante knew, actors' quarters up top, a studio in the back, but that arrangement had fallen apart, as tended to happen, and Ricci owned the property now. Over the gate hung an iron sign.

THE SAN FRANCISCO TROUPE
The Play's the Thing

Dante went through the gate and into the yard. In a little while, Annette Ricci herself opened the door.

Her hair had been restrained under a scarf, pulled in tightly, and this had the effect of accentuating the rawness of her features and a certain imperious beauty. She did not seem surprised to see him, but instead smiled easily—though she was an actress, of course, and thus possessed a plasticity of expression.

"Come in. But I have to warn you, we have a rehearsal in a little while."

"This won't take long."

"I can give you a few minutes now. Or if you'd rather come back later?"

"Now's good."

"I'll tell Juan to begin the warm-ups without me."

She left him alone in a small parlor decorated with kachina dolls—a considerable number, actually, all arranged rather precisely, too precisely—and also memorabilia from the troupe's earlier days. Ricci had been there from the beginning, he saw. She'd joined the troupe in the late sixties—a renegade from her father's ranch in Wyoming—a gangly young woman whose eyes in the photos glimmered with the air of the prankster. In person, the mischievousness had a harder edge—he'd seen that edge at the party—but he'd seen also her ability to act quickly, and the comfort she'd given Marilyn. Even so, as she walked into the room now, she held her head a bit too high, and he could see again in her the need to control.

"So what can I do?"

"Mostly," he said, "I was hoping you could help me with the discovery material. There are a few witness names here, on the prosecution list, we haven't been able to identify."

"You used to be a cop?"

"It shows?"

"I heard a rumor." She laughed. It was a charming laugh, vulnerable. "And so why did you leave the force?"

She arched her eyebrows. She had switched roles, making him the subject of the questions. Partly it was her desire to be in control, but in these situations the behavior wasn't unusual. People often felt more comfortable answering questions if you gave something up first—some small piece of yourself.

"I had an opportunity. Corporate security," he said. The statement contained an aspect of truth, more or less, but he had no intention of elaborating. There were things about his past he kept to himself. No different from Owens, he supposed. No different from a lot of people. "Nothing too glamorous, I'm afraid." Then he handed her the list. "You'll see the prosecution has listed your name as well."

"As an unfriendly witness, no doubt."

"Have they talked to you?"

She shook her head. "Thirty years ago I gave them a statement. If they intend to take Bill to trial, I imagine I'll hear from them."

Dante had been through the discovery material and he knew the substance of that statement. Her own involvement with the SLA had never been so firmly established as Owens's. A government informer, working at KPFA, the underground radio station, had identified her as an insider. A surveillance photo had caught her on the steps of the SLA safe house in Berkeley a few days before the robbery, standing alongside her boyfriend at the time, Naz Ramirez: an SLA recruit with a dope habit—who years later told a cellmate that he'd been in the bank with the group on the day of the robbery. But Naz himself was dead now, and that kind of talk, retold by an ex-cellmate currying favor with a parole board, didn't carry a lot of weight.

Anyway, according to her own statement, Annette Ricci had been out in Aptos the day of the robbery, working with Cynthia Nakamura on a theater project.

"Cynthia was painting backdrops for us. That's how we knew her. Her parent's place in Aptos, there was an old barn," she said. "Jan and I went down there for a few days to help with the backdrops. Bill came along, too."

"Was she active politically?"

"Not really. She was just a painter."

"Did you meet Kaufman?"

"Cynthia's boyfriend? The poet?"

"Yes."

She smiled. "We took a walk on the beach."

"What did you talk about?"

"It was a long time ago."

"Did he mention Leland Sanford?"

She bent down then, all of a sudden, tugging at her shoes, tucking her finger in the area behind her heel. Something about the gesture, her discomfort, did not seem altogether genuine. "I met Lee a couple of times," she said.

"According to the report, after Sanford disappeared, you went down to the radio station with a tape of Sanford. Some photos. But it wasn't clear if these were from before the shootout in LA, or after."

"Why are they going down this road again?"

Dante wasn't sure, but the broadcast of that tape, together with the confusion over the dentals, had contributed to the mystery of Leland Sanford's disappearance. That confusion had ultimately undermined the government's case.

"Some of the old affidavits, they imply you orchestrated all that confusion. Blackwell and some of the others—"

"Blackwell is a snake," she said. "A prick with two heads." It was clear she enjoyed insulting the man, and enjoyed, too, the bawdy language. "Pull his tail in Washington, one of those heads—it pops up out of a hole on Larkin Street."

"The confusion over Sanford, did you orchestrate that?"

"Whose side are you on?" She laughed again, and this time put a hand on his arm, leaning into him—dropping her guard just for a moment, holding her head in that imperious way, eyes flashing, wanting him to know her role, to see her cleverness. "I never saw Lee again, after the awful business in Los Angeles, if that's what you mean. But I wouldn't doubt he's still alive. In spirit, if not in reality." Dante glimpsed for an instant the same disdain he had seen in her face, that moment at the party—and on her current boyfriend's face, too, the Sandinista, when he had asked about their upcoming play. Dante had a question, regarding the day at the house, but decided to save it. Instead, he returned her attention to the names on the prosecution witness list.

"Do you know any of these people?"

"It's a long list."

"If you could just look through?"

He let her linger over the list, talking up the people she knew. She was chatty on the surface but in the end didn't tell him much he didn't already know. He directed her attention toward the unknowns. Ringers, he guessed, thrown in by the prosecution to keep him occupied, but it didn't mean there wasn't something hidden there.

"Cynthia Nakamura—did she remarry?"

She shrugged. "Not that I know of. Are they trying to find Cynthia again, is that what this is about?" Dante saw, for a moment, he thought, the same slackness he'd seen in Owens's face. "The feds, they put some pressure on her back then. They didn't like her story."

Outside, in the backyard, the players had gathered. Dante could see them through the window—Juan the Sandinista dressed up in a cardboard outfit with giant wings, an airplane with a bomb strapped to his belly. A woman in a suit and tie, holding a remote control.

"I would ask you to stay, but we keep our rehearsals closed. You know, we like it to be a surprise."

"You'll be in Washington Square, on Columbus Day?"

She shook her head, correcting him.

"Native People's Day."

"Yes," said Dante. "That's what I meant."

At the door she embraced him, holding him a little closer than he expected, pressing her cheek to his, like he was on old friend, someone whom she was not quite ready to let go.

"I appreciate what you are doing for Bill."

"I'm being paid."

"Have they found anything—on what happened to Marilyn?"

"Not yet. But the police, they don't talk to me much."

"How is she?"

"I am going back to the hospital just now, for visiting hours."

"She's such a lovely thing." Her eyes watered, and he saw something like compassion, but there was again also the plasticity of expression.

"One more question."

She looked at him, puzzled.

"At the Owens's party. Why did you lock the back door behind you, before you came into the yard?"

"I like a captive audience. I wanted everyone to see the play." She said it shyly, as if embarrassed at her vanity. At the same time engaging him with her smile.

"The tamales?"

"Pardon?"

"Wrapped in banana leaves. In the kitchen, Jill said—you and Juan, you brought them early."

She nodded, pleased. "You liked them?"

"There was another man with you."

"Oh," she said, wincing, bending at the knees.

"What's the matter?"

"These new shoes, they are just too tight on my feet."

"The man?"

She looked at him then. "He was an immigrant. Doing delivery work, that's all. A man without papers. The police had the same idea as you—find a Latino to blame. They've already arrested several from what I understand."

"Where can I find him?"

"You won't."

"Why not?"

"Without papers," she said. "Would you stick around? No, he's long gone by now. Picking somebody's fruit. Mowing someone else's lawn."

The Torino had not moved. Sorrentino sat as before, leaning back, his head just visible above the wheel. Overhead, the sun was going down. Dante glanced toward his car across the way, listing toward the curb, then back toward Sorrentino. He was tempted to let the man stew, but he wanted to see Marilyn—and he did not want Sorrentino following, waiting in the hospital lot.

He headed toward the Torino.

Up close, he noticed the car was not as well preserved as he had thought. The carport in San Bruno had protected the paint some-what, but the vinyl top was peeling. Still, the car fit Sorrentino. He sat behind the wheel with a certain pleasure, like some kind of bull-dog prince, feigning indifference as Dante approached.

Dante circled around to the passenger side and opened the door. The seats were green leather and had weathered reasonably well. In-side, though, was the vague smell of spoiled milk.

"I knew you would walk over here," said Sorrentino.

"How did you know?"

"It's your generation. You like to talk about things. All those psy-chologists."

Sorrentino snorted.

"Why are you following me?" asked Dante.

"What's this? You can do as you please, you rifle through my busi-ness, but I have to stay in my shell—that's how it goes?"

"All right," said Dante. "Now we're even." He reached for the door handle.

"I'm not finished," said Sorrentino.

"What is it you want to tell me?"

The man snuffled, eyes flashing, as if he did not really know what he wanted to say. "You're on the wrong side."

Dante didn't feel like listening to this kind of thing.

"Why help Owens and those sons of bitches—after they murdered that woman in cold blood?"

"You don't know that."

"I know, and so do you. Underneath all your shit, you know."

"My fiancée—"

"She's not your fiancée," Sorrentino interrupted. "You haven't given her a ring. You never asked her to marry you."

It was true, but it made Dante angry to hear it from Sorrentino.

"I know things, too. You poke in my life, I poke in yours," Sorrentino barked. "But it wasn't Elise Younger who firebombed that house. You got everything back assward. Your father—"

"Don't talk to me about my father."

"You're on the wrong side," Sorrentino said again. "That girl lost her mother."

"That's not why the government's on this case. That not what this is about anymore."

"Maybe not to you. Where's your conscience?"

The remark got under his skin. Some other time, maybe, some other universe, he and Sorrentino might have been *paisans*. They might have worked together. But if this conversation went on, he was going to haul off and slam the guy. Meanwhile Sorrentino regarded him with a new scorn. Dante felt something inside, like a coil tightening. "Get out of here," said Sorrentino—but there was a tremor beneath the bravado. His jaw quivered. "I don't want to talk to you anymore."

Dante nodded. "Nice car."

As he walked away, Dante waited to hear the Torino's engine fire up, but the sound didn't come. His own car, it listed too heavily toward the curb; then, walking to the other side, he noticed what he had missed before: His back tire had gone flat. Across the way, Sorrentino sat with his arm out the window, just sitting, watching. Dante bent to his knees and saw the stem had been slashed.

He was tempted to walk back across the street, to yank Sorrentino out of the car, hold him by his neck like a fish on the wire.

Dante's plan had been to return to the hospital—and he could still do so. Pull the spare out of the trunk. Change the flat. Drive to the station on Twenty-fourth for air, even if he had to ride the rim.

Sorrentino fired the ignition.

Dante pulled out his keys and went over to the trunk and hesitated over the lock. The Torino drove by slowly, but Dante did not look up, he did not turn his head. He waited till the car crept by, resisting the temptation. He kept his head down and his eyes on the key slit on the trunk.

The lock had been filled with putty.

TWENTY-TWO

So, we'll fix you up, you can ride with us on the Columbus Day float," said Beatrice Prospero.

"Not with this face," said Marilyn.

The medical cosmetician had arrived some time ago, and Marilyn watched as she rearranged her creams on the tray by the bed. Then Marilyn jimmied the controls so as to bring herself further upright, into position. Meanwhile, Beatrice sat in a chair with her legs crossed.

"My father will be insulted, you do not ride."

Beatrice Prospero was a big woman with pomegranate hair and a husky voice. She smiled slyly, but it was true what she was saying. Her father had a float, and he ran it every year in the parade, loaded up with staff Realtors and their families, and he did not care how they looked, so long as they wore company blazers.

"I don't know," Marilyn said.

Dante had been by earlier, Marilyn knew, and had promised to return. She wondered how she would look.

"Wait till you see how we get you looking," said the cosmetician. "There's no reason to keep yourself locked up."

"That's right." Beatrice had gone shopping for Marilyn, and herself as well, clothes from Dazio's, and the bags lay clustered at her feet. "There's plenty of ugly people walking around. Take Mollini's wife. You don't see her staying at home, do you?"

"I thought she had died."

"I'm talking about the daughter-in-law. She has the face of a dog."

"Tony Mora, he used to date her."

"See what I mean? Anyway, it doesn't matter. My father will insist you ride on the float."

The cosmetician began applying Lycogel. "You are healing well," she said. The nurses had told her the same. They had started applying the Lycogel almost immediately after the surgery to oxygenate the skin, and the cream hid the scars. Even so, Marilyn knew she was not a pretty picture. The grafts were still raw, and the way the stitches turned gave an ugly twist to the corner of her mouth. The worst part, though, was her right eye. The lid was deformed, the eye itself discolored, and she could not bare to look at herself in the mirror. The doctors were not sure yet whether it could be saved.

"We start by building a base."

The cosmetician showed Marilyn how to thicken the base to cover the scars and how to mix the Lycogel with color so that the flesh tones matched. It was a time-consuming process, like theatrical makeup, and was not without pain. Marilyn had suffered burns on her arms as well, and on her hands, and so had difficulty imitating the procedures. The cosmetician applied the special lipstick, feathering away the scar, painting in eyebrows where they had burned away.

"You'll get the hang of it," the woman said. "What color eye patch would you like?"

"Color?"

"The new patches, they breathe really well. And there's quite an array." The woman had a box full.

"Am I going to look like a pirate?"

"Don't worry. You see it in all the magazines."

"Give her that one," said Beatrice, "with the sequins."

The cosmetician positioned the patch, then started examining her hair. It had been burned to the dander on one side and hacked by the emergency crew. A stylist had spent some time with it earlier, but the cosmetician wasn't satisfied. She worked at reshaping, leaving the hair relatively long on one side, cutting it short on the other.

"This look is in fashion."

It was true, Marilyn understood—a flapper look, but more drastic, edgy, not something you saw on the street but on the runways, with high-fashion models, and even the patch some way fit in.

If you used your imagination—and ignored the mottled scalp.

The cosmetician had an answer for this as well, a way of folding the scarf and tying it under. By the end of the session, Marilyn was exhausted, but there were still the clothes. She had sent Beatrice to Dazio's, and she knew what was in those boxes. A chiffon blouse, black slacks. A carmine-colored shift. A pair of red flats.

She knew, though, even before Beatrice took them out of the boxes, that she would not be wearing the slacks. Her thighs were burned, and her abdomen, and she could not wear anything that clung.

She got out of bed, standing flat-footed on the floor, and the women helped her into the shift. Then they admired her. They went on and on. She was beautiful. She was a doll. The shift was of a thin material that let the light through, so she was a rose in the field, said Beatrice, it was impossible to take your eyes away.

It wasn't quite true, Marilyn thought.

She did not look like herself. She looked fragile and somewhat silly. The material chafed. Still, she would keep the dress on until Dante arrived. He should be here before long.

Beatrice lingered.

They talked property values, how the market was still ascending. They talked about the Columbus Day parade. They talked about how Rossi's Grocery was closing down because the Rossi kids had decided enough was enough, and they could do better selling the property.

"It's a good thing," said Beatrice.

It was her mantra, learned from her father—the salesman's mantra—everything was good, everything an opportunity. If the market was up, this meant ascending values. If it was down, it meant a buying opportunity. There was always a light in the distance, a lining around the clouds.

The nurse entered. "Someone is here to see you. He has flowers."

Marilyn smiled. She couldn't help herself.

"Good timing," said Beatrice. "You look wonderful."

Sitting on the edge of the bed, in her loose dress, belted at the waist, with her eye patch and her new lashes, Marilyn wasn't so sure. She felt nervous, like a bride. The makeup had an unnatural look, she feared. In a certain light, you could see the crosshatching from the sutures, the mottled skin. It was easily mussed and would take hours to put on.

She heard the nurse go away and then other footsteps approaching, but knew it could not be Dante because he did not make that kind of shuffling noise, but came up on you softly. And she was right. It was the other man—with his millions of dollars and his many houses.

"Flowers," said David Lake.

"How beautiful."

Though she gushed, and Beatrice did, too, she had no doubt David Lake had sensed her surprise at his sudden appearance. He smiled anyway, clean shaven in his white shirt, boyish, and she saw at once both his charm and his vulnerability—the manner of a man who knew the limitations of his charms but was going forth, anyway. She was, despite herself, happy to see him. Meanwhile, Beatrice Prospero watched. Marilyn could all but hear the woman's brain clicking, and in that brain, Marilyn knew, Beatrice was adding up the man's worth, putting it alongside Dante's, comparing the one against the other.

Dante would lose.

"I was just leaving," said Beatrice.

"Not yet."

"Yes. You've got to get ready for tomorrow. So I'll let you two visit."

Usually visitors could stay till nine, but she had a procedure early in the morning, one last examination before the doctors signed her out. David Lake sat with the flowers between his knees.

"I am afraid I have delayed the sale of your property," she said.

"It's not the most important thing in the world. Are you comfortable? Do you want to lean back?"

"Yes."

He used the buttons to lower the bed into the reclining position, then helped her scoot back, so she lay faceup with her hands at her sides. She still wore the colorful shift.

"I suppose I should let you rest."

"You can get someone else to represent the house—Beatrice would be glad to."

"No, I signed with you. I can wait."

"You'll miss the market."

"Close your eyes."

He was a goof, but she did as he said. She closed her eyes. He did not leave, and after a while the phone rang.

"Should I get that?"

"No."

It was Dante, she guessed. Something had happened on the case; no doubt he'd been delayed. He'd been here almost every day these past weeks, but not today, not now. The phone stopped ringing. She felt guilty, but it wasn't her fault. She should open her eyes, she should say something to her guest, but she liked the quiet. It was good, just lying in this room, eyes closed, with him in the chair, those flowers in the vase by the bed.

Later, she heard him leaving.

Felt him hovering over her bed before he left. Or imagined it, at least. David Lake watching her as she slept, then brushing his lips against her cheek. She resisted the urge to kiss him back.

TWENTY-THREE

J ensen's law offices were on Larkin, in the Henderson Building—
the Gray Matron, as it was known: a squat, aging edifice on the
edge of the Tenderloin. They were not fancy offices, and sometimes this bothered clients—or a certain kind of client, anyway;
though those who knew Jensen, and his reputation, realized it was his
philosophy to focus his resources on the case itself, not appearances.

Still, it created for some, not so much an air of the social
underdog—an aura Jensen cultivated—as one of desperation, of a
seediness that a certain kind of client would have nothing to do with.

The man who had put forth Owens's bail, William Sprague, was
supposed to be the kind of man who did not care much about appearances. Regardless, he did not appear comfortable. Or Owens did
not think so. He was a white-haired man, ruddy and thin, a man who
had done well over the years but nonetheless possessed at the moment a disjointed and uncomfortable air.

"Jan would have liked to have been here," said Sprague. "She
would have liked to see you, but she had to speak at a foundation
meeting. Back East."

Owens didn't believe it. Jan had no desire to be here, to see him. Rather, Sprague and his attorney had come to address again the thing that had been left unsaid at the earlier meeting, at the prison, and which still hung in the air.

"As I mentioned during our last visit, we are concerned," said Sprague's attorney, "very concerned, about the way these terror laws are being applied here—and the manner in which these old cases are being resurrected by the government as a way to discourage future dissent. As you know, Walter is willing to help—to provide full assistance to the defense. Our only condition . . . ," the attorney paused then, significantly. "His only condition is that the defense be equally committed."

The attorneys looked at each other and then at him and the thing that went unsaid remained so. Owens tried to hold his mind empty, but despite himself he pictured that dance inside the bank almost thirty years ago, the people in masks, the line of customers weaving behind the velvet ropes, the tellers backing off—and the shot ringing out. The incident had been recreated in the media, choreographed on television, using extant footage of the shootout in Los Angeles, of Leland Sanford brandishing a rifle, the real and unreal superimposed, so it did not matter if Owens had been there or not, or what had happened—it unreeled in his head like a recurring dream. He thought of the dead woman. Of Eleanor Younger moaning on the floor— and how her death was being used—and he felt anger where others might want remorse.

"No plea bargaining. No offer of information in exchange for sentences. This is about an innocent verdict—about pursuing that innocence. And if you lose," the attorney turned toward Owens, "your wife, your kids—Mr. Sprague will stick by your family financially . . ."

"That's correct," said Walter Sprague.

"One small detail," said Sprague's attorney. "The bail Mrs. Sprague put up for Bill—we'd like to have that secured."

"All we have," said Owens, "is the house."

"It's a formality."

"I understand," said Owens.

Owens knew it was more than that.

Sprague would hold the deed to the house. And his family would lose everything if Owens betrayed his trust.

Jensen leaned back, ran his fingers through his sideburns. Owens had seen the gesture a thousand times. The mutton chops were out of fashion, but Moe Jensen still had them, and somehow he carried it off, that and the small ponytail: radical chic, attorney of the left, patron of the poor and oppressed, though he had crossed the line, it was true, defending scumbags and opportunists, same as everyone, and had looked, at times, pondering in front of the jury, like an overweight cocaine dealer. Jensen had been divorced several times, on account of his weakness for paralegals, and Owens sometimes wondered about Jill, who'd started as an intern at the firm.

Owens felt for a moment that paranoia he'd seen in criminal cases, when the defendant becomes suspicious of his lawyers, realizing the attorney's ambitions might have little to do with his own. No doubt Jensen had been brokering with Sprague before this meeting.

Jensen leaned over, staring at him with those hazel eyes.

"What do you think?"

And Owens remembered that moment a long time ago, in that basement in the Haight, when he'd confided more than he should have. So they both understood Sprague's interest in the case. In exchange for financing the defense, he wanted a certain kind of silence.

"I appreciate Mr. Sprague's idealism," Owens said.

"Yes," said his attorney.

"Jan," said Sprague. "Jan and I both—we've always been committed to the higher good."

"As are we all." The attorney pushed the consignment papers across the table. The places where he needed to sign were marked with a plastic arrow.

Owens signed.

TWENTY-FOUR

L ate that evening, from the window of Marilyn's apartment, Dante saw a woman walk by, and he saw her again—the same woman, he thought—maybe a half hour later, lingering in the shadows on the corner. When he stepped outside, she turned away. Later he would tell himself that he had recognized her—or should have, perhaps. And it was true, for an instant he had thought of Elise Younger and remembered how they had faced each other out on Judah Street—and remembered, too, how Owens had seen her lingering in front of his house. But then, no, this woman was just a passerby, most likely, and he, himself, was spooked by all that had happened, jumpy from that business with Sorrentino, feeling out of sorts because by the time he'd reached the hospital Marilyn was asleep, and he'd been unable to see her. And at any rate, the woman was soon in her car. Her taillights brightened. The car pulled a circle and went down the hill.

Dante walked. He walked for a long time. Annette Ricci had not told him the name of the Honduran restaurant, but the truth was there were only so many places in the Mission, and he'd been to them all. He had nothing to go on, no face, no name, so he had just sat and watched the dark faces and listened to the music. He did not trust Ricci, no. Or Jensen. But he did not trust those on the other side either.

Soon it was late. The bars had closed, and a patrol car circled Washington Square, sweeping it with a floodlight. On Grant Street, meanwhile, a woman pushed her cart away from the park. Coit Tower gleamed atop Telegraph, a white spike in the fog, and no doubt there were people sleeping under the scrub pines along the terraced hill, along the steps to the WPA murals depicting the triumph of the workers.

Voices carried from the apartments above. Indecipherable voices. Somewhere along here Kaufman had gotten drunk, written his poems.

Now the cop car swung back, and Dante found himself caught in the white blaze. They held the lamp on him for a long time, then a cop got out and studied his identification.

Just routine, apparently.

Part of the new routine, the new drill.

Soon he would deliver a report to Jensen, detailing everything he had learned so far, but he had not found Nakamura either.

The cops let him go, and he went back up the hill and stood for a while looking out where the woman had been standing. Then he went back to bed. In the morning he would go pick up Marilyn. He had missed her tonight but tomorrow he would go pick her up. She would be waiting for him in her bright-colored shift with the belt cinched loosely at her waist. She would have her makeup on, and he would help her out to the car, and she would lie next to him in this bed.

Outside there was the sound of a foghorn, and a car rumbling up the hill, and then footsteps growing fainter.

He closed his eyes.

He saw himself and Marilyn together, how it would be. They'd drink dark coffee. She'd sit with him for a long time looking out at the bay. They would wander down the streets in anticipation of the parade.

TWENTY-FIVE

The festival went back to the turn of the previous century, when the flat-footed boys in their knickers and suspenders would line up along the piers, feet dangling in the water, to watch the blessing of the fleet. It was an elaborate business. Out in the harbor, three fishing skiffs floated in the shallows, decked out like galleons, and on the lead boat, leaning over the edge, that would be Columbus and his Sicilian buddies, surveying the New World. Onward they came, smelling like fish, like wine, to stumble at the bishop's feet.

Part of the ceremony then had involved the Modoc chief, down from Yreka, who came with his dark face and black eyes to exchange gifts—and to dance with his tribe the dance of dirt and feathers. A skid-row Indian, no chief at all, pulled at random from the Bowery along with the other chiefs, all shuffling and shaking along the wooden planks in their ceremonial clothes while the Italians watched, chewing on crab legs and tossing the shells where the Indians danced.

The procession ended at the Italian cathedral. Who marched

where, in what position, who were the legitimate Italians, the pre-tenders, was a matter of squabbling now like then—so that it ended up being not just one procession, but many. Little groups winding down from Goat Hill, from Washerwoman's Lagoon, from Cow Hol-low. The celebration would go on all night and into the evening. There were booths up and down Grant Street and a cacophony in the square—street performers and mimes, Indian drumming, Chinese street toughs watching all the while, monopolizing the benches on the south end.

Today was a warm day, unseasonably so, and the old Italians gath-ered in a red tent at the center of the square. A group of tables close to the stage had been roped off for the local dignitaries, for the Ital-ian Auxiliary. Prospero had bought those seats, reserving them. The other tables were largely unoccupied, despite the crowd streaming by the tent.

Dante was there. Marilyn, too. She had ridden on Prospero's float, and the crowd had waved at her, knowing her story, pressing close to get a look at the woman in the white blouse and company blazer. Everyone was outside. Dante had glimpsed Owens along the route, out with his family, watching the parade.

Now Prospero leaned toward Dante. "Your girl, she's more beau-tiful than ever, don't you think?"

"Yes," said Dante.

"You shouldn't drag her anymore places, that business you do."

Prospero always attracted the local dignitaries, and they came up now, the members of Il Cenacolo, with their Italian sausages, their finger food, their glasses of wine—and each of them stopped to talk to Marilyn. She wore a scarf, loosely veiled, but still you could see the mottling on her cheek. She'd always had the air of a wanderer, a Sephardic beauty, and maybe it was this that had kept her apart. Now, though, she was the center of attention—and seemed comfortable in their midst.

Others came, crowding into the area between the ropes. Rossi, who had been mayor two decades past. Father Campanella. Gucci, from the mortuary. Frank Angelo, deputy to the chief of police, who had been Dante's partner. And a gaggle of old-timers up from Burlingame. The gang from Serafina's was here, at Prospero's behest. Besozi, with her cane. Pesci, with his cigarettes. And Stella, of course, hands on hips.

"This stage," Stella said. "Why is it empty?"

"There is an accordionist coming soon. And later, opera," said Prospero, ever ebullient.

"There is hummus in the sauce."

Stella's voice was accusatory. Father Campanella had hired a chef from one of the new restaurants—a dark-skinned boy with effeminate gestures. Prospero looked at his plate, confused. "I don't know what you mean."

"All these empty tables. What is the problem here?"

Father Campanella glanced away. There were rumors about him and the boy, but there were always rumors about priests. "We have done our best," the priest said. Still, it was a sore spot. In the old days they had had Frankie Valli here in the tent. Antonio Benedetto, too. And that one time Liza Minnelli, her mother drunk in the audience. Now the place was not even one-third full. The passersby glanced at the white tablecloths, and kept on walking.

In the next stall over, in a booth for the Wu Benevolent Society, Dante saw Leanora Chin mingling with a group of Chinese cops and firefighters. Her companions had marched in the parade, from the looks of them, one of those contingents that marched down from Chinatown. Chin herself was dressed for the weather, shorts and a sleeveless shirt. He was surprised to see her, but maybe he shouldn't have been. She used to work at the Columbus Station and had grown up around the corner.

"Why all the empty tables?" Stella repeated.

"Demographics," said Prospero. "Times are changing."

"This is not it," said Stella. "People walk by. Calzones. Pizza."

Rossi, the former mayor, piped in, speaking loudly, as he always did, with the air of an insider. "The problem is not here. It's out there."

Rossi pointed outside, at the stage at the other end of the square. From where he sat, Dante could see deep into the crowd. The San Francisco Troupe had its truck parked next to the outdoor stage, all decked out in medicine-show colors, and people were gathered on blankets. The troupe had a history of staging plays that mocked the festival. "To keep the agitators off our stage, we have to say this is a church benefit," Rossi said. "Then to do that, it means charging admission."

Across the way, Chin had seen him, too, Dante realized. She still lingered.

"The cook's name is Ahmed," Stella said. "This is the problem. You have a cook named Ahmed, he puts hummus in the sauce."

"There is no hummus in the sauce," said Father Campanella.

"In the past, we charged admission to our tent, no problem. But people, they smell the hummus in the sauce, they go elsewhere."

Prospero, though, had returned his attention to his plate, eating with gusto, lips smacking, a napkin tucked into his shirt, old-style. "I think it's pretty good," he said. "Maybe you should get the recipe."

Stella picked her fork out of the linen. Dante thought she was going to stab Prospero in the eye.

Instead she glared at the priest. "This utensil is dirty," she said. "No wonder no one eats here."

D ante stepped outside.
    The San Francisco Troupe was onstage now. The fights between the community boosters and the troupe were old hat, he knew, and went back even further, to the days when the *buffo* used to mock the *prominenti* in clownish skits, full of pratfalls and goose steps, stage pranks and trap doors—less than subtle, but the kids liked it, and part of the attraction for the adults was to see how it might offend the status quo.

On stage:

Two agents on a special mission from the president. Stumbling clownlike out of a whirling, whizzing machine. Back to the time of Columbus—to nip terrorism in the bud.

They sought an enemy agent by the name of Disappearing L, played by Annette Ricci.

Slipping the Indians from their chains on the Santa Maria: Escaping Then pushing forward through time, pursued by government agents in their machine.

Meanwhile, the cops were out, walking in pairs—part of the security detail patrolling the square. A stepped-up detail, including plainclothes, on account of the holiday. Dante got a glimpse of Owens in the crowd, sitting on a blanket with his family. Though the man was still living in his house on Fresno, Dante had not talked to him lately. Partly this was on Jensen's insistence. There had been more threats, and the lawyer worried someone would follow Dante to Owens. Dante understood the need for precaution, but he suspected also that Jensen did not want him talking to his client unsupervised.

When Dante turned, he all but bumped into Leanora Chin. She stood in front of him in her blue shorts and her sneakers, but a glance at her, the way she stood, he knew, she was never really off duty. She was a lithe woman, with gray eyes that tended to hold you once they had gotten your attention. Those eyes regarded him in a way that was neither malicious nor particularly friendly.

"I hear you had a confrontation with Sorrentino, out in front of Annette Ricci's."

"I didn't know you two were in touch," said Dante.

"Police people talk, like anyone else."

Back onstage, the play spun forward through time. A slave rebellion, a union meeting, Latino workers in the field.

Chin nodded toward Annette Ricci, in costume, up onstage.

"You were out to her place."

Dante said nothing.

"I thought you'd like to know, Ms. Ricci's boyfriend, Juan—one of his associates was in town recently. Luis Montoya. Montoya's wanted on extradition charges, by the new government in Nicaragua. Luis and Juan, they did a lot of work in the old days. Burning the capitalists out of their homes."

Dante understood the insinuation. The noise from certain quarters had grown louder, pointing the investigation into the firebombing back at the people who had been in the house. A political move, Jensen would say—government proxies attempting to blame the victims, suggesting they were bombing themselves.

"I thought it was drug related?" He said it with a smirk.

Chin didn't seem to notice. "I know Owens is your client. But if you run across something, the information would be appreciated."

She nodded toward Marilyn inside the tent. "I know you have an interest in seeing someone apprehended."

Dante understood what Chin was trying to do. Cops did it all the time, working with private detectives. Reminding them of their legal responsibilities—the hazards of withholding evidence. But if the cops had anything on Montoya, they wouldn't be coming to him. No, Chin was just fishing, he thought. Two steps behind, after all that delay in Oakland. Grabbing at straws—and doing it in a way that would turn the defense against itself, blaming friends of the accused.

Now, on the stage, the time machine veered out of control, slamming into the Twin Towers.

"Oh, no," the agents turned to the crowd in mock chagrin. "What will we do now?"

"Who can we blame?"

The pair looked at each other, as if they both had the same idea at once: "Terrorists!"

Mostly, it was not a government crowd. People laughed, jeering at the agent. Others, though, got up to leave, offended.

"I'm glad to see Ms. Visconti is doing well," said Chin.

Dante glanced at the cop. He studied her face for the suggestion he'd seen often these last weeks: that he himself was somehow responsible. Often, beneath those expressions of sympathy lay disdain and mockery.

Meanwhile, the play moved toward its conclusion. The troupe almost always ended its skits with an escalating moment, when the boundaries between the audience and the actors broke down. Onstage, the agents were dragging old hippies from their homes. Now they bounded into the audience, making mock arrests. The real cops at the edge of the crowd, the plainclothes, hesitated, not knowing who was in the play and who was not.

Annette Ricci appeared onstage, pulling the shackles off the imprisoned.

"There she is!"

Annette Ricci stood center stage, Liberty herself, torch in hand, the minions around her freed. The agents lunged.

She disappeared in a puff of smoke.

When Dante returned to the Italian tent, the accordionist had at last taken the stage. The crowd had filled out to some degree, and a man he did not recognize sat chatting with Marilyn. The way the man leaned toward her, though, the way she smiled—he had a notion who the man might be. Dante felt a spike of envy. As he stood there, the old Italians were watching him, he knew, their eyes running back and forth between himself and Marilyn at the table and this new man next to her. This new man had a wholesome look, disheveled hair. Dante knew what would happen next. He would follow Chin's lead despite himself. He would head up to Cicero's office and run an Internet check and likely pull a photo. But first he would walk over to Marilyn, and she would introduce him to David Lake, and the three of them would sit too long at this table, making small talk, smiling, the two men politely waiting each other out.

The next day Dante drove to the Tamale House. He'd already been there before, but now he had a photograph in his pocket. He ordered a beer and a tamale and showed the photo to the Latino kid behind the counter.

"No conosco," the kid said.

The kid did not look comfortable. After a while Dante showed the photo to the waitress, and the cook, and a dark-skinned man who emerged from a tiny room in the back. It didn't take Dante long to figure out they were all related. The dark-skinned man was the father, and when Dante asked the question, he responded that his wife was from Honduras and he himself was from Mexico, and they generally did not get involved in Nicaraguan politics.

He spoke with a little too much of a grin, condescending, as if Nicaraguan politics were for idiots.

In the end, Dante could not tell whether the man was telling the truth or not. He motioned to the man that he wanted to speak in private, and together they went into a small room with a tiny desk and miscellaneous shelves and a couple of mop handles in the corner.

Dante put some money on the table. The little man looked at the money in confusion, still shaking his head, and Dante grabbed him by the shirtfront. Thinking of the old Italians and the looks in their eyes, and how it was his fault and he'd been unable to find out a goddamn thing. Thinking of Marilyn and her ruined face. The man tried to wriggle free. The shirt buttons tore, and Dante thrust him on the floor in the tiny room, so he lay trapped between Dante and the door. Dante grabbed one of the broom handles and started poking it at the man, jabbing, hitting at the wall near his head.

"No conosco!"

Someone was lying. Ricci or Owens or Chin or this Mexican on the floor. Maybe all of them, for all he knew. Meanwhile the man's wife and kids were pounding on the door behind him. A siren started in the distance, but there was always a siren in the Mission. Dante threw down the broom and left the restaurant. Out on the street, no one looked at him, no one met his eye. He, himself, was thinking of David Lake, how when he had been sitting across from the man, there inside the Italian tent, he would have liked nothing better than to take such a broom handle and drive it into his skull.

PART FIVE

The Ancient Rain

TWENTY-SIX

I t was hot, the Day of Remembrance, unseasonably so. Elise Younger wore her yellow dress, and it was soaked through with perspiration, wet under the arms, before the march had managed five blocks. The marchers had started at the Sacramento River and would end with a gathering on the north steps of the State Capitol.

Up ahead, the road narrowed, and the marchers funneled into a bike lane. At close quarters like this, she caught the odor of sweat in the air, not a healthy sweat, but rancid. Although Elise had had three tequilas the night before, she told herself it was the man beside her who stank.

The man was Mike Iverson, Blackwell's assistant prosecutor. Blackwell had planned to be here himself but something had come up in San Francisco. So Blackwell's man walked alongside her, at the head of the march, and on the other side was Barbara Golan, an assemblywoman facing a stiff challenge in her district. Elise had visited the assemblywoman's office some years ago, unable to gain an audience, but things were different now, and the woman had embraced her today like an old friend.

"You are a brave woman," said Golan. "Your endurance is admirable. An example to us all."

"Maybe I should run for office."

When the assemblywoman laughed, tilting her head under her straw hat, Elise saw the woman's teeth. Iverson took Elise by the arm as if to guide her away. His touch was gentle, but there was a pained look on his face. The smell, she thought, definitely came from him. Everywhere the junior attorney went, he wore his prosecutorial outfit—his black slacks, his suit coat—as if he were stepping out into the Civic Center Plaza, into that gray wind that blew down Van Ness. But there was no breeze here in Sacramento, not today—only the Indian summer heat and the glimmer of the capitol up ahead.

Yes, it was Iverson who stank.

Elise had been to a number of these events over the years. Too many, perhaps. Her ex-husband had grown to hate them after a while and would not let her take the kids. But the early marches had been smaller, there had been a camaraderie. Now people came by the busload, it seemed, from all over California. From the Delta. From Shasta and Riverside. Here in their baseball caps, their stretch pants, their bright blouses. Here to spend the night in the Holiday Inn, to lobby for the dead. For victims or relatives of victims. Little girls who had disappeared from front yards. Boys gunned down on street corners. Women raped, dismembered.

The marchers held placards. They carried pictures. Their numbers extended back several blocks through the capitol mall.

What do they want? she remembered her husband pleading. *What do they expect anyone to do now?*

Though this march was bigger than the others, she felt more alone. For one thing, Guy Sorrentino was not here, walking alongside her, as he had been these last few years, and she missed his presence. Also, she marched at the head of the crowd, and though this was the envied position—it meant your case was a cause célèbre—she felt cut off. Isolated by Blackwell's people and the coming trial.

And she herself was scheduled to speak.

But it wasn't just those things. There was a buzz in the air, a hardness. There were more flags. There were soldiers and firemen and a man upfront, walking with his two children, whose wife had been killed in 9/11.

Everyone was a victim now.

"*Newsweek* is here," said Assemblywoman Golan. She had dressed more practically than Iverson, a cotton blouse—bright red, for the cameras—but a touch prim, buttoned-up. Even so, she was sweating, too. "They are running a story."

Iverson tipped his head toward Elise. "Remember, it's wiser if you don't talk to the press." He spoke to her as if she were a child. "With the trial approaching."

"I understand."

"You have your speech?"

"Yes."

"You don't want to deviate."

"I won't be a problem."

"I'm not worried, Elise. I know you understand. The press likes you, because you shoot from the hip. It makes for a story. But it's just not wise."

They had been through this more than once—and it was true, the press sought her out. Just a few nights ago, a reporter from the *Chronicle* had called, wanting to know about her friendship with Guy Sorrentino. Despite the continual admonitions, she had talked to the reporter for a while—until suddenly, out of nowhere, the man raised the question of money, wanting to know if her investigation had been privately funded.

It spooked her and she hung up.

She hadn't told anyone other than Sorrentino about the money, twenty grand, sent anonymously, a donation to the Eleanor Younger Justice Fund, set up twenty-seven years ago by her father—all but bankrupt these many years.

"Stay with the script," Iverson said.

She had been in front of crowds before. She often went with notes, things she wanted to say, but she could not be bound by them. She was not a professional speaker. She stammered, she twisted in midsentence, she strayed from her notes. To make contact, she had to look into the eyes of someone down there in the crowd. It was in those moments, those hesitations, that she felt the upswelling of words. If her words then came spontaneously—if they were ugly and jagged and if she offended the newspapers or some person in an office someplace, some lawyer—then at least they were real, and sometimes they got to the heart of the matter. But her spontaneity, she knew, frightened Iverson, because part of his job was to make sure she did not talk to the press. *There is a trial approaching.* There were more people listening now, and the case was on its way. *You don't want to look foolish, you don't want to look rash.* There were reporters, always circling. One of them was talking to the man whose wife died in 9/11.

"Why is he here?"

"Who?" asked Iverson.

"What does he want, the man whose wife is dead?"

"The same thing as you. An investigation. Justice. We can't let the bad guys win."

She couldn't argue with that, but it was a different thing somehow.

The police chief, the war veterans, the men with flags on their lapels—they were here for other reasons. Still, if this is what it took.

The reporter eyed them now, looking Elise up and down in her yellow dress, but Iverson steered her away. Behind her, Assemblywoman Golan stepped into the brink. "It's about self-sacrifice," she was saying. "It's about standing together. All of us." Elise saw Iverson cast an envious glance backward. He was ambitious, she knew; he wanted his moment. Regardless, when the reporter came, Iverson sent him away.

Iverson had his fingers on her forearm. It seemed they were always there. "After you speak at the podium, the press is going to come at you again. Tell them no comment."

"All right."

"You don't want to say anything to jeopardize the case."

"Okay."

"I'm glad you understand."

Though the distance was not far, the group crawled slowly in the October heat. Cars honked, people waved. Pamphleteers worked through the crowd from the opposite direction, slowing them down, handing out religious fliers. When they reached the stairs at last, there was a podium set up already, a microphone, but Elise and the others had to wait for the rest of the crowd to catch up. How many there were, she didn't know; several thousand, perhaps. The sun was hotter now, and the sunlight gleamed off the marble, and Elise smelled the stench again and felt the dampness of the yellow dress where it clung to her arms, to her stomach. Her perspiration would leave salt rings, she feared, all over the yellow dress.

The governor's man had come down and was waiting to say a few words.

Elise had been inside these halls on more than one occasion. The officials and their secretaries had dealt with her politely, at first. When she persisted, though, when she returned, they regarded her as a nuisance, it was clear—as someone who did not understand social boundaries. Someone who had been damaged in some way, but for whom their sympathy had worn out. Someone who did not understand the limits of what could be done.

The speech she had prepared was not long. It told of her struggle, a struggle that went back to that day twenty-seven years ago . . . but it told the story with the anger trimmed out because the people who had ignored her once, they had taken on her cause now, they had chosen to listen, and she could not afford to make them angry. It was a speech that thanked all of those who had stood beside her for so long; but it was a lie.

No one had stood beside her these last few years. Only Guy Sorrentino. And him, she had been forced to push away.

She had another speech inside her head, different from the one on paper.

The crowd had gathered, and the governor's man was at the podium now. "This day, this gathering, it really isn't about our grief. Or even about those whom we have lost."

Then what's it about? What?

For what reason had she been shuffled from office to office in these halls? For what reason had she suffered the condescending stares of secretaries and the condolences of people who squeezed her in between appointments? Why had she listened to a counselor saying it was time to go, to move on—to the implication that after a point the problem was not what had happened to her mother, no, but instead an indication of a problem within, a deformity, an inability to cope, a flaw that needed to be healed. They all stood behind her now, but she was the one who had broken down, who had been reduced to following Owens and his wife in a shopping mall, full of some awful revenge.

What was it about, then?

She knew the answer. It was not about her mother, no. It was not about herself or the people in the crowd. The governor's man was right about that.

No, it wasn't about us, it was about them.

About the prosecutor and his promotions, the newspaperman and his story, the next election and the allocation of the budget. About this assemblywoman whom she would never see again, more than likely, once this march was over.

Elise stood at the podium.

The people were below her, on the steps, gathered along the sidewalk, standing in the grass, under the sun. There was a line of trees in the distance, and the sun came hard over the buildings. For an instant, she remembered old Sacramento; she remembered the heat and dust and her mother's face as they drove along Interstate 99 through the tomato fields. Now she squinted into the light. She shielded her eyes, but it was hard to see their faces. She could no longer make out the writing on their placards, or the pictures of their loved ones.

"My mother," she said. "Twenty-seven years ago, she was my age. She walked into the bank . . ."

She paused.

Iverson looked at her with a glimmer of panic, worried she was about to stray.

She searched the crowd. There was a girl in the audience below, off to the side in the shade, a small girl, maybe ten years old. She had brown hair and was wearing a white hat and held in her hand a photograph. Elise lowered her eyes, trying to glimpse the face in the picture—a parent? a child?—then all of a sudden, without explanation, Elise began to sob.

Then Barbara Golan was at her side, and despite herself, Elise tilted toward the woman. The assemblywoman put an arm around her, and for an awful instant Elise sobbed into the woman's shoulder, into her bright red blouse. The woman smelled of perfume, of dry-cleaning fluid. Elise could hear the cameras clicking, she could hear the stirring of the crowd. She tried to pull away but the assembly-woman held her close.

"Just read the speech, honey," she whispered. "Just read what's on the page."

Afterward, lying on the bed in her hotel room at the Sacramento Sheraton, still in her yellow dress, unbuttoned now, she did not remember the details of what had followed so much as the sensation: the feeling that something had been let loose in the air as she stood at the podium. She had stayed on message, as the expression went, but the truth was she did not remember speaking. She did not remember the moment so much as the moment after, the applause, Iverson nodding his head, Golan smiling, the people pressing around after she was done, and the feeling of celebrity, later, as she walked away, head down, and Iverson led her through the crowd.

So now she lay on the bed, exhausted, arms at her sides.

She had a tremulous feeling and remembered how it had been at the time of her breakdown. She felt that feeling again now, the root-lessness. A week ago she had seen that man Dante Mancuso at the side-walk memorial in front of the construction site. She had seen him kneel down and pick up the portrait of her mother, the flowers that had been knocked over by the wind on the corner out in the Sunset District. What right did he have to touch her mother's memorial? That had been her first thought, and when their eyes met, perhaps he'd seen that in her posture. But there was something else about the man, too.

There had been something gentle in the motion, something sad. His fiancée had been injured in the bombing, she knew that. For an instant, she thought, perhaps he is not the enemy. Then the anger got ahold of her . . . and she found herself in the darkness again, watching from the shadows. Mancuso worked with Owens. Likely he knew where the man was staying now. Likely they met for coffee, for lunch . . .

She knew where that train of thought was leading, but she had a hard time pushing it away. If she was not careful, the feeling grew. Sorrentino had kept her grounded, in some odd way. She fought the panic in her chest, breathing deep, like the psychologist said, then pulled one of those little bottles of Cuervo from the minibar by the bed.

Later the phone rang. It was Blackwell, back in San Francisco. There was something unpleasant in his voice.

"You spoke with the *Chronicle*?" he asked.

"Iverson was with me the whole time, I didn't speak to anyone."

"That's not what I mean and you know it. The *Chronicle*'s breaking a story, in tomorrow's paper."

Again, there was the scolding tone, as if he were talking to a child. She had had enough, really.

"You should have been here," she sneered. "You could have your picture in *Newsweek,* too. Instead they're running Barbara Golan, standing with me out on their platform."

There wasn't any truth to it, so far as she knew, but speaking to him like this gave her a momentary satisfaction. Then he was silent, and his silence made her uneasy.

"The breaking story, it has to do with your finances," he said at last. "It has to do with you and Sorrentino."

"What finances?"

"It has to do with the fire bombing over at the Owens house."

"What?"

Her uneasiness turned to dread. She thought of the anonymous donation, and it occurred to her that she'd been duped. Guy had been right. There were strings attached to everything, everyone had a motive.

But who? Why?

"I am taking a drive down there. Soon as I get there, one o'clock, two, I'm coming over to your hotel room, and we'll stay up all night if we have to," Blackwell said, and she could hear his contempt, his utter lack of regard. "I am going to stay there until you tell me who you are in bed with."

"I don't know what you're talking about."

"I want to know where you've been getting the money. I want to know what the hell you've been doing."

TWENTY-SEVEN

That same evening, Guy Sorrentino spent some time with a girl he'd picked up at the Belmont Flats, a lackadaisical young woman whose face he forgot almost as soon as she'd left his room at the Lamplighter Motel. It was not a very rewarding encounter. Sorrentino had drunk too much beforehand and afterward had trouble sleeping.

He'd left his apartment at twilight, first buying a pack of Parliaments and a pint of Dewar's at Ace Liquors, then driving to the mudflats next to the 101. He'd checked for Dante in the rearview mirror, but the man was off him now, and anyway, what did it matter?

He cruised slowly. The Flats was a mixed neighborhood of warehouses and two-story apartment buildings not too different from the one in which he lived, only these had been built on bay fill and were inhabited by immigrants sleeping six or seven to a room. Girls walked the streets, runaways mostly, loitering in the driveways, and it was surprising how many of them were white. A lot of the girls gathered in clusters, but Sorrentino avoided them. It was too conspicuous, and he didn't like having to pick one from the others as they pushed at the car.

Up ahead, a girl in a blue T-shirt stood alone in the middle of the block. He pulled to the curb and waited for her to stick her head in the Torino's window.

Sorrentino allowed himself these encounters every few weeks, for the liquor and cigarettes as much as anything, because the encounters themselves were seldom satisfying. Officially he did not smoke anymore. Officially he did not drink. But he allowed himself on these evenings out. Then in the morning he would empty the rest of the bottle into the toilet. He would save a single cigarette for later, after breakfast. The rest of the pack he put under the faucet, filling it with water—so he would not be tempted to take it with him. Then he would not smoke again, he would not drink, he told himself, until his next visit. It was his way of keeping his vices under control.

Last night, though, he had bought himself a second pint and had smoked most of the pack. Now his stomach was queasy, and he could hear the traffic throbbing on the El Camino. His hangover reminded him of the old days, after his dismissal, when he'd spent all that time in Cholino's Bar in the Tenderloin.

He looked for a paper, but it was midmorning now and the box was empty.

Inside the café, there was a waitress about his own age. She had large breasts and dyed red hair and maybe she had been good-looking once. She was nothing special, but he fantasized about her sometimes as he lay on his back in the Lamplighter, with a girl straddled on top of him. It was not unusual for him to fantasize during sex, to think of different women, never really settling. His ex-wife—no. Elise— for a moment, maybe, but no, she was like a daughter to him. Stella— no. Absolutely not. The waitress in her ochre uniform . . .

The waitress asked for his order. She did not smile. She wore blue eye shadow and she was all business. You would not know that he had been here a couple dozen times before, and that she had taken his order in just this way, and that the order was always the same.

"A paper?" he asked.

"In the box."

"It was empty."

"You can check the counter."

She said it without looking and he thought of the girl then, in her pale T-shirt and her thin hair, hovering over him, eyes fixed on the wall.

Not seeing him. Guy Sorrentino. An old man full of rage and grief.

Part of the reason he checked the paper these days was for news of the Owens case—to watch the dance in the press. Lately the story had dropped back to the middle of the paper, and often there wasn't anything at all. He unfolded the paper, preparing to leaf through, then noticed with a flush of panic the headlines on the front page, just below the fold:

QUESTIONS ARISE IN PROSECUTION OF OWENS CASE
Funding Links Victim's Daughter to Right-Wing Violence

The newspaper reporter, through an unnamed source, had managed to trace activity in Elise Younger's bank accounts, and apparently she had received a deposit for twenty grand via money order just a few weeks back—the money order itself having been purchased via traveler's check in Palo Alto. And that traveler's check had originally been issued to an Ed Metzger of Yreka.

Sorrentino sickened.

He blamed Mancuso, the goddamn defense, dragging names out

of nowhere, nosing in his past. He had known Metzger, sure—he'd had a brief encounter with the man some half-dozen years ago, down at Cholino's, but so had a lot of people in the department. Metzger was a former revenue agent who had been dismissed for laundering money on behalf of a survivalist group suspected in the bombing death of a liberal judge in Humboldt County.

Though the article didn't say so directly, the inferences were clear—that Metzger had been behind the bombing out at Owens's house, and that his group was giving money to Elise, to assist with her case: "According to bank records, money from the Eleanor Younger Justice Fund was used in part to pay for a private detective named Guy Sorrentino, who had done the groundwork for the prosecution case. Sorrentino, like a lot of other San Francisco police at the time, had an association with Metzger in the midnineties. While details are not clear . . ."

Sorrentino cursed. It was the kind of thing defense lawyers did all the time, impugning the prosecution, but Owens and his bunch were clever bastards. They had their friends at the paper . . . No scruples in the world . . . And that son of a bitch Mancuso . . .

The waitress came with his order, and he felt himself redden, worried that she had seen his picture in the paper. She had the same crooked smile as always, the same dark eyes. She put down the eggs, she poured the coffee, but did not give him a sideways glance. He looked around the restaurant. There was a man reading a paper on the empty table across from him, people at the counter. No one paid him any mind. Still, people would see the paper: his ex-wife, friends from the old days, men on the force, Stella, the old fools at Serafina's, his obese neighbor, the apartment manager. There would be strangers looking at his picture, shaking their heads, amused smiles, clucking tongues.

He was in no mood for breakfast but he ate, anyway. Because it was in front of him. Because he needed to fill the emptiness. The food did not go down well, but he ate it greedily. When he was done, he did not wait for the bill but scattered money over the table before going to the restroom and evacuating everything all at once, all of it streaming through bowels already inflamed with nicotine and alcohol.

His cell phone was in the Torino.

People had called, left messages. Blackwell himself. The feds' press liaison. Some joker from the newspaper.

And Elise.

He dialed her number.

"Where have you been?"

"With friends."

"Your ex-wife?"

She asked him this sometimes. He had hinted once at the nature of his nights out, in an odd, self-revelatory moment, but she had misinterpreted it—deliberately, perhaps—to mean he and his wife got together sometimes. It was better, he guessed, than having her think he was with a prostitute.

"I don't talk to my ex-wife, you know that."

"That's what you say."

"I have other friends."

She lowered her voice. "I've been trying to call you, that's all. I tried your house, your cell. Blackwell even sent someone out to your place, and when they couldn't find you . . ."

"I just now read the paper," he said. "This man Metzger, he was the one who sent you money?"

"The donation was anonymous, I told you that."

He stood with his cell to his ear, feeling fat and foolish. A gap had been growing between them for some time, and in the silence now he felt that gap grow wider, filling with suspicion, as she wondered what machinations he'd been hiding, and he wondered the same about her.

"You know Metzger?" she asked.

"The newspaper . . . the reporter, he didn't even contact me. What kind of journalism is that?"

"The money was anonymous," she said again. "There was no name on the check."

"What does Blackwell want?"

"He wants you to call him, right way. There's going to be a press conference."

"He wants me there?"

"No. But he wants to talk to you. And he wants you to stay away from the press meantime."

Sorrentino knew how these things went. The prosecution was going to get in front of the microphones and read some kind of prepared statement, controlling the damage. Meanwhile they would need a scapegoat, someone to blame, and he already had a pretty good idea who that might be.

"I'm worried, all this publicity. It's going to hurt the case."

"It'll be all right," Sorrentino said, though he had his doubts.

"We shouldn't have taken the money. You told me."

"It's not your fault," he said.

"This man Metzger . . . why would he do this?"

"Maybe it wasn't Metzger."

"What do you mean?"

Sorrentino didn't know for sure, but it didn't feel right to him. Metzger wouldn't be so foolish as to leave his name all over the receipt. And even if he were, how would the reporter have found out so soon?

"All the things in the article, the personal stuff—about me, about you?" She asked. "How did they find out about that?"

"They hired an investigator."

"The one from North Beach? His fiancée—I saw her once . . ."

Later, Sorrentino would wonder if he should have paid more attention to Elise then, that sudden lilt in her voice. He knew how much the case meant to her, how fragile she was. But he was thinking about himself. He was thinking ahead to the conversation he would have with Blackwell. It was not going to be pretty. And chances were Blackwell would not talk to him alone; no, there would be others there, they would be pressing to see if he were involved in some way with Metzger, they would push him hard. They would find nothing of course, but that wouldn't matter. Iverson would ridicule him. He had done what no investigator was supposed to do: He had become part of the story. No matter that the story was a lie.

"I'll see you," said Elise.

"Yes."

Truth was, Sorrentino did not think he would be seeing her soon, and expected Elise knew this as well. Blackwell would not want him at the press conference, and it would not be wise to return to his apartment. The press would be hovering. No, his job now was to lie low, here at the Lamplighter, in the motel room, and wait for Iverson and Blackwell and the rest of the squad.

He went back to the lobby desk and asked for a cheaper room.

TWENTY-EIGHT

The street was unusually quiet, the sky unusually black. There was no moon, and a dark fog lay over the hill. Dante could not shake the feeling, as he stood at Marilyn's window, studying the empty street, that something was about to happen. *La Seggazza,* in the language of the crones: the wisdom, so-called. The old woman's name for that certain intuition, that feeling of inevitability that overcame a person sometimes—standing on a street corner, maybe, hesitating in the market—the notion that some secret was about to be revealed. Something set in motion.

Often as not, nothing came of the foreboding. An illusion, perhaps. Some chemical loose in the brain.

Behind him, Marilyn sat on the sofa. She had put on music, an opera—an obscure aria Dante could not put a name to—from the CD that the man David Lake had given to her. She had been listening to the music a lot lately, the choral swellings, the strings low and brooding, building in intensity, falling away—then all at once, the solemnity giving way to something that sounded like hysteria. The soprano in the throes of death. Followed by the chorus, a long, mournful note.

Marilyn had gone inward since her return home from the hospital. She had lost weight and her clothes were loose. She resembled from certain angles a younger version of herself—gangly, uncertain, on the verge of transforming into someone else.

"Come away from the window," she said. "Come sit with me."

Straight on, her looks were disconcerting. Without the makeup, without the scarf, he could see the sutures and the places where the skin still puckered. It was healing nicely, the doctor said, but she would need more grafts, and the surgeon could not guarantee there would be no scars. Her right eye was covered with a vermillion patch. Marilyn had an assortment of these patches—pink, carmine, blue. Her skin had begun to itch—a good sign—but there was still sporadic pain, unpredictable, damaged nerves inside the muscles on her forearms and thighs.

He went to her on the couch.

They kissed—a lingering kiss, gentle and tender, but with something fierce in its tenderness, controlled but not controlled. Then, fearful he might be hurting her, he pulled away. She did not look at him, and he could not escape the feeling that he was losing her: that whatever had been between them was slipping away.

"I love this music," she said.

"My mother—she used to sing sometimes, walking up and down the stairs."

"Have you been over to the house?"

"Owens moved out," he said.

It had happened quickly. There were reasons for being surreptitious, keeping the family's movements out of the public eye. And reasons, too, for not informing him of the Metzger story before it appeared in the paper. Still, he felt shut out.

"Jensen found them another place."

"It's empty?"

"All their things are gone."

After the Metzger story broke, Jensen had made a motion for dismissal, but the judge denied it. Blackwell quickly distanced the prosecution from Sorrentino, then fought back in the press by claiming the story had been planted, implying the information had come from Jensen as a way of discrediting the case and smearing Elise Younger herself.

In fact, much of the information had come out of the file Dante had collected. Not the financial stuff, though, not the bank records or the alleged stubs connecting Metzger to Elise. You had to have insiders for that.

Sprague's people, Dante guessed.

The whole business made him uneasy, as if he were back working deep cover, in that underworld where intention and action, means and end, became increasingly difficult to sort out. He liked to think that kind of ambiguity had disappeared when he'd left the company.

"It all comes back, doesn't it?" she said.

"What do you mean?"

"The things we do."

"Maybe. But sometimes it's just happenstance. Sometimes it's being in the wrong place at the wrong time."

"Like me at the window."

"That wasn't your fault."

"Maybe not. I would not have gone, if not for you." She said it without resentment, at least on the surface. But Dante had thought the same thing. If he had never answered the phone that gray morning . . . if he had not taken her out to pick up the kids . . .

The music swelled again, male voices, rival suitors. Their voices rose, and then there was a lull—the soprano from beyond the grave.

"Do you believe in anything?" she asked.

"I don't understand."

"Everywhere, it's one group against another. You can't untangle it."

"You have to take a stand," he said, but then he realized it was the same nonsense everyone spouted these days. *We can't let them get away with this . . . we have to stand firm, or else everything we believe in . . . all our stuff . . .*

"Beatrice Prospero goes to church every Sunday, you know, she and her father."

"They're fishing for clients," said Dante. "Weddings and funerals. The exchange of property."

"It's something, at least."

"Isn't that where they found Mr. Lake—after his wife died?"

"You don't have to be so cynical."

Outside, the blackness got blacker. The soprano's voice grew more angelic, ghostly, fading as the tenors renewed their battle. Fiercer now, louder. *Do nothing.* But it was impossible. Things had their own momentum once they got going. People wanted vindication, they would not let you stay out.

"What are you thinking about?" she whispered into his ear. He felt the brush of her lips against his cheek.

"Spain?" she whispered. "Barcelona?"

He was filled with longing, regret. He thought of Cicero on his boat.

"You remember the hospital?" she asked.

They had discussed this once, her delirium at the hospital, and he had humored her, lightheartedly. A game. He was surprised now that she would go back to that moment.

"Yes," he said.

She knew it wasn't true. She had to know it had not happened. That he could not have made love to her that way, on the hospital bed, so soon after the fire.

"Let's go upstairs." She smiled. "Let's do that again."

She took his hand, and they went upstairs, and he lay beside her on the bed. He touched her face, put his fingertips on her cheeks, his lips to her scars. He kissed the eye patch, then ran his fingers over her body, over the places the fire had touched, following the gasoline, the trails of grease and tar. He ran the tip of his nose along the scabrous tissue. Her legs widened. "I don't know," he said, but she pulled him toward her. His chest grazed hers. She winced painfully but did not let him loose. She had described to him that imaginary moment in the hospital, but this moment was real, he could feel the rawness of her body, the wounds oozing, the scabs. He felt the fierceness in her, or perhaps it was within himself, trying to possess something that had already slipped away. He wanted to believe that there had been such a moment between them. She arched toward him, she shuddered all over—and then he, too, let himself go.

In a little while she fell asleep. She lay there on her back, snoring in her nightgown, the bandages disarranged, her eye patch a bit too low.

He walked about the house, turning out the lights, then stood a long time at the window staring out at the darkness, and he entertained for a moment the idea that life was somehow normal—that he and Marilyn might somehow be all right. Then he checked his phone, looking at himself in the reflection of the window as he did so—at the small blue glare of the cell reflected in the glass.

He dialed up his voice mail.

Elise Younger had found him. She had tracked him down through the office and left a message on his cell.

TWENTY-NINE

Dante met Elise Younger the next day at Nico's, a Japanese restaurant at the back of a strip mall beneath a yellowing hill on the outskirts of Vallejo. The place was just off Highway 37, not far from the Napa junction, but not so close that a tourist was likely to stumble upon it.

Elise lived in an apartment not far away, and he guessed that must have been the reason she had asked to meet him there.

She was not there when he arrived, so he waited in his car, half thinking the meeting might be a ploy. In a little while, a late-model Toyota pulled into the lot. Elise Younger climbed out and stood with her purse held in front of her. It was a small black purse, and Dante noticed how she played with the metal catch. He kept an eye on her hands.

She stood very straight, stiff-backed, her hair curled tight. She wore slacks and a blazer cut in the nautical style, but her clothes were somewhat rumpled. Up close, he noticed the array of freckles across her cheeks, unusual in a woman her age. Her skin was sun damaged, her eyes bright. A girlish, scattered look.

"Dante Mancuso?"

"Yes."

Inside, the restaurant wasn't particularly fancy, but it was nicer than he had expected. There were paper lanterns on the wall, and the tables were clean, and Japanese beer was on the menu.

They sat in a booth, and she set the purse on the table, just letting it lie there. Dante had looked into her background fairly closely these last weeks. He remembered how, at the time of the breakdown, she'd filed the paperwork to buy a gun down at Vallejo Gun & Sport, but had never picked up the weapon.

It was possible she'd been back recently, he supposed. Possible, too, she'd found some other way to secure a firearm.

"I saw you out on Judah that day, at the sidewalk shrine."

"I noticed you as well."

"You were rearranging the flowers."

"It's windy out there, one of the vases had fallen over. So I picked it up."

"Does that make you feel better about yourself?"

Dante let the remark pass. He had all but stumbled on the sidewalk shrine: the yellow flowers and the placard with her mother's picture; the candles and the glass statues and the newspaper articles; the paper hearts trimmed with lace. He'd bent over all that to put the vase upright.

"You gave Jensen information for the article, didn't you?"

"Some of it."

"The way that story was put together, the innuendo, it's not true . . . The aim—it's to poison the case . . ." She moved the purse off the table, putting it on the seat next to her.

"I didn't write the article."

"So what else did you find out—about me, I mean? Did you talk to my divorce lawyer, my psychiatrist?"

She was baiting him, trying to find out just exactly what he knew, maybe, and how he had discovered it. It was possible Blackwell had sent her out on a kind of mission, but he doubted that. It would not be a wise thing to do.

"How can I help you?" He heard the good cop in his voice, the man who had come to listen. It was not convincing. "Why did you call me out here?"

She leaned forward, and the way her chin jutted, and the shape of her head, the manner in which she wore her hair, the curls permed tight against her crown, reminded him of the picture of the dead woman at the center of the shrine.

"Guy Sorrentino is a sweet man," she said, squaring her shoulders, as if to challenge him in some way. "Before my breakdown, I ran into Owens at the mall. But you know that. The rumors, how I followed Owens and his family." She peered across the table. "But the thing is, I was this far away from him. He looked right at me, right into my eyes. With that empty look of his. Like I wasn't there. Like he didn't see me."

He knew the look she meant—the way Owens retreated, the seeming vacancy behind the pale eyes. But what had she expected from such an encounter?

The waitress brought their drinks and some appetizers arranged on a plate. Elise did not seem much interested in her food. She was drinking gin, and it occurred to him then that this wasn't her first drink of the day. She had her hands on the table, and the small black purse remained out of sight. He kept an eye on her hands.

"Why did you call me out here?"

She hesitated. "I wanted to tell you I didn't have anything to do with the firebomb," she said. "I'm not saying I don't hate Owens, I'm not saying that there haven't been times when I would do anything—I admit it. But I wouldn't go after those kids. And I didn't have anything to do with what happened to your fiancée. I didn't know Metzger, and Guy only knew him in passing."

"The money came from somewhere."

"I'm not naïve," she said. "I know people are using this case. Using me. But there are people using you, too."

She gave him an odd smile, waiting for his reaction. She believed what she said, maybe, or wanted to believe, but he could see that the recent fuss in the paper, all the publicity, the trial—the whole business was caving in on her. "Owens was staying for a while in North Beach, around the corner from you and your fiancée?"

Dante didn't answer the question, but he wondered how she knew this. She'd learned it from Sorrentino, maybe, or slipping around the streets on her own.

"I know lots of little things," she said. "Benny's Café—that's one of Owens's hangouts isn't it, down off Third, by the old wharf? He likes to meet people there, to slum it and show what a guy he is. But that work you're doing for him, Owens and his attorney are using it to make it look like *he* is the victim. Maybe it will work. Maybe he can hide the truth in that empty face of his—but not forever. It will be revealed."

She didn't sound entirely certain. He thought of all the times she had spent with Sorrentino, and the time they had spent nursing each other's grief.

"You live with your fiancée?" she asked.

Again, he didn't answer.

"Or does the question bother you? Does it make you suspicious—me rummaging around in your life? Like you out there, at the shrine."

"You've made your point—if that's what this was all about."

"No, I wanted you to tell Owens something." She tilted toward him now, her eyes bright, a bit too much so. "I want you to give him a message from me. There was a time when I told myself I wouldn't be satisfied until he was in jail. I wanted him punished. I wanted him in a dark hole, and I wanted him to know he would be in that hole in hell till he died. I wanted him punished, that's what I thought. But I was deceiving myself."

"Yes?"

"The reason I want him in jail, the reason I want him locked away, it's because—I'm afraid of what I'll do. If he stays out here, I'm afraid I'll become just like him." Dante thought back again to their encounter the moment on that sidewalk. He had felt sympathy for her then, but at the same time he knew he couldn't let that sympathy sway him. She might be dangerous. If not to him, then to someone else.

"We've all lost people," he said.

"You don't know anything about it."

"I know something."

She bit her lip.

"You need to be careful," he said. "This trial's going to last for a while. It may not go the way you want it to go."

"You and Sorrentino, you're not so different as you think."

She reached down beside her then, picking up the purse. Her fingers played with the clasp.

THIRTY

When Dante found Cynthia Nakamura, it was not through his own brilliance, or a sudden revelation, but on account of a certain long-nosed tedium—examining for a hundredth time the growing list of witnesses the prosecution had submitted as part of the discovery process. It had occurred to Dante that the prosecution might be hiding Lady Nakamura among the stiffs—and the list was rife with these, with misspellings, dropped surnames, people who had witnessed the crime but had since passed on or were otherwise incapacitated. Through this process he came back to a name he'd crossed off before but now examined again. Another name in the slough of names:

Johnson, Robert. 350 Fourth St., Union City. Eyewitness, deposition forthcoming.

The death certificate, however, suggested that Mr. Johnson wouldn't be testifying anytime soon. Died April 20, 2002. Cardiac arrest. Unmarried. Sixty-eight years old. Identify verified by an estranged son.

Dante phoned the son and discovered the dead man had a

common-law wife, going by the name of Cynthia Johnson. According to the son, Cynthia had taken up residence at Hamilton Care Center in the South Bay: a state-funded holding place for the terminally ill.

But Cynthia Johnson was no longer in residence there, either.

Some weeks before, she'd been moved all of a sudden to a much better facility in San Francisco. So at the end of the day, Dante found himself standing in front of the receptionist's desk at the acute care facility in La Honda.

"Whom may I say is visiting?"

"Dean Johnson," he lied. "I'm her stepson."

The receptionist buzzed Mrs. Johnson to make sure it was all right, then directed him down the hall.

"But don't keep her up too late. She has chemo in the morning."

The hallway was long and wide, freshly papered, with handrails for the infirm and small alcoves that looked out toward Lake Merced, here on the gray side of the city, with the ocean just beyond those row houses on the other side of the trees. The place was a notch or two above the place where Dante's own mother had spent her final days, but he did not want to think about that. When he rang the door, no one answered. So he tried the handle.

It was a small apartment, a hospital efficiency, and he found the woman on the balcony, along with her oxygen tank. The evening fog had come in off the ocean and was settling over the lake, bringing a chill with it. The woman had a blanket draped about her shoulders and across her chest but showed no inclination of wanting to move.

"You're not Dean," she said.

Her voice was hoarse and scratchy—a strained whisper forced up through what remained of her voice box.

"No, I'm not."

"I didn't think he would come," she said. "We weren't close."

"The prosecution—they didn't make it easy to find you."

"Yes. The prosecution. I don't care for them. I don't much care for your side, either."

"I can understand that."

"My voice."

"It's not so bad."

"It's hideous.

Dante had done his research and he knew Cynthia Nakamura had grown up in one of the garden houses along the Filbert Steps. Her parents had retired to the place down in Aptos, but the house on Filbert had remained hers for quite some time—a lush area, hidden on the west side of the cliff next to the concrete stairs, where parrots scurried helter-skelter among the trees and people left their screen doors open and drank wine on the steps. Or that's how it had been back then. Some time after the robbery, she'd sold it and moved away. Now her hair was gone from the chemo, but Dante had seen photos of her as a child. She had been small and delicate even then, a Japanese girl with skin the color of sand and eyes like glass. In the picture of her alongside Bob Kaufman, her hair had been long and black, and she stood leaning against him, a cigarette at the end of her nervous hand.

"Kaufman, he knew Sanford?"

"He wrote about him," she said.

In a halting voice—hard to understand, bits and fragments—she told him more or less the same thing he'd heard from Owens. How the police had raided the place on Filbert and arrested Kaufman, confusing him with Sanford because they were both African American. There'd been rumors of a correspondence.

Did they know each other?"

"Bob corresponded with a lot of people." She grimaced as she spoke. The muscles at her neck tightened, but eventually the words forced themselves through. "Those he didn't know . . . he talked to in his dreams. Nixon . . . Chairman Mao . . . Rimbaud . . . He talked to all of them. But if he met any of them, it wasn't in my presence."

She laughed, and a wheezing sound came back up her throat. Inside the apartment the phone rang, or something like the phone but with a higher pitch, a sharper nag. "The steward," she said. "He will be coming to tuck me in. There are people who don't want me to die."

"That day," said Dante. "In Aptos . . ."

Dante paused. This was the core of it, he knew. That day, twenty-seven years ago.

"I lied."

"The alibi?"

She looked suddenly exhausted. "It was a lie."

"Why?"

"I was a believer."

"And now?"

"My cancer has metastasized."

Dante thought of the figure this woman would cut in the courtroom, retracting her statement of long ago. Nakamura was in her midsixties, but looked yet older, unwell. The defense would not look good going after her on the stand—such a sick woman. "The prosecution—you've done a deposition?"

She stared at him blankly, a distracted expression that would be easy to attribute to her condition. Except he'd seen the same distracted look in the photo from long ago.

"Maybe I thought there was a greater truth. Back then, when I was young. Or maybe I was just following the crowd. But now . . ." She paused. Her head wobbled and she closed her eyes. "I don't want to do this, either way . . . I don't know what the fuck happened . . ."

"So Owens and the others, they weren't in Aptos the day of the robbery?"

"Only Rachel."

"Excuse me?"

"His ex-wife. Sobbing night and day. She'd come a few days before. She wanted out. Bill was sleeping with one of the others."

"Who?"

She shook her head. "Rachel was supposed to drive getaway but she wouldn't do it."

"Who drove?"

The woman's eyes went black then, and Dante wondered how closely her recollection could be trusted, how much the prosecution had talked to her. Not just Sorrentino, but those who came afterward—people like Blackwell, more skilled in gaining a certain compliance, in shaping memories. It could be, too, that the woman was just buying a little comfort with her tongue, a softer pillow on which to expire. It was a nice facility.

"Leland Sanford was a pawn. All of us, really. Bob understood that." The woman's eyes were wide. The doorbell rang. "The steward . . ."

Unlike Dante, the steward did not hesitate long at the door. "Visiting hours are over," he said to Dante. "What are you doing here, Mrs. Johnson, what are you doing out on the balcony?"

The steward spoke quickly, in a manner that suggested neither affection nor its opposite, merely that he had a job to do.

"Time for bed, Mrs. Johnson. We can't be sitting out here in the cold." He turned to Dante. "You must leave now, sir. Before your mother catches her death."

Dante was about to correct the steward, but didn't bother. Cynthia gave him a smile.

"They're torturing me with the chemo," she said.

THIRTY-ONE

It was the next day. The sun had been out earlier, but now clouds scudded overhead, and the tide pushed toward the seawall at Ocean Beach, on the western edge of the city. Anyone who had grown up in San Francisco knew how dangerous this beach could be if you turned your back: how the rollers swelled up out of nowhere. It wasn't quite riptide season, true, but there were stories every year about dabblers along the water's edge, people swept away without warning.

"This is a treacherous stretch," said Owens.

"Yes," Jensen agreed.

The attorney was a big man, but he could modulate his voice, so that it was at once both soft and expansive, reassuring. *Humoring me.* His wife and daughter were walking along some hundred yards behind. Zeke, his son, had yet to emerge from the Cliff House. The boy had lingered behind at the restaurant with Jensen's paralegal.

"Don't worry," said Jensen. "She's going to bring him down the other way, along the seawall. They'll meet us in the lot. It will give us time to talk."

Owens and his family were living now in a place Jensen had

found for them, in Outer Richmond, not too many blocks away. Jill felt less cooped up there than on Fresno Street, but they still had to take precautions, and so did not go out much. Today Jensen had stopped by and insisted on taking them to lunch out at the Cliff House, and afterward this walk on the beach. He and Jill had worn their sloppies, as they called them—faces hidden beneath ball caps and wide-rim shades, dressed in sweatpants and Alcatraz T-shirts so as to fit in with the tourists. No one had turned a head. But then he'd always had that ability to blend in.

Inside the Cliff House, Zeke had become obsessed with the seals. They could be seen from the huge glass windows, out there in the ocean. Then, on the way out, the young woman had lingered with him so he could study the fish in the restaurant's aquarium. Owens worried now that this had been a mistake, but he had been eager to talk with Jensen regarding Dante and the man's conversation with Nakamura.

"I got a call from the prosecution," said Jensen. "From Blackwell's man, Iverson."

"Did you mention Nakamura?"

"No."

"That's a violation of discovery, keeping her hidden the way they did."

"Maybe. But that wasn't our focus. With a trial approaching, they want to know if you're going to pursue a plea."

"What did you say?"

"I said I didn't see any reason for you to change your plea. But that I would present the notion to you."

"Eight years?"

Jensen shook his head. "Twelve to fifteen."

"That's not what they said before."

"Blackwell's got a hard-on. He wants vindication. He wants it so bad he can't see straight. And the higher-ups are pressuring him. But the reality is, they don't have much of a case."

Jensen might have his interests at heart, but Owens did not altogether trust him, because he had seen how the man slanted things when he talked to clients, to push them toward the action he thought best. Jensen had money troubles as well, all those wives, all those kids. The firm had been walking a tightrope lately, financially speaking, and only stood to gain if the trial continued, now that Sprague was paying. Then there was Jill. Those two had worked together for years. Late hours. Off to conferences. He glanced back again at his wife and daughter on the beach. Then strained ahead, trying to spot Zeke and the paralegal along the seawall.

Perhaps he was being overly edgy, but there had been a car lingering out front yesterday evening, despite the care they had taken to keep the move secret. Protective surveillance, maybe, but that had been curtailed since the move off Fresno Street.

"The ocean's a bit rough today, I can't tell if the tide, if it's coming in or out," said Jensen. "Do you hear the seals?"

Owens listened. The rocks where the seals congregated were on the other side of the Cliff House, but somehow their racket carried, and he could hear them barking between waves. His son had been very curious about the seals.

"Relax," said Jensen.

"How do you think the case will play with the jury?"

"You know my feeling. The case is mostly circumstantial. The evidence isn't there. And as far as the press goes, the prosecution has looked pretty foolish," Jensen said. "But as your attorney, I would be remiss if I didn't let you know that anything can happen once we get to court."

Owens understood, too, the deal the prosecution wanted to make, and he understood that there were reasons to take it, guilty or not—and part of him was tempted to grab it. You couldn't tell what a jury might do, or what a witness might say, even a friendly witness, and the public mood could always shift. All the things that had been going wrong in the paper for the prosecution—all the news that was not supposed to impact the trial but ultimately did— all that could change. There was a war in the offing, a certain hysteria in the air.

"There's the principle of the thing, I suppose, and your agreement with Sprague. It's important to take a stand."

"I don't know if I care about principles anymore," said Owens.

They headed across the sand toward the parking lot, then stood waiting on the concrete promenade, behind the seawall, watching his wife and daughter make their way across the sand, heads down, both of them with their honey-colored hair whipping behind them and their round shoulders slouched against the wind.

Jensen, too, glanced back at Jill.

"As far as the things you care about, eight years is the same as thirty. You go to prison. Everything will be different when you get out."

The remark angered him, but he understood. Not many relationships survived a prison term of more than a couple of years.

"What about Nakamura?" Owens said.

Jensen's eyes penetrated him. He knew what the man was thinking.

"We can undermine her testimony if we have to. Her age, vulnerable, dying woman, manipulated by the prosecution. The care she's getting, the few extra months—she has reason to say what they want to hear. From what Dante said, she might have been coerced."

"Is that what he thought?"

"She might not be as cooperative as the prosecution thinks. And if she is, it won't be hard to slice her up."

"I don't know. Are you going to ask for pretrial access?"

"Yes and no."

"I don't understand."

"I'm going to ask for it, but I don't really want it."

"What do you mean?"

"The way they've handled this—burying her in the list. That's not going to look good."

"People do it all the time."

"She's not going to last forever . . . And if we delay . . ."

Owens understood this, too. Jensen was full of tricks—ways of casting doubt through procedural delay—but sometimes these tricks could backfire.

His wife and daughter came up the stairs now, onto the promenade. Jensen's assistant appeared at the other end of the parking lot, coming alone down the walkway from the Cliff House.

"Where's Zeke?"

"I thought he was with his mother."

"What?"

"I went back upstairs for my coat."

Jill stood with them now. "Zeke's not with you?"

The young woman tried to explain it again, how she went back for her coat, assuming Zeke had gone with his parents down the steps to the beach. Owens felt himself panic. His life had been riddled with such moments lately, when the kids slipped from his sight.

"Call the police."

"What?"

"I said call the goddamn police."

"Don't panic."

"What do you mean, don't panic?"

A glance fell between the assistant and Jensen, and there was something in the glance Owens did not like. As if he were someone to control. He'd heard the insinuations in the media—government proxies, talk-show hosts, right-wing columnists who said the kidnapping threats, the firebombing, all of that was coming not from the prosecution but from the defense camp: stage-managed crimes designed to get sympathy for the defendant. *They did it thirty years ago, and they're doing it now . . . Annette Ricci and her guerilla politics. Jan Sprague and her husband's money . . . the same lousy crew . . . Meanwhile our boys are packing up for overseas . . .*

"You know how Zeke is," said Jill. "He's probably back up there somewhere. He probably just wandered into one of the other rooms."

"I don't see how you could let this happen."

"Me?"

Jill had her hands on her hips now, arms akimbo, and the gesture made her look older—the way her belly pushed out. She wore her sloppies now, but at home the night before, in her pleated pants and gold sweater, she'd made the same gesture, and suddenly he'd wanted nothing to do with her anymore. He'd felt this kind of disgust more than once, not just for her but for himself as well, their whole middle-class life. He hadn't wanted all this, but now he couldn't let it go. The fear shot through him.

"Bill, you can't blame this on me."

He wasn't listening, but was instead already headed toward the car. Jensen was almost as quick and got into the passenger seat beside him. Owens veered onto the Great Highway, jackknifing over the curb, up the hill toward the Cliff House. The restaurant was less than a mile from the lower lot, but he could not restrain himself.

"Easy," said Jensen. "It's not going to help if we run over someone."

The admonition only made him more reckless. At the top of the hill, he pulled wildly across two lanes of traffic, ignoring the crosswalk. A startled family jumped back from the curb.

"What's the matter with you?" yelled Jensen.

Owens strained forward. A car blocked the way, and he leaned on the horn. Then he shouted at Jensen, "What's the matter with me? Don't you think I see what you're doing? You and the rest?"

"I don't know what you're talking about."

Owens felt himself shaking all over, losing control. Him, the conspirator, veteran of the underground. The same man now, wild, out of control, puffing middle-aged fool, inarticulate as could be, suspicious of everyone.

He thought of the woman cut in half on the bank floor.

"Everything's a publicity stunt with you, everything's a way of getting attention for the case."

Jensen's lips turned up. They were both thinking the same thing, maybe: back again to that moment in the dark, heads down, in that basement on Haight Street, whispering. *The shotgun, short barrel. Sawed off so it fit sideways into a straw bag. The trigger, hair trigger, filed too sharp . . . I told Jan to be careful, but she took it, anyway . . . Annette stuffing it in the bag . . . I told her . . .*

"I wouldn't get so pious, Bill," said Jensen. "Not if I were you."

He left the car now and stormed into the Cliff House—calling more attention to himself than he should. He searched the bathroom, the gift shop, the dining room where they'd eaten lunch. Then he burst back through the doors onto the sidewalk.

He could hear the seals. A tourist bus had parked in the easement, and over the crest families headed toward the Sutro Baths. Children straining toward the cliffs. Past the signs warning of crumbling rock. Unroped paths that snaked out toward the vista.

Down the other way, Jill and his daughter came toward him along the seawall, working their way up from the lower lot.

He ran down the path, dodging the families.

The Sutro Baths had been built over a hundred years ago—a public bathing house overlooking the water, brine pumped in from the ocean. The baths were famous in the city's mythology, a place lost to fire, demolished in the sixties, but the truth was they had been unsanitary, and there had been a lot of illicit behavior. Politicians sucking cock, making deals. Now the building was gone, and all that remained was the foundation down there in the rocks, a few stubborn walls, concrete, rusted pipes, the old pumping station out there at the edge of the tide, moss and rocks, a cracked basin filled with water. It was in some ways the bleakest corner of the city, the place where the edge of the peninsula jutted into the ocean, and the wind seemed always hard, the sky always black and gray.

And then Owens saw his kid.

Around the bend, standing at the vista. Zeke stood in the midst of strangers, other families, a bit too close, not reading the social cues. Fascinated by the seals. Thrumming his fingers. Listening to that gadget in his ears.

Owens stood in the middle of the path, looking at the boy. In a little while, Jill and the others came up behind him. Jill brushed past without speaking.

Jensen put a hand on his shoulder.

"It's all right," he said. "These kind of things happen. People lose control."

Owens watched Jensen head toward his son, his family. He felt his suspicions again. Unwarranted, maybe. But natural enough. He knew Jensen was right about one thing: Eight years was the same as thirty. He had to push his memories back there into the dark. He would lose everything if he went to jail.

THIRTY-TWO

The day before the trial started, Sorrentino went down to the North Beach Library. His tape had arrived. Despite the enthusiasm of the boho couple at the bar, the tape came with no special restrictions. It was a rare item, maybe, but the source library in Minnesota did not seem aware of the fact, and the North Beach librarian handed it to him without any particular fanfare.

Kaufman reading: May 13, 1975.

Sorrentino took the cassette with him. He had not been to the Beach since the Metzger story had broken, but today he went down to the Serafina Café. Stella emerged from the kitchen looking pretty much as she had the time before.

"What do you want?"

"Spaghetti."

Despite her age, Stella did not have much gray, and her breasts did not sag. She wore an underwire, maybe, and she dyed her hair, who knew? But it was a black mop nonetheless, thick as ever, and he remembered how surprised he had been at the way it felt when he'd finally gotten his hands into it: not soft, not luxurious, but coarse and wiry.

"Water?"

"No, wine."

She made no remark but instead brought him the wine, as if she had no idea about his problems with the grape, and even if she did, it was a few dollars more in the register. He pulled the pack of Parliaments from his pocket. No one cared if you smoked in Serafina's, and he had given up the pretense. He smoked as he pleased.

He put the tape on the counter.

The television was turned to one of those afternoon shows, but the volume was down low, and no one seemed to be paying much attention. The place was all but empty. It was just Johnny Pesci over there in the corner, his head tilted toward the wall, sleeping, a dead cigarette between his fingers. Just Johnny on one side of the room and Julia Besozi upright by the window, a smear of sauce on her lace collar, mincing at a plate of pasta, twirling it over and over with her fork, then putting it down without eating, sipping at her glass of port. None of the others, just these two, the oldest of the old—Pesci with his walker and Besozi with her cane. Just these two—and those shadows in the corner.

"Play this tape for me."

"There's a show on already," said Stella.

Sorrentino glanced at Pesci, his head against the wall, dozing on his afternoon wine. Then at Besozi, gaze forward, blind as a dog underwater.

"At the break then," he said. "During the commercial."

"This is why you came? You could not watch this at home?"

Stella turned the tape over in her hand, and the way she did, Sorrentino could not help but feel as if it were himself being examined. He glanced away, down the glass countertop, into that sea of faces in the photos embedded under the glass. Meanwhile he could hear the Chinaman in the back cleaning the dishes.

"So they gave you the bump," Stella said. "You helped that girl, and they're done with you."

"You could put it that way."

This was the kind of thing to expect from Stella: for her to remind him of his humiliation. Maybe that was why he had come down here. To get it over with, one way or the other. Here, in Serafina's, in front of Stella, with all those pictures as witnesses. The dead ones in the shadows no doubt were enjoying this, too.

"The other one, they will give him the bump, too. From the other side."

"Which other one?"

"Dante," she said. "Mancuso's son."

"He's nothing."

"It's just business. You shouldn't be so sensitive."

Maybe she was right, but he had no love for Mancuso. And not much for the rest of them, either. Blackwell had raked him harder then he needed to, taking a special pleasure in it, Sorrentino thought, Blackwell and Iverson both, looking for links to Metzger, to the fire-bombing, threatening to charge him with conspiracy, with obstruction of justice, knowing of course there were no links there—that Metzger himself could not be tied to the money, or to the bombing, most likely because Metzger had had nothing to do with it. It was a set-job, somebody playing bingo with the press, same as the Hearst kidnapping thirty years ago, Leland Sanford's resurrection from the dead, all that absurd theater in the street—but the feds couldn't figure it out, and now they were looking like jackasses all over again. The prosecution needed someone to humiliate, for business reasons, sure—but it was beyond business with Blackwell and his cronies. They'd taken a special pleasure in it.

Still, he'd gotten a dig back. "For that bombing, did you check

out the Sandinista?" he'd asked them. "Did you check out his buddies? They're the ones experienced at this kind of thing." But he'd
seen at a glance—the way Chin hung her head—they'd played jurisdictional games too long. They'd let it slip, the trail was cold. Blackwell and his arrogance.

Now Stella put the tape in.

It was an old cassette, a redub onto video of film recorded three
decades back. The colors were washed and faded. It had been shot
inside the Caffé Trieste. The owners of that place, they'd always
played it both ways, even back then, hosting the old-timers with their
accordions, their swelling violins, the local diva at the mike alongside
a brick mason as fat as Caruso—but this night, the place had been
packed with bohemians, gathered elbow to elbow at the long tables,
glassy eyed, arrogant, pretending they were in the East Village, or
Paris, lounging around in a movie of the sort no one with any sense
would want to watch.

The camera work was amateur. It zoomed about in jerks and stag-
gers, skimming the audience, holding on a face here, there. The date
was not too long after the robbery—after the FBI had raided the Aptos property but before Owens had turned himself in. It could even
be that Owens was in the audience. Nakamura, too. The video cut all
of a sudden, catching Kaufman midsentence at the podium.

Kaufman had a beer bottle in one hand and fumbled around like
a man with the shakes. He wore a turtleneck underneath one of
those hippie vests, a white turtleneck, and his skin was leather-dark.
After all Sorrentino had heard, he'd expected a more electric presence, but Kaufman was shy, stuttering, his voice high and unsure, and
the crowd—smoking cigarettes, swaying, nodding, hands on their
goatees, on one another's legs—had, underneath it all, that bored-to-
death coffeehouse look. Kaufman held some scraps of paper in his

free hand, and after a while he fumbled the beer onto the podium and began to snap his fingers, leaning into the mike, muttering in a singsong voice Sorrentino found hard to understand.

Something about the ancient rain.

About Russia, China.

The entrails of America on a slab in ancient Greece.

The rain was a mist of blood. It was fragments of bone, a sky full of ash, and it had been falling for a long time.

It wasn't going to stop falling anytime soon.

Why should it?

Kaufman snapped his fingers out of time. He took a drink, lost his place in the papers, then lost his rhythm altogether as one of the scraps fell to the floor. He shuffled through the words. Bits of tissue, colored paper, shopping bags, napkins, he let them slip through his fingers—reciting from memory now. Making it up as he went along.

He let the paper fall and reached for the beer.

The gasoline that is eating your car. The wife with the high hair who is not really there.

His mouth sounded as if it were full of sand. He jittered about behind the podium, graceless. He slobbered and lurched. The crowd looked as if they had seen it all before. I spoke to Leland Sanford the other day, he said. He told me he was dead. He told me strangers had inhabited his body in the moment of its demise. But do not listen to them because they are dead, too.

The revolution is dead.

And the ancient rain is still falling.

I hunt myself on the savannahs and kill myself in the streets.

I am a soldier in a ditch at the end of time.

Kaufman went on. Describing the corpse at the end of time, a corpse that lay in the sand. The rain that fell like sand driven by the wind until the bones were ground to dust. The sand red like blood. Yellow like a Chinaman. Black like rain.

The rain does not purify anything but keeps on falling.

The rain falls in my mouth as I die. The rain of vengeance. The rain of purification. The rain that sets nothing right.

Now it is raining television sets, bits of glass. Severed hands.

Ash.

The old rain, the endless rain . . .

Kaufman went on. And then on some more. It was time to give it up, but he kept on going. He laughed. He dropped his beer. Then there was a smattering of applause, and the video flickered out. Johnny Pesci, the old black shirt, had not stirred, he was still sleeping, and Julia Besozi, whose husband had been interned with the Japanese, took another sip of port. Stella had left halfway through the man's rant, retreating to the kitchen, but returned now at the sound of the static to eject the tape.

Nonsense, Sorrentino thought. The tape had told him nothing. Or almost nothing.

Only that he had been suckered. By the rumors, by that hoax and nonsense Ricci and her like had put out, tapes, stories smeared all over the press, making connections where they didn't exist, sending the feds scurrying this way and that. They'd done it back then, and they were doing the same thing now.

No, Sanford was long dead, Sorrentino was all but sure. Or if not dead, insignificant to the matter at hand.

Blackwell, he guessed, had already figured this out. Blackwell wanted Owens—for his own lousy reasons, maybe, nothing to do with Elise—but Sorrentino could not see how he meant to get him. He could not see Blackwell's angle.

If Sanford had not been with Owens the day of the robbery, then who? What four people? But it didn't matter. It wasn't Sorrentino's business anymore.

Sorrentino looked along the counter and felt his eyes welling. Stella slid him the tape but he did not look up because he did not want her to see. He leaned over and picked up the tape. Then he just stood there, head down, staring at the counter.

He looked at the photo.

Himself and the kid, smiling. Father and son. Arm around Dad. A string of fish hanging on a line at the dock. Mountains behind.

He felt a cry rise from his diaphragm, involuntary. An ugly noise, strangled in an old man's throat.

He pushed the front door out into Chinatown. He was weeping now, and could not stop himself, not even in front of these yellow men and their families, these Chink bastards, these faggots and Jews.

My son. You killed my fucking son.

Down at the Embarcadero, he put his hands on the railing and let himself go. The tape had told him nothing. A dead lead. His weeping had nothing to do with the man on the tape, he told himself, nothing to do with his meandering poem. It was of no value to the case, no value at all.

He looked over the pier into the water. He looked at the water for a long time. Then he dropped the tape into the bay.

PART SIX

The Trial

THIRTY-THREE

The trial would bring certain things to light. Or that was the idea. What had happened that day in the bank, it would be revealed in the courtroom, with the jurors watching from their box, the press reporting, the cameras peering. In reality, though, there was a door at the back of the courtroom, leading to a corridor, and that corridor in turn led to another room. Inside that room, the judge sat in her chambers. And the truth was, not everything emerged from chambers. Not everything made its way down the long corridor back into the light.

In chambers, at the moment, the defense sat to one side of the judge, and the prosecution to the other.

"I am going to address this question to the prosecution," said the judge, and she glanced toward Blackwell, the federal prosecutor.

Blackwell was not well liked. He knew this. Mocked in the press, distrusted by his underlings. Despised by the defense, of course—but also by Elise Younger, who shrugged away from him as if he were some kind of reptile. Disdained, too, by the honchos at Justice, who worried he would botch the government's case.

He'd read the recent spate of articles, seen the media portrayals contemplating his motivations, picking at his biography—or the bones of it anyway, the barest facts. He'd read the descriptions of his ranch house in San Mateo, of his fundamentalist daughter and wild son. Of his long career as a nose-to-the-grindstone investigative attorney, a cool shell with a hot exterior, perennial second in charge. The government's hit man, angry in the shadows.

Well . . .

Maybe he was a son of a bitch, but the world was full of sons of bitches. Like a lot of people, he had a wife and family. And like a lot of people, if anything happened to them—if someone with a cockamamie idea blew apart his life—then he would want someone like himself to do just what he was doing now.

"Yes, Your Honor," he said.

"In regard to Cynthia Nakamura—this issue of the discovery material?"

"Ms. Nakamura has been available to the defense for some time."

"That's not true," interjected Jensen. "The prosecutor has been playing a shell game."

"Your Honor, Ms. Nakamura was listed initially under her husband's name. As soon as we realized the potential for confusion, we corrected the problem. The defense has been provided with her deposition."

"Her illness precludes our speaking with her," said Jensen. "And the deposition has obviously been heavily coached. Your Honor, we must insist this witness be disallowed."

This back and forth had been going on for some time, since early in the trial, and Judge Jackson looked weary of them both, but seemed particularly impatient with Jensen, Blackwell thought. The defense attorney had lost his touch. He was loud, inelegant. His skin had grown splotchy, and he touched his beard too often. There was something decidedly syphilitic in his manner.

"Your Honor," Jensen continued, "if it weren't for the current political environment, we wouldn't be here. This case is the same one that was too weak to go to trial three decades ago. So far, the government hasn't brought anything new. And now they want to bring forth a woman who has obviously been coerced on her deathbed."

"You've made your point," said the judge.

Regardless, Blackwell knew that his case so far hadn't done much to tie Owens to the crime. He'd introduced the new forensics, true, connecting bullet casings at the bank to weapons found in an SLA hideaway. But Jensen would counter that by challenging how the evidence had been stored these many years. Other than that, Blackwell had spent much of his time with witnesses who could establish what had happened in the bank. An aging woman who'd been working as a teller that day. The security guard who'd seen the shooting. The insurance salesman who'd dropped to the floor at the robbers' commands, and who had lain beside Eleanor Younger as she died.

The only thing that had taken the defense by surprise, perhaps, was when he'd called Annette Ricci and Jan Sprague. Both of them well spoken. Ricci with her theatrical smile. Sprague with her cashmere looks, her pearl necklace, her well-cut jacket. His questioning of the two women had been brief and without incident. He'd asked them where they had been the day of the robbery. In Aptos, they told him. And Owens, they said, had been there, too.

The press commentators had derided the seeming purposelessness of his approach, how he'd been outclassed by the women, but this didn't bother him. He had his own strategy, his own plan.

As for Judge Jackson, Blackwell had been in front of her before. Antonia Jackson was African American—a severe, dark-eyed woman of liberal reputation, but she was no knee-jerk liberal. She had a brother who'd been killed in a robbery and a son who worked as a prosecuting attorney. And she, too, like everyone, had her own considerations.

"How ill is this woman?" she asked.

"She's terminal. But she has recently taken a turn for the better. If I can point out, our handling of this is well within the boundaries of the new legislation, which grants the state considerable discretion in matters of protecting witnesses."

Jensen went off on a howl then. Complaining about the abuse of the system. About the trumped-up nature of the case. About the state expanding its powers to coerce witnesses and bring in pretty much whomever they pleased, violating the rules of discovery. Most of it was noise. The rules had changed recently, but underneath it all, there were other reasons for the fuss. He could see the worry in Jensen's eyes.

Antonia Jackson shifted in her seat, uncomfortable in her robes, her eyes running from one of them to the other. She was in a hard place herself. The administration was going after certain judgeships. And the public was in a lousy mood. Once you got past the noisy ones and the fools, the protestors in the street, people weren't game for letting killers go.

"I don't see the reason to exclude this witness," she said at last.

"Your Honor," Jensen objected, "the state has taken multiple depositions from Ms. Nakamura—all riddled with contradiction. Either she is not altogether competent, or the state is coaching—"

"The defense will have a chance to point out these contradictions during cross-examination," said Judge Jackson. "In the meantime, let's proceed with Ms. Elise Younger. I believe she is next on the prosecution's docket."

There was often a certain theater, an electricity, to the moment when the aggrieved took the stand and peered down from the witness chair toward the table of the accused. Elise Younger had waited for it, Blackwell knew, with considerable hunger. After weeks of proximity, watching Owens from across the aisle, brushing against the family in the corridors, hours on the hard benches, Elise shifted in her skirt now, rising at the sound of her name. Owens, meanwhile, sat with his hands together, maintaining his posture, neither particularly attentive nor dismissive. Most of all, refraining from the impulsive gesture. The shaking of the head. The twisted smile. Anything that could be interpreted as arrogance in the face of grief.

He had been carefully coached, no doubt, as had Elise.

Blackwell knew that verdicts were often handed down on the basis of moments such as these—by personal associations the lawyers ultimately could not anticipate. By the fact that Elise Younger, perhaps, reminded the juror in the second row of his high-school English teacher. That Bill Owens's son resembled a brother who had died years ago. That a flicker in the lighting overhead gave Blackwell himself the appearance of a perpetual scowl. Like other attorneys who worked in this building, he sometimes patted his face with a faint powder.

Some people might mock him, but it wasn't his fault. He hadn't invented the fluorescent light.

Blackwell wore his bluest suit. He had thick hair, and he was fit, but not too fit. The imperfection helped, he knew, because people did not trust anyone who looked too good. Jensen, on the other hand, tipped too far toward the slovenly these days. His Nordic looks had grown too jowly, too thick.

Blackwell started by projecting a map onto a screen, showing the path Elise and her mother had driven to the bank that day. He had an evidentiary purpose, but another purpose as well—to capture for the jury the texture of the day, the girl riding on the hot vinyl in the Ford Falcon down Judah Street, the mother with her hands on the wheel, the big purse on the seat bench between them. He wanted the jury to see the mother in the checkered blouse, adjusting on her face the horn-rimmed shades that would later tumble from her fingers in the bank.

"You entered the parking lot from the north side of Judah, as shown on the map."

"Yes."

"And you waited in the car."

"I was listening to the radio."

"So, as to the events of that day, is it true you delivered an account to the police at that time, and identified, with the aid of a sketch artist and file photos, two of the suspects in the robbery?"

Jensen objected, as Blackwell expected he would, challenging a childhood memory from almost thirty years before: an eyewitness account blurred and faded by time.

Judge Jackson overruled. She motioned for Blackwell to continue.

"What happened next?"

"We pulled into the parking lot, and there was a woman sitting there, on a bench. I noticed her because of her hat—a floppy hat, like people were wearing then, with the big brim."

They dwelled on the woman for a while, seated as she was on that bench, situated as it was, affording a view of the street corner, of the parking lot, and of the bank itself, front entrance and side. The bench sat some forty-odd feet from the parked car, but not so far that Elise couldn't see her mother exchange pleasantries with the woman on her way to the entrance. After her mother had entered the bank, the woman on the bench suddenly rose to her feet and started to wave. She wore dark glasses and her features were hidden in the long shadows of her hat.

"I thought she was waving at me," said Elise. "She was making some kind of sign, the peace sign, I didn't know, I just waved back. But then I looked behind and saw these people, four of them, coming out of an alley." Elise paused then, as if she were peering into that alley. "The woman on the bench . . ."

"Yes?"

"She was Japanese, I think."

"Objection," said Jensen. "This is speculation on the part of the witness."

Jensen was right, of course. Blackwell himself, years ago, odd as it seemed now, had missed the significance of the woman on the bench. But Elise's description had not much changed.

"How many people, did you say, were in the alley?"

"Four. Dressed in camping clothes, or that's how it looked to me. And one of them gave the sign back. And the woman with the floppy hat, she went off in the other direction then."

"This Japanese woman . . ."

Judge Jackson hit the gavel, cautioning Blackwell now for deliberately leading the jury, since the ethnic identity of the woman had not been established. It was true, the slip had been deliberate . . . planting a seed . . . preparing for things to come . . .

"These four people, what did they do next?"

"They headed across the parking lot toward the bank."

Elise described the figures, all dressed like men on a hunting trip, in clothes too warm for the season: camouflage jackets with big pockets, baggy pants, and hunting caps. She had thought they were all men at first, but when they came closer, two were women, she was pretty sure, one with a mop of frizzy hair crammed up under a baseball cap, and the other, more slender, her hair tied up off her neck, carrying a straw beach bag with something inside it. The bag swayed as she walked.

They not did head toward the front entrance, where her mother had gone. They went instead to the glass doors fronting the parking lot. Because they walked so quickly, Elise did not get a good look at their faces, not on the way in to the bank.

She did not see either their transformation on the other side of the glass doors—the instant in which the androgynous figures suddenly appeared in the bank lobby as if out of nowhere, ski masks yanked tight, pistols drawn, a sawed-off shotgun emerging from the straw bag.

Blackwell allowed the pause to lengthen—a moment for the jury to imagine the chaos inside the bank.

Ninety seconds.

That's how long the robbery had taken, more or less. Blackwell had been over the details with earlier witnesses, recreating the scene inside the bank.

A minute and a half.

Right now, though, he wanted the jury to think about that girl inside the car, with the AM Radio on, listening to Tommy James and the Shondells, or the Boxtops, or some damn thing, slouching in the vinyl seat, half bored, watching the cedars shift in the nagging breeze that blew off the ocean.

"What did you do after they went inside?"

"I was just sitting, waiting for my mother."

Blackwell glanced at his watch for effect.

Inside the bank, first thing, the security guard had dropped to his knees. Blackwell had gone over this in court with the guard himself, now retired: The gangsters had pointed their guns and he'd dropped at their command, lying facedown on the tile, arms spread, letting them take his weapon. One of the intruders had started counting backward from ninety. *In and out, ninety seconds! Eighty-nine! That's all the time we have. Eighty-eight!* Other witnesses had mentioned the counting as well, and when they did, Blackwell had paused—glancing first at his watch, then at Elise Younger—so the jurors would follow his gaze to the woman in the courtroom and feel the inexorable draw back to that moment, when the woman had been a girl inside the car waiting for her mother. While she'd waited, the voice inside had gone on counting, and the figure at the center of the bank waved the shotgun in a wild arc, shouting orders. *Everyone down, on the floor, before my friend counts off one more number!* The two voices, the man and the woman's, intertwined. *Eighty-four!* The one voice urgent, impatient; the other harsh and mechanical—a clock ticking backward. In the midst of the confusion, the girl's mother, Eleanor Younger, not understanding, maybe, panicking . . . *seventy-eight!* . . . grabbing at her purse as it slid from her shoulders . . . *seventy-seven!* . . . the shooter pivoting . . . *Oh my god!* . . . Now everyone was down on the cold tile, everyone except the tellers and the robbers . . . *sixty-three!* . . . the tellers doing as they were told . . . *fifty!* . . . emptying their money drawers, filling the straw bag and another sack as well. Then pretty soon the tellers had been forced down as well . . . *nineteen!* . . . as the numbers all but expired, and the sounds dwindled . . . rushing footsteps . . . a woman moaning on the floor.

"What did you see next?"

"Those four people, they came running across the parking lot."

"All four at once?"

"There were three up front, and another trailing behind. They wore masks now, the first three did. They had to run right past our car to get to the alley."

"So you didn't see their faces?"

"Not the first three."

"And the fourth?"

"He came out after the others. He scampered over between the cars, low to the ground, and disappeared for a second. When he stood back up, he didn't have the mask on. Then he walked more slowly, calm now, like nothing had happened."

"Did you see his face?"

"He walked right past the car. I was on the passenger side, and the window was down, and he looked right at me when he walked by. He seemed surprised to see me, but he just kept walking."

At this point, Blackwell submitted into evidence the drawings made by the sketch artist who had sat with Elise Younger the day after the killing.

Jensen objected once again, but to no avail. Judge Jackson was letting it in, leaving the jury to decide.

Blackwell put the first set of likenesses on the overhead: a sketch of the woman in the floppy hat. It was a full-length drawing, of a woman at a distance. Looking at it, you saw the wardrobe, the stance, the slightness of the figure. There was the sense that it could have been anyone, true, but Blackwell wanted the jury to see it for later reference.

Then he put up another sketch, a young man with a beard and glasses, a man with unremarkable features. And beside that, a mug shot bearing a striking resemblance.

"Did you also consult with the sketch artist on this drawing?"

"Yes."

"And did you make an identification based on the photos in the police file book?"

"I did," she said.

"Do you remember the name of the man whom you identified?"

Elise had waited a long time for this. She waited an instant longer, as if examining the moment in front of her, the whole business compressed into this particular instant, held in suspension. She glanced toward Owens. Blackwell had worried, but Elise held her composure. She was not overeager. When she finally spoke, her voice tremored, but the anger, the grief, it did not overwhelm the moment.

"Bill Owens," she said. "That was his name. The man at the table."

The defense went after Elise in the cross-examination in the way Blackwell had anticipated, challenging not only her immediate testimony but what she had witnessed in the past, suggesting that the police sketches were based not on what she, herself, had seen, but on photographs the police had provided.

Jensen attacked her testimony in the same way he might attack that of a child witness.

The girl had not been lying, but the testimony was a lie nonetheless. Because the authorities had manipulated the distraught child into describing the people they wanted to arrest. And so Elise's memories of the event, these many years later, were likewise distorted.

As the cross wore on, Jensen harrowed her on other matters as well: her mental health, her obsession with Owens, the pretrial insinuations that she and Sorrentino had somehow been involved with the violence at Owens's house.

Though Jensen was a large man, with a reputation for defending the disenfranchised, his size at the moment, as he stepped toward Elise Younger, gave him the aura of a bully.

"Isn't it possible," said Jensen, "that you have been led horribly astray?"

"No," Elise said. "I saw him. I saw him very clearly. And then I walked over to the bank door—and I saw my mother." She paused, as if about to describe her dead mother. But she refrained, as Blackwell had told her. They had autopsy photos for that. "So it's not something I have forgotten. Those moments—they are indelible in my mind."

Jensen pushed some more, hoping she would crack in the way she sometimes did, but Elise did not explode. Her testimony, on its own, would not be enough to sway the case, Blackwell knew; but Elise was, in her own way, convincing. Jensen did not relent. He started after her again, but the more he went on, the more the jury disliked it. Jensen had crossed the line, so that it was not the woman he was bullying, but the young girl peering through the glass of the bank door at her dying mother.

When cross-examination was over, Jackson put the court into recess until the following Tuesday.

Blackwell would have preferred to have put Nakamura on the stand immediately, but it had been a good day. Not perfect, but Elise had held her own. He'd seen, too, at the end of the day, as Jensen gathered his papers, the brooding look on Owens's face, his distraught wife, then the big attorney turning toward his clients with his best smile.

I have disarmed them, Blackwell thought.

Thirty years ago, he had thought Leland Sanford was the key. For that reason, he had never been able to identify the four people in the alley. This time around, he let the defense believe he was pursuing the same angle, but no.

Now he knew the identities.

Owens—counting backward. Annette Ricci and her young friend, a Chicano kid—Naz Ramirez, he was all but certain, the one who'd later died in prison—those two had been the ones with the paper sacks, going to the tellers. And the fourth one, carrying the straw bag out in the lot, the one with the trigger filed a hair too fine—

Jan Sprague.

How Blackwell knew—it was on account of number five, the fifth wheel, the young woman who'd been recruited to stand lookout. The Japanese woman, in her floppy hat. Who'd sat on the bench on Judah Street and met the gang later, at the mouth of the alley, driving getaway, taking them to Aptos in John Panarelli's station wagon.

Cynthia Nakamura, the woman in the sketch.

So when Blackwell left the courtroom, he felt good about his chances. Maybe even a little smug. The case wasn't won, by any means, he knew that. The defense would try to discredit Nakamura. But if nothing else, he would pull Ricci and Sprague back on the stand. Go after them for perjury, lying about their whereabouts. The whole dynamic would change. A little pressure and they would unravel, he was all but certain. But the following afternoon, as he sat with his wife in San Mateo, on the patio, trying not to think about the case, working a crossword instead, he got a call from Laguna. Cynthia Nakamura had taken a turn for the worse, a respiratory infection, early-stage pneumonia. "I think she'll recover from this," said the nurse. "With antibiotics. Though it might take some time." Blackwell started to work immediately, repositioning his witnesses, filing for delay, but in the end it didn't matter. The next day, before he could put a motion to the judge, the nurse called him again. Cynthia Nakamura had expired in her sleep.

THIRTY-FOUR

On the day of the closing arguments, Dante ran across Guy Sorrentino on Larkin, on the edge of the Tenderloin. Dante had been in the Civic Center, delivering some documents, and had walked outside into the plaza. The scene was not unfamiliar. It was just past lunch, the office workers returning, clerks and lawyers in scattered pairs, while a woman from Code Pink stood on the steps, just outside the security perimeter, in a pink shirt and black tights, handing out pamphlets. Farther on, at the center of the plaza, a trio of young men, all dressed in gray suits, tossed dollar bills into the air, play money, while a clown balanced himself on an oil barrel, and a woman in fatigues waved a plastic carbine. Street theater, lunchtime entertainment—but the sky was drizzling a slow and steady rain, and the audience was small and laughed a bit too hard. A group of homeless loitered by the trees under a sign that read FOOD NOT BOMBS. There was in the air a simmering anger, righteous, frustrated. Around the corner, out in front of the Federal Building, a different group, in JAMS and polyester, baseball caps and pleated skirts, carried signs that read JUSTICE FOR ELEANOR YOUNGER. There was the same sense of injury here, the same sense of justice unsatisfied.

After Nakamura's death, Blackwell had struggled to make his case. Judge Jackson had allowed the jury to watch the depositions, but the videos were contradictory, not altogether cogent. Still, the verdict wasn't in, and it was hard to say what a jury might do.

Dante spotted Guy Sorrentino from a distance, halfway up the block, emerging from Cholino's, a dive frequented by vice officers and washed-up cops. The man wore his sports jacket and a white shirt, and his belly hung over his gray trousers. Hatless, with his balding pate and winged hair, he resembled an overweight parrot whose wings had been clipped—a grayish bird in a dirty white shirt. When he recognized Dante, he gave his fellow investigator a look of disgust. They had not encountered each other, face-to-face, since that day in the Mission.

"So—you have made your slander."

Ordinarily, Dante would have ignored such a taunt, but he was tired of Guy Sorrentino. The man had a little American flag on his lapel and smelled vaguely of beef.

"You like to ruin people," said Sorrentino.

"I didn't ruin you."

"Anything but the truth. But you know that. You just pretend not to know."

Dante knew he should walk away, but something held him there, listening to the old man. It was a dirty street, noisy with traffic, horns wailing up and down, and the people you saw, hurrying along, chests forward, looked to have come from some fresh argument.

"Don't you have any conscience in all this? Things you do—your father, he would be ashamed."

In reality, Dante's father had not thought much of Sorrentino. The man had worked at the Mancuso warehouse for a summer when he was young, and Dante remembered what his father had to say: good shoulders, but not much brains and a bad disposition. "No," Sorrentino said, "he told me once, your father, about all the expectations he had for you. About what you were supposed to be. But after the kind of things you pull, your line of work—I mean, maybe you should be the one in the paper."

Sorrentino had been drinking, it was apparent. Cholino's was the place old cops came to hang out when things went bad, mingling with vice officers who had a few bucks to dish out if you were willing to play the mark: drinking all night in the Tenderloin and coming back with a list of low-level creeps to help the squad boys make quota. Down the street, at the moment, some uniformed officers sat parked in a cruiser, watching the street action, but neither Dante nor Sorrentino paid them any mind.

"To hell with you, Sorrentino," Dante said, and he was about to say more, to tell Sorrentino what his father had really thought about him, but he looked at the old man's bull-dog face and felt something like sympathy.

Sorrentino himself was not so restrained.

"To hell with you!" he countered. The man took him by the arm. "Let me tell you one thing. You are a selfish pig. You left that girl years ago for New Orleans. She waited for you." Dante tried to pull away but Sorrentino had his fingers in the fabric. "And now she's blind, and it's all because of you."

Sorrentino had his lips pursed in a look Dante hadn't seen since he was a kid, on the faces of the old Italians when they were filled with disgust—when they wanted to indicate that you were a person beneath contempt. They puckered their lips up like one monkey telling another monkey to kiss his ass.

"And your mother . . . and your beautiful mother, if she were still alive . . ."

Dante had had enough. His sympathy and pity gave way to something else. "Let go, old man," he said again, but Sorrentino only tightened his grip. So Dante came around with his other hand and knocked himself free. He could have walked away then but something got into him. Or maybe this was the reason he'd hung around, waiting. He grabbed Sorrentino by the collar, the same way he'd grabbed the Mexican at the Tamale House, but Sorrentino was strong, built like an ox, low to the ground, and he did not move easily—and Dante did not protect himself. Sorrentino attacked low, hitting him in the solar plexus. Dante felt himself doubling, and the old man hit him again. The blackness veered up, and in that blackness Dante came around with his elbow, smashing Sorrentino in the jaw. He planted a side kick at the knees, trying to knock the feet out from under him.

Sorrentino did not fall. There was noise farther down the sidewalk, footsteps approaching, men hollering. Dante hit him again, low, hard in the stomach, and saw the old man's jaw drop and his eyes glaze. The temptation was to go harder now, to beat Sorrentino until he fell down, and he would have done so and kept on going, but the cops were on them.

They pulled Dante off, and as luck would have it, one of the officers knew Sorrentino from the old days.

"What are you doing hitting an old man?"

Dante shook his head.

"He's a bum!" yelled Sorrentino.

Dante was not sure which of them had gotten the worst of it. His hand hurt and his ribs were sore, but he could see that Sorrentino was breathing hard and bleeding from the mouth. Dante worried the old bastard would have a heart attack. The younger cop walked Sorrentino over to the cruiser, and the other one stayed with Dante.

"So what was this about?"

"We were talking," said Dante.

"About what?"

"The weather."

"The weather?"

"About the rain. He told me it had been raining for a long time, and I told him it wasn't true."

"I can see why he doesn't like you. What I want to know, I want to know why you hit this old man."

"I didn't like the way he was talking to me."

"So you hit an old man."

"I did."

A couple of cops appeared at the corner and another approached from across the way. They stood awhile, listening to this exchange.

"Put the locks on him for me, will ya?" said Sorrentino's buddy, "while I go down and talk to Guy."

Dante stood on the sidewalk with the cuffs on. The Federal Building towered over the block and below that was Civic Center Plaza. The streetlight changed, and he could see city workers in the crosswalk. Civil service employees, lawyers, local politicians, and clerks. People on jury duty, office girls, litigants, court reporters, small-time criminals. A few glanced his way, but the neighborhood went bad fast, and most did not give a second look at the man standing there with the cuffs next to the parking meter.

All this while, the older cop was talking to Sorrentino, getting his side of the story. Sorrentino was loud and Dante could catch bits of what he was saying, laying out the Owens business for his buddy, complaining how he, himself, had been served up to the press by prick-face over there, by that little donkey with the hook nose. In a little while they led Sorrentino across the way, back into Cholino's. Sorrentino, despite his infamy, still had friends on the force—which was more than Dante could say. It wasn't unheard of for the uniforms to consort with the undercovers, for them all to mingle a little here at the edge of the Tenderloin on a Friday afternoon.

Now the older cop came back. His name was Officer Allen. He and a Chinese cop took Dante over to the cruiser. The car was parked in the mouth of an alley and they walked Dante past the car into the alley itself.

"I been on the horn. Seems you have a little bit of a history with the force."

"Yeah."

"We're going to let you go."

"That's kind of you."

Officer Allen, however, did not move, and he made no attempt to take off the cuffs. Dante stood with his back to the car, his thighs against the rear fender. His departure from the force, his adventures since, this particular case, none of these things had made him popular with the SFPD.

"Arrogant fuck, aren't you?"

"I don't know. Depends on how you define arrogance."

"You're backing the wrong horse. Kicking an old man around. Helping a criminal get off."

Officer Allen stood there, and the other one, Lee or Wu or Yang, whatever his fucking name was—stepped away. Dante had an inkling of what was coming now but there was nothing he could do. Officer Allen drove his fist into Dante's stomach and then hit him again. Dante fell to the ground. The cop let him lie there for a little while, nudging him with his toe. Dante rolled over, faceup, staring into that great fog overhead, not seeing it, not feeling, really, the drizzle that fell on his face. The cop nudged Dante's cheek with the toe of his shoe and put his heel on Dante's nose. He put his weight a little harder on the nose, enjoying himself.

"Allen," said the Chinaman.

"It's okay. I've got permission."

The Chinaman said nothing.

"Everyone says San Francisco cops are soft. We're not soft." Allen leaned forward now, pressing a little harder with his heel. "If you want to make a police-brutality case, go ahead and report it, okay. We'll see what kind of publicity you really want, Mr. Investigator. Mr. Attack-an-old-man-on-the-street. I'm sure you'll find lots of people on your side, an upstanding man like yourself."

Dante said nothing. He was not quite conscious.

"Roll over."

Dante grunted. Allen kicked at him, and Dante rolled onto his side. Then the other cop, the Chinaman, unfastened his cuffs.

"You're free to go," said Allen.

PART SEVEN

Epilogue

THIRTY-FIVE

After his father's death, Dante had lived for a while in a cold-water flat on Columbus Avenue. In fact, he had not given the place up. He still stayed there on occasion, more so these last few weeks since Marilyn had gotten out of the hospital. She had needed him at first, close by, but he sensed in her a growing remoteness. Also, more practically, he was keeping late hours on a new case, and she needed her rest, she needed to heal. So he had stayed at the place on Columbus a few nights this week. Maybe it didn't make sense, since the house on Fresno Street was empty, but he had mixed feelings toward his parents' house.

Now Dante walked down the hall, to the shared bathroom, and examined himself in the mirror. Despite the beating he had gotten the day before, he did not look too bad. His nose was swollen, but it was not broken. His elbow was sore and his chest hurt and occasionally he felt a sharp pain shoot up his side, but he was not pissing blood, and he figured he would be all right.

He walked uphill to Marilyn's apartment at the top of Union

Street and rang her bell. Marilyn took a while to come to the door, then regarded him as if examining a puzzle.

"Did you lose your key?"

"No."

"Oh."

"I didn't want to startle you."

"That's considerate."

He followed her in. There was an awkwardness between them, a separation. "I came to see if you wanted to go out to dinner."

"What happened to your nose?"

She stepped closer, examining him. She still wore the eye patch but he had grown used to it. The way she touched him, the look on her face, for an instant, he imagined they could step back in time.

"I tripped on the sidewalk."

She looked skeptical. "That doesn't sound like you."

"I'm getting clumsy I guess . . . For dinner, I was thinking, if you want to join me, the U.S. Restaurant?"

She shook her head, and moved away with a nonchalance that made him uneasy. The jury in the Owens case was still out, but they did not speak about this.

"Didn't I tell you? I have to go out tonight."

"Maybe you did tell me."

"I don't want to go, it's a client thing for Prospero."

"Where are you going?"

"To the opera. Prospero has a box, and he takes turns inviting his employees."

"That's good. It's good for you to get back into the business."

"I suppose."

"Why don't you stay awhile?"

She got dressed then, and he watched her. It was part of their routine. He watched her standing there in her slip as she studied herself in the mirror. He watched the serenity with which she made up her face. He watched her put on a pastel skirt and a white sweater and some new pumps, and then take them all off for another outfit. She still wore the patch, but she had gotten better with the makeup, and the grafts were healing. She moved with her familiar adroitness. Even so, there was something different about her, something changed. She put up her hair, letting the tendrils fall about her cheeks, then changed into darker colors, a silk blouse and also a pair of pearls that, he knew, had once belonged to her mother.

It wasn't Prospero, he thought.

"I wish you could come."

"You look good. The patch becomes you."

She walked over and kissed him, as if experimenting with an idea. Then walked back to look in the mirror.

D ante ate dinner at the U.S. Restaurant. The place was popular with the old-timers. It had changed locations recently, and for a while had tried a new menu, hoping to attract a younger, more affluent set—pasta al dente, designer sauces, specialty risotto—but the young people did not come and the old ones complained. The regulars wanted their soft noodles, their dark sauce from the can, their bread with the hard crust and their meatballs held together by eggs and cheese.

Dante ate his meal, then went to the house on Fresno Street.

Owens and his family had cleaned it up pretty well, putting clean sheets on the beds and sweeping the floors, leaving their trash cinched in a plastic bag on the back porch. The only evidence of their having been here was a discarded Game Boy disk. Regardless, the place had an empty, deserted feeling. After the trial started, the defense had had little use for him—and he had not talked to Owens for some time. They had used him, there was no doubt, but that's what the defense did. Dante went into the closets and took out some of the old things, the old pictures, that had belonged to his mother and father. He hung up a painting of the Amalfi coast, one of his father's favorites, and a photo of the Mancuso warehouse, and gathered from an old box pictures of his family on the wharf, his grandfather, his uncle Salvatore, his mother in a thin white dress.

There were more pictures up in the attic, he knew, boxes in the garage, photo albums and bundled letters: pictures of relatives back in Italy whose names he no longer remembered; a portrait of the Virgin; Holy Communion cards; business ledgers from the past half century, numbers written in a careful hand, column after column.

Listen.

He remembered his mother, beckoning him. *You can hear, I know you can.*

La Seggezza, as it was called. The intuition—a special power. His grandmother had had the gift, apparently, and his mother as well.

Then came the voices.

They had taken her to Agnews first, the state asylum, in the South Bay; then up to Sonoma County. But there was nothing they could do for her. The whisperings of the doctors, the numbers on the calendars—messages in code. She was in touch with the other side, with something haunting her, but whatever it was, it never became manifest; it would change shape before she could pin it down.

Dante lay on the couch, in the old television room, with the big RCA. A wire ran from the rabbit ears on the roof to a plate attached to an old-style antenna, but the antenna itself had long since been taken down. The couch smelled of cigar smoke and wine, of his father's last years. Dante dreamed as he slept, and in his dreams there were people saying things he could not quite hear. It was raining. On the roof, there was the noise of the rain, the noise of leaves, the sound of his grandparents singing, the aria of the fishing boats, of trash cans rolling up and down the street. The noise of his father coughing and the squeaking of bedsprings, of his mother sighing. It was the noise of the fog; of those poets hollering in the street; of the accountants on their adding machines; of Italian radio; of Marinetti and Johnny Pesci arguing over who was stupider, the Sicilians or the Calabrians; over whether it was Mussolini who ruined Italy, or Hitler, or Roosevelt; over politics and issues of importance that no one remembered . . . *Do nothing* . . . And in the morning he awoke with a headache, as with a fever, the feeling of having eaten too much, hungover, his nose still sore, and the image of something in his head that he could not quite remember, that would not come to consciousness, of children he would not have—of Marilyn whispering something to David Lake, maybe; of Elise Younger in the shadows; and then he was on the mudflats again, and the sky that had been so dark with birds was empty now, and gray, and the cliffs were barren. The tide was coming in, and there was nowhere for him to go.

Dante got out of bed.

The phone was ringing.

He did not recognize the voice at first. It was Cicero, back from his cruise. The jury in the Owens case had finished its deliberations, the old man said. That was the inside dope. They could expect a verdict later that afternoon.

THIRTY-SIX

There was a mist in the air, a primordial grayness—a dampness that was not quite rain, but almost, as if the water were seeping through the air. The fog muffled the sound so that there was a kind of intimacy, a closeness. It was not a closeness that made you feel comfortable or cozy, but rather one that constricted the vision to a field of gray, so you were not sure what would come out of that grayness. Dante walked out of that gray field down Telegraph Hill toward Cicero's office.

Cicero had been mistaken.

The verdict had not come in that afternoon, but came several days later. Dante had seen the television footage—the thin, exhausted smile on Owens's face, while across the room Elise Younger let out a moan—and then the camera caught her as well, the anguished look, her head falling forward into her splayed fingers.

"Not guilty."

Now, three weeks had passed. The case was not so much in the news anymore, and Dante walked up the long stairs to Jake Cicero's office. He had a check to pick up, and also a report to pass along concerning a case involving a man who had held up a bar down on Columbus Avenue. Dante's job was to find some mitigating evidence, but there had not been much.

"How's Marilyn?" asked Cicero.

"She's fine."

"Healing up?"

"Last I saw."

Cicero gave him a curious glance, but he did not press the matter. He leaned back in his chair, with his feet up on his desk, and his Genovese eyes staring at him, brown eyes, the color of the dirt. Cicero had gotten a tan out there in the Mediterranean, and he looked good—though Dante knew the man was worried about his heart and had lingering concerns about his marriage and the way his wife, a younger woman, had behaved on the boat. Still, he seemed happy to be back, with his line of bocce trophies on the wall behind him, and on his desk a picture of the stripper Carol Doda in her prime. Tits like melons, the big ones that had been genetically altered.

Perfect shape, perfect size. But touch one, put it in your mouth, and then you'd know it wasn't the real thing.

That was the joke, anyway—the one Cicero liked to tell.

Outside, a light had begun to shine beyond the mist, as if the sun might break through.

"Do you think it's going to clear up?"

"No," said Cicero.

"I think that's the sun up there."

"I don't know why everybody is so in love with the sun."

"Not everybody is."

Outside, there was a peculiar stillness. Cicero's place was on the third floor of a building that tilted precariously over the Broadway Tunnel. They were on the lee side, however, away from the traffic, and given the way the mist muted the noise, the rise and fall of the sound of cars rumbling in the tunnel, the grayness of the sky, the gulls squawking on the rooftop, it felt as if they were on a cliff at the edge of the sea. "Owens returned your call, by the way. He says he'd be glad to meet with you."

"My call?"

Dante found this curious, as he had not called Owens. When he told Cicero, the man shrugged his shoulders.

"What does it matter? Go talk to him. All this attention Jensen's gotten with this case—he's going to be bringing in clients. Sooner or later, they're going to need us again."

"I don't know."

"You prefer the city case—this mugger? He's a better class of clientele?"

Cicero looked at him with his brown eyes, and it all passed between them in an instant. Dante could tell him about his reservations—how the information he had given to the defense had been manipulated, how he doubted Owens's innocence, how he felt somehow used—but they both knew this was part of the game, that your job was to collect information and let the lawyers figure out how it played.

"It could be Nakamura was lying."

"Which time?"

Cicero shrugged once more. He was a relativist, so long as he got his money. So they talked of other things for a while. Cicero's cruise. The house on Fresno Street. The price of real estate. At length, there was another pause, and Dante feared the man would ask him about Marilyn.

"All right," Dante said. "I'll go talk to him."

Cicero handed him the note—the time, the place. But it was not for the sake of recruiting business, Dante told himself.

No—it was because Dante had questions of his own. Loose ends to tic up.

Outside, the sun had retreated again. The fog was thick. People, cars. Shadows, moving this way and that, at purposes hard to determine. Dante joined them, walking along in the mist.

A t the appointed time, Dante headed out for Benny's to meet with Owens. Benny's was an all-night hash house out on Third Street, close to the water, halfway to Hunters Point. It was a working-class place, tucked in between the railroad lines and the piers, not so much a neighborhood as a tangle of truncated alleys—a handful of derelict Victorians standing among Quonset huts and corrugated shacks. Something resembling a main road led down to an old cigar factory that had been converted to general storage, and Benny's was there, on a little rise across the way from a makeshift church with a sign calling attention to the coming rapture. An old union hall stood nearby, its windows busted out, and there was a bar farther down, men loitering, and also a woman in an old raincoat, sunglasses, a red scarf covering her head. She shunted away at the sight of him.

The wisdom.

A moment when the heart stills and the voice within suddenly goes silent, and there is the feeling of prescience, as of something about to be revealed.

Do nothing.

Benny's itself was a lively place, drawing a mixed crowd— dockworkers from the surrounding area, delivery drivers, hardcore regulars, as well as men from the flophouses nearby.

Dante found Owens inside sitting at one of the linoleum tables, wearing a baseball cap. He had on a pair of shades as well, and a work shirt. If Dante had not been on the lookout for the man, he would not have noticed him. It wasn't that Owens blended in with the clientele, that he resembled a worker or a transient. He was just somehow non-descript. Your eyes tended to skim past him.

Owens greeted him warmly, but there was at the same time a sense of reserve—of something held back.

"How are the kids?"

"Good," Owens said. "But homesick. We had to move again. After the verdict."

"Threats?"

Owens looked away. "Some people, they make up their minds—it doesn't matter what the court says . . . It's something you can't escape."

Dante did not know how much sympathy he felt. He thought about the man's kids and his wife, and he could see that Owens was trapped in his own way. His house out in Berkeley had been boarded up for the time being, and his family had no real home.

"We've been thinking about Florida."

"Florida?"

"It's just a thought. Jill has an opportunity."

"What about her job with Jensen?"

"I feel like I've gotten a second go at life. Also, the kids, the publicity—it might be better to get away."

Dante had a hard time imagining Owens outside the Bay Area. He was too tied to the streets, to a certain way of being. Like it or not, he would not find someone like Jensen to give him the work he did. He could not see the man in Florida.

"You were in the bank that day—you were part of the robbery?"

Owens said nothing.

"Who fired the gun?"

Owens shook his head. The man has to realize, Dante thought, what I have come to suspect. The prosecution hadn't been too far from wrong. The fire bombings, the threats—all of it an elaborate bluff, designed to impugn the prosecution's case, to create sympathy for Owens.

He tried to read the man's face but got no further then he had before.

"Is this why you called me?" Owens asked.

"I didn't call you. You called me."

Owens smiled—the same empty, soft look that had so infuriated Elise Younger. Everything was a dodge. But why this? Pretending it was Dante who had called to set this meeting up? Dante thought again about the way it had been arranged and how he'd felt driving up—an instant of prescience, the woman in the red scarf, back turned. An explanation occurred to him, or almost occurred, but then the thought scuttled away.

Do nothing.

"I appreciate everything you've done. If it wasn't for you, and all the other help I've gotten . . ."

The waitress brought their food. It was good food—fried chicken, hush puppies, collard greens cooked with ham. The last time they'd been here, Owens had told him the history of the place: started by a man out of prison, out in South City. How he'd eaten here once upon a time with Leland Sanford, years ago, not long after the man escaped from prison.

"There were things that happened a long time ago—and maybe I regret them," Owens said. The words had a familiar ring, too familiar. "Maybe we were young and a little bit stupid, and there was a way of thinking in the air."

Owens hesitated, then he fell silent, and Dante realized this was as much as he was going to get. Owens shook his head again. "But there are still demons out there. The same demons . . . and innocent people get hurt. When you fight back, innocent people get hurt. I don't know how much any of us can be held responsible for that."

This was the moment. If he had a card to flip, he should flip it now—something joining together the cause and effect.

Dante thought of the dead woman. He thought of Marilyn. He thought of Sorrentino's son.

Wrong place, wrong time.

Unintended victims. Collateral damage.

He took out a picture of Montoya, the Sandinista's buddy, specialist in putting Molotov cocktails through enemy windows. Dante had found pictures, but not the man. Not just one picture, but several, from different angles. Some of them were not so recent, but between them all, you got the idea.

"Do you recognize this man?"

"No."

"Annette and the Sandinista—he was with them, the day of the party?"

"I've never seen him," said Owens.

"How about I ask Jill?"

"Why would you want to do that?"

"How about the kids? They might remember?"

There was the slightest tic in the man's face, maybe. Or maybe not. He looked for signs of remorse or regret but there were none of these. A wistfulness, maybe, a look Dante could not penetrate, but which he saw again a few minutes later, after they'd finished eating, as they stood on the street corner, preparing each to go his own way. Dante did not know whether to despise him or admire him.

"You're right. Jill and I aren't going anywhere. We'll stick it out here. Jensen needs another investigator. And I have debts to pay."

The man put out his hand.

Dante shook it.

Dante headed toward his car, parked down the rise that opened up toward Third Street. He did not glance back at Owens, though he did glimpse, perhaps, the figure hovering at the edge of his vision, the woman on the sidewalk.

He did not walk far before he heard the shot.

Dante turned, and he saw them, Elise Younger and Owens, and for an instant, the way they stood, facing each other, it was possible to mistake them for two people engaged in conversation. Then Owens staggered on his feet, backing away. Elise stood in front of him, in the long raincoat, her hair under the red scarf. She fired again, then a third time, point-blank. Owens fell onto the broken sidewalk. And the woman fired one more time.

Elise Younger stood maybe fifty feet away from Dante, across the street, and Owens lay on the sidewalk beneath her. She glanced at Dante. A group of African Americans on the corner had seen the whole thing, but they did not move. Neither did a woman sitting on the church stoop. They all stood as if frozen.

He could have charged her then, he supposed. But his instincts told him that if he did not rush her, she would not shoot. She had not come for him, and anyway she was already in a kind of reckless motion, trotting sideways toward her car.

It had been Elise, he realized. She'd set up the meeting, posing as the secretary on the phone. Arranging for the two men to meet. Because Owens had been incognito since the trial, still in hiding, and it was a way she could flush him out. Now she was in her car, veering toward Third Street. The light had already turned red, but she did not slow, trying instead to dodge the traffic, but it was a busy street, a hard turn across four lanes, and she did not make it. A pickup smashed into her from the side, and the little Toyota jackknifed, spinning into on-coming lanes, and then was hit again.

On the sidewalk, on the other side of the street, a crowd had started to gather around Owens. A man stood over him with a cell phone. On Third Street, traffic backed up behind the wreckage. In another minute, Dante would start in motion, glancing first at Owens, dying on the sidewalk, then toward the accident, where he would find Elise Younger, her legs crushed, wailing in misery, the gun just out of reach on the seat beside her. In another minute the sirens would be wailing, and everything would start in motion. There would be the notification call, and the memorial speeches, and the widow at the funeral, and after that, preparations for another trial, Elise Younger in a wheelchair, the families in the courtroom, the chil-dren who would grow up without their dad, forever returning to this moment. But none of that had started yet. For now, it was just Owens on the sidewalk, and the car at the other end of the street, gushing steam into the air. It was the instant before the sirens, and the question of what had gone wrong, who had done what to whom, who would be punished—none of that mattered quite yet.

Meanwhile, the rain was falling. It was an old rain. Blood puddled in the rain along with the oil. There was the smell of gasoline in the air, but it didn't matter. It was a rain that had been falling for a long time. It didn't clean anything, but it kept falling anyway.

AUTHOR'S NOTE

This novel takes its title from a poem by San Francisco poet Bob Kaufman, "The Ancient Rain," which appeared in a volume of poetry by the same title, originally published by New Directions in 1981. The brief appearance of Kaufman himself in these pages, and the videotape described, are apocryphal renderings and should not be regarded as biographical fact. Also, the activities of the Symbionese Liberation Army, and the events leading to their apprehension, have been fictionalized for the sake of this drama. This book is a work of the imagination, and all characters are fictitious.